D0875228

The Spiderling

Also by Marcia Preston

The Wind Comes Sweeping

Trudy's Promise

The Piano Man

The Butterfly House

Song of the Bones

Perhaps She'll Die

The
Spiderling

Marcia Preston

THE ROADRUNNER PRESS
OKLAHOMA CITY, OKLAHOMA

Published by The RoadRunner Press
Oklahoma City, Oklahoma
www.TheRoadRunnerPress.com

Cover Design by Jeanne Devlin

First edition published November 3, 2020.

Library of Congress Control Number: 2019952240
Publisher's Cataloging-In-Publication Data on file
(Prepared by The Donohue Group, Inc.)

Names: Preston, M. K. (Marcia K.), 1944- author.
Title: The spiderling / Marcia Preston.
Description: First edition. | Oklahoma City, Oklahoma : The RoadRunner Press, 2020.
Identifiers: ISBN 9781937054588 | ISBN 9781950871056 (ebook)
Subjects: LCSH: Preteen girls--California--Fiction. | Mothers and daughters--California--Fiction. | Murder--California--Fiction. | Abusive men--California--Fiction. | Escapes--California--Fiction.
Classification: LCC PS3566.R4123 S65 2020 (print) | LCC PS3566.R4123 (ebook) | DDC 813/.54--dc23

10 9 8 7 6 5 4 3 2 1

To Army brats everywhere and to their parents

Chapter 1

Wild Horses

AROUND MIDNIGHT, Libby stopped the car on a rocky cliff and sailed the gun as far as she could out over the ocean. It disappeared into the black sea two hundred feet below. She stood on the brink with the wind at her back, listening for the splash, but heard only the rush and crash of the surf. She climbed back into the Mustang and drove on.

Fog crept in from the sea, covering the road in thick patches that blocked her headlights. The steep curves looked surreal in the dark. She strained to see the white line that marked the shoulder and tried not to picture the car crashing through the guardrail and plummeting over the edge. That might be the best idea, but she couldn't make that choice. She glanced into the back seat and then kept going until San Jose was far behind.

The next morning, coming down a staircase behind the motel, Libby paused on the landing to look out over the Big Sur River that ran along the back of the property. Twig chairs sat in the shallow stream. She inhaled the smell of forest and damp earth and imagined sitting there with the ache of icy water on her bare feet.

She zipped her hoodie and descended to a cracked sidewalk that led around to the front of the building. The motel and café shared the parking lot with a gift shop and gas station. It was a downscale tourist place, nearly deserted at this time of year. She had counted on that when she chose the coast highway instead of the interstate. The black Mustang sat alone where she had parked it in the night, dew condensing on the windshield.

On the terrace outside the café, canvas umbrellas hugged their masts. Libby pulled the door open, setting off a wind chime that chattered like glass birds. The place was empty, a lounge at the back cloaked in shadows. But the dining section was lighted, and Buddha Bar music floated in from a sound system. She took a booth by the window and found a menu behind the napkin holder.

In less than a minute, a woman bearing coffee pushed through a bead curtain from the kitchen. She was lean and ageless in a gauze skirt and no makeup, with sunspots across her cheekbones. Her name tag said *Sara*. She poured coffee into Libby's mug without asking. "Good morning. Need a minute?"

"No, I'm ready," Libby said. She kept her eyes on the menu, not wanting a conversation that the waitress might remember. "Two scrambled eggs and a short stack, please."

"Coming right up," the waitress said and disappeared behind the clacking beads.

The music's synthesized rhythm thumped like a migraine. On the wall, a row of large photographs showed the Big Sur coastline Libby had followed in the dark. She almost overlooked the naked woman in each photo, softly focused and exotic, with her back to the camera. Libby shivered and grasped the mug to warm her hands. She noticed a faint stain of someone else's lipstick on the rim. She turned the cup around and drank anyway. The coffee was scalding and strong, exactly what she needed.

Across the highway from the café, sunrise crowned the brown hills. Libby watched a silver pickup pull off the road and park on the gravel beside the Mustang. She could see the driver checking out the car even before he opened his door. She tensed as the man walked a slow circle around the Mustang before moving toward the café entrance. Police?

2

Or worse, maybe a friend of Rocket's. Her eyes slid back to her coffee; her hands tightened on the mug, her heartbeat rabbiting.

The man came in and sat at a table across the room with his back to the wall. He wore a leather bomber jacket and faded jeans. Sara emerged from the kitchen to take his order. When the waitress turned away, the man glanced toward Libby as if ready to speak, but she didn't look up. She sipped her coffee and watched from the corner of her eye as he took off his jacket and tossed it on a chair.

Sara returned with Libby's breakfast. "There you are, Hon," she said, setting down a pitcher of syrup. "Anything else I can get you?"

Libby's mouth watered. She hadn't eaten since yesterday morning. "A warm-up, please."

Sara refilled her cup and moved on. The music shifted to a breathy female singer with the same monotone beat. Libby felt the man's gaze as she smeared butter on the pancakes and drenched them with syrup, shoving the scrambled eggs to the rim of her plate. Stay calm. Don't look at him. Still, her hand shook as she forked a bite of eggs.

"That your Mustang outside?" he said.

Here we go. Libby didn't hurry to answer him, steeling her voice to sound matter-of-fact. "You see anybody else in here?"

The guy grinned, trying too hard to be friendly. His teeth were straight and white. "I collect old cars. Always wanted a Mustang."

She noted the black motorcycle boots, expensive, and a complicated watch below his rolled-up sleeve. Too well dressed for any cop she'd ever known. The tag on his truck wasn't from Santa Clara County either. Aging rich kid, she diagnosed, with more money than he deserved. Definitely not one of Rocket's friends.

She relaxed a bit and concentrated on breakfast. The pancakes were perfectly browned.

"That's a sixty-four-and-a-half, isn't it? A classic," the man said.

"Ummm."

"Not many of those left. Looks like it's in great shape. How's it run?"

She glanced at him. "Like a Mustang."

Before he could respond, his breakfast arrived, and then Sara swung by Libby's booth again.

3

"I'll need a breakfast burrito and an orange juice to go," Libby said.

"Sure thing, Hon."

The man called to the waitress. "Ma'am? I asked for sunny-side up, and these eggs are hard." He sounded disappointed.

Sara walked over and glanced at his food. "They sure are. Sorry about that." She swooped up the plate; the crystal beads clacked behind her as she disappeared into the kitchen. Libby heard her talking to the cook, louder than before.

For a few minutes, Libby ate in peace while the other customer drank his coffee. Then he turned toward her again, long legs set apart on the wooden floor. "Don't suppose you'd be interested in selling your car?"

Was he kidding? She stabbed the last bite of pancake. "Then I'd be on foot with no way to get out of here."

"I could drop you somewhere."

She gave him a look, and he laughed. "Okay. How about I trade you, then? My truck for your old Mustang."

Libby glanced out the window at his Silverado pickup. Chrome running boards and fancy hubcaps. A gas hog in ecocountry. This guy was no local. She felt him watching her. She was thinking fast but kept her face blank.

"Straight up?" she finally said.

"Straight up."

He was serious. The Mustang must be worth a lot of money. And there could be an APB on it right now. If he was a collector, maybe he'd take it off the street. Not even tag it.

She waited a few beats and then shook her head. "I'd have to have some cash."

He perked up, having fun. "Really? Do you know what pickups cost these days?"

"Nope, and I don't care."

The perfect teeth flashed again. "Fair enough. How much cash?"

"How much you got?"

He looked at her as if she was crazy, his smile pulling to one side. Already thinking about how he'd tell the story to his friends, Libby bet.

He stood up and dug into his jeans pocket. His wallet was tooled leather. He began to count hundred-dollar bills onto the table. "Three, four, five, six, seven. You gotta leave me something to get home on."

The waitress came out with Libby's to-go box and a small carton of orange juice; she put them in a sack and brought the sack with the check to Libby's table.

"Breakfast's on me," the guy said.

The waitress looked at the stack of hundreds in front of him. She glanced from the man to Libby and back at the money. "That my tip?" she said dryly on her way back to the kitchen.

So much for Sara not remembering me, Libby thought. She needed to get out of there fast.

The man brought the bills over and laid them on her table. He was taller than she had first thought. He put his truck keys on top of the money and picked up her breakfast check.

"Title's in the glove compartment and the gas tank's full. We got a deal?" He stood beside the booth, waiting.

This was all too easy. They should be signing over titles. But if he didn't care, why should she? Guys like him could pay to take care of such things, and she had bigger worries.

Sara reappeared and set a plate on his table. "Here you go, mister, sunny-side up. You could drink 'em with a straw."

Libby pulled a car key from her jacket. She held it for a few seconds, running her thumb over the wild horse emblem on the ring, waiting until the waitress disappeared again. Then she dropped the key on the table and slid out of the booth. She pocketed the truck keys and shoved the cash into the sack with the burrito. "Title's in the glove compartment," she said, "and the gas tank's empty."

Outdoors, the air was fresh and cool. She crossed the parking lot quickly, glancing inside the Mustang to be sure she'd left nothing behind. Then she aimed the gizmo attached to the man's keys and pushed a button. The truck's door locks clicked open.

Libby jogged around the building and up the wooden stairs of the motel. She turned left and continued down the outdoor walkway to Number Nine, unlocked the door, and pushed her way inside.

"Kiwi, wake up. We have to go."

In the rumpled bed, a small tween body twisted beneath the covers. Libby pulled off the sheet, revealing a little girl with hair tangled around her head like brown Silly String. "I gotta pee," she said.

"Bathroom's in there. Brush your teeth quick, and I'll get your clothes. I brought you some breakfast for the road."

Kiwi slid out of bed and trudged toward the bathroom. Her bedraggled stuffed dog remained among the covers.

Libby found her daughter's jeans from the day before and a clean T-shirt. She tossed the few things they had taken out of the suitcase back inside and zipped it shut. Kiwi came out of the bathroom, and Libby went in, giving orders over her shoulder. "Stick your toothbrush in the side pocket and grab your pillow—don't forget Moxie."

When Libby returned, Kiwi was dressed and holding her pillow under one arm, a Moxie-sized lump inside the pillowcase. Her nose was stuck inside the paper bag. "What's all this money?"

"I'll explain later. Let's go." *Before the guy finishes his runny eggs and changes his mind,* Libby prayed.

Kiwi trailed her mom across the parking lot. "We've traded cars," Libby said. "We're taking this truck."

Kiwi didn't even register surprise. Libby unlocked the cab and tossed her blanket inside. Kiwi stepped onto the chrome running board and climbed in. The suitcase would be fine in the bed of the truck as long as it didn't rain.

The pickup had bucket seats and lots of leg room. Libby adjusted the seat and mirrors and studied the dashboard controls.

"This thing is a battleship," Kiwi said, still holding the pillow and sack, her briar-patch hair catching the sun through the windshield. "Are we stealing it?"

"Of course not," Libby said. "Buckle up." The gas gauge showed full. She turned the ignition and the engine rumbled. "Put that money in my purse and eat your breakfast."

She backed up slowly and steered the truck onto the highway, adjusting the seat forward again. After the Mustang, the truck was like driving a house.

In the rearview mirror, Libby watched the black Mustang shrink into the distance and disappear. It felt as if she and Kiwi were doing the same thing. She wondered if the Mustang's title really was in the glove compartment. She hoped not; it would have Rocket's name on it, his legal name. He'd go ballistic if he knew she'd traded off his car.

But he never would.

"There's a brush in my purse," Libby said, driving south again. "You need to work on that hair."

"After I eat," Kiwi said with her mouth full. She had made a nest on the wide seat and sat cross-legged with a napkin over her lap, finishing breakfast. Except for the comment about the truck, she hadn't asked one question since they'd left San Jose. This was not normal for a girl who could ask twenty questions in the course of a trip to the grocery store, and it worried Libby.

For two hours, they drove the winding highway along the ocean. It was foggy and slow going at first, but the marine layer gradually receded, and the sea turned brilliant blue. Boulders jutted from the water like icebergs, their tops whitened by generations of bird dung. Then the coastline flattened. They passed a place where elephant seals covered the beach, stinking of fish. The fence was lined with tourists. Kiwi wanted to stop and look at the seals, but Libby said no. They needed to keep moving.

They lost almost an hour midday clawing their way through L.A. traffic. Libby wrapped both hands around the wheel, her neck tense. After that, the towns ran together. They got lunch at McDonald's and kept driving until a road sign showed fifty miles to the Mexican border. Libby knew nothing about Mexico and didn't speak Spanish.

Near Oceanside, Libby turned inland. Not going somewhere, just going. Kiwi was reading a book she'd retrieved from the suitcase. The child was obsessed with books the way some kids were with video games, a healthier escape from reality than the methods Libby had chosen as a kid. Miles later, Kiwi closed her book. Watching her stare out the window, Libby wondered if Kiwi was reliving those last hours in the apartment and whether she always would. She didn't ask. Maybe, if they didn't keep the images alive with words, the memory would fade. Like so many things Libby wanted to forget.

They were driving through open country when Kiwi sat up straight and pointed out the window.

"Look, Mom. Wild horses!"

A dozen animals, all different colors, were galloping across the hills between patches of forest. Something must have spooked them. Or maybe they just liked to run.

"I doubt there are wild horses anymore," Libby said. "They must belong to someone."

"No, we read about them in school," Kiwi insisted. "People protect them so they can stay wild. See, no fences."

The ponies ran parallel to the road at a distance, their manes and tails streaming.

"You couldn't ride one, though," said Kiwi. "They're too skittish."

Skittish, Libby thought. How many kids her age used the word *skittish*? She'd known since Kiwi was five years old that her only child was smarter than she was. And Libby was proud of Kiwi's intelligence, although sometimes it stood like an invisible wall between them, leaving Libby feeling overmatched.

When the horses were out of sight, Kiwi got out the notebook she called her journal and began to write. Libby wondered what she was putting down this time. Kiwi had insisted that a journal was private and Libby must not ever peek. Touched by how much it had seemed to mean to Kiwi, Libby had agreed. And she had not broken that promise.

They drove on in silence. Soon, however, Kiwi propped her pillow against the armrest and curled into a tight ball on the seat. Car rides always made her sleepy. Libby glanced over at her in the fading light: pink-and-green striped socks, baggy at the toes, the ragged Moxie, a refugee from an Army garage sale, crushed to her chest.

This child was all she had left of Deacon, the soldier husband who'd saved her from herself. In sleep, Kiwi's face looked smooth and innocent, like any other little girl's. But Kiwi wasn't any little girl. And Libby had no clue how to be her mother.

What will become of her? My daughter, the murderer.

Chapter 2

The Sleepy Iguana

LIBBY TURNED OFF THE highway toward a pink neon lizard glowing in the Mojave dusk. She'd been driving since daylight. They had spent the night in the pickup, with one blanket stretched over them and the halogen lights of the truck stop glaring through the windshield like an alien sun. By then, her eyes were sandy and her back ached from hours in a hollowed-out seat built for men. She would have traded her soul, what was left of it, for a cold beer.

She hadn't seen the name of the town. Maybe this place was just a highway junction. All she needed—besides a beer—was a cheap motel and some decent food for Kiwi. She still had most of the cash from the sale of the Mustang, but it might have to last a long time. The damned truck sucked gasoline like a sinkhole.

Approaching the lizard sign, she saw the curved spine of the reptile formed the letter S in Sleepy Iguana. Coors and Corona signs blinked in the window. Libby could taste the cold bite of a draft beer sliding down her throat. She turned into the parking lot without hesitation.

Kiwi was asleep again, balled up on the seat with Moxie in an arm-lock. Libby left her there, locked the truck, and went inside.

The interior of the tavern was so dark she had to pause in the doorway to let her eyes adjust. A jukebox played country music but not loud. One customer sat at the bar, no one at the tables. A bartender was stocking bottles. Along a back wall covered in cheap paneling, a staircase bent upward into darkness.

The only other customer was a woman. Libby took a seat three stools down, and the bartender dropped a coaster in front of her. He had a brown ponytail and spooky eyes, tats on both biceps. In the bar light, his skin looked bronze.

"All drafts are two bucks for ten more minutes," he said.

"That'll work." While he pulled the beer, she glanced sideways at her fellow drinker.

"Evening," the woman said, nodding her head.

Libby nodded back. "How ya doing?"

Libby guessed the woman to be in her late thirties, maybe forty, about ten years older than herself. The woman had a mannish haircut and remarkably straight posture.

The bartender set Libby's beer on the coaster and went back to polishing glassware. She sipped from the skin of foam, then took a long drink. The icy cold beer left a satisfying ache behind her right eyeball.

"Been on the road all day, I bet," the woman said.

"Good guess. I must look it."

"Nah, I saw your truck come off the highway." The woman smiled. "Besides, if you were local, I'd know you."

Her hair was black and peppered with gray. She wore an inexpensive pantsuit, rimless glasses, and no makeup. Probably had just gotten off work. The jukebox stopped and an unnatural silence fell over them, but it didn't last long.

"You ready for another one, Myra?" the bartender asked.

"In a minute," the woman said good-naturedly. "Don't rush me."

The bartender smiled and walked down the bar to fiddle with the remote on a wall-mounted TV. "What channel's the game on?" His back was turned as he watched a slide show of images flicker across the screen.

"You're the bartender, you're supposed to know these things," Myra said. "ESPN2, I think."

Libby turned slightly toward her on the stool. "Is there a military post around here?"

"Closest is Edwards Air Force Base, but it's still quite a ways. You looking for a PX?"

"Yeah. Pharmacy, actually. My daughter's allergic and I need to refill her prescription." What she was actually after was sleeping pills for herself, if the druggist wasn't a hard-ass about a doctor's permission.

"That's a long drive for a cheap drugstore," the woman said. "We got a Walmart over in the next town."

Libby nodded and drank her beer, the cold and heat streaking toward her empty stomach.

"I was in the military once," Myra said.

Libby had suspected it from the posture and haircut.

"What branch?" she asked.

"Army."

"So was my husband. Until he got killed."

Myra winced. "Accident or combat?"

"Combat. Iraq."

"That's rough. I was in before 9/11, so I escaped the Mideast thing."

"Good timing."

Myra signaled the bartender with a raised glass. He nodded and drew another, sweeping away the empty one when he set it down. A football game came on television, the sound like white noise in the background. "How old's your daughter?" Myra asked.

"Eleven. Going on forty."

She smiled. "Like most military kids. My dad was a lifer. But I just did one tour."

Libby finished her beer. She felt better except for a pinching at the crown of her head. The bartender cocked an eyebrow toward her empty glass, but she waved him off. She dug in her purse and placed a few bills on the bar.

"Could you recommend a cheap motel?" she asked the woman.

Myra shook her head. "There's the Frugal Javelina, but it's a hooker hangout, and I heard it has plumbing problems. The Sand Dunes Suites up on the highway is new, but it's kinda pricey."

Libby sighed. "I guess we'll get some food and keep driving. Surely there's a decent restaurant in town."

"Sure is. Bunch of them right down the road." Myra tipped her head in the opposite direction from the interstate. She watched Libby a moment, frowning. "There's no place to stop for a lot of miles out here. You and the girl could crash at my place, if you want. Shaun here can vouch for my character."

The bartender smiled. "Pillar of respectability, our Myra." Then he held out his palm as if she owed him. Myra slapped it and laughed.

"Seriously, Myra's okay," the bartender said straight-faced, like he was giving a testimonial.

What kind of woman invited strangers to stay with her? Libby wondered, but she wasn't in a position to be choosy. "I appreciate that," she said, "but right now I better get my daughter some dinner." She slid off the stool.

"I'll still be here if you change your mind," Myra said. Her eyes stayed on the TV screen as Libby left.

Kiwi was sitting up on the truck seat, her white face reflecting light from the bar sign through the windshield. Her eyes looked scared, but she didn't say anything as Libby unlocked the door and climbed into the cab.

"Let's go get some dinner," Libby told her.

They drove slowly down the line of fast-food restaurants, a pizza joint, and a pancake place.

"You pick," Libby said.

"Pizza."

"Okay, but you need to have a salad with it."

They helped themselves from a lukewarm buffet and sat on plastic chairs near the window. Libby could feel the rapid cooling of the desert night through the glass.

"Are we going to sleep in the truck again tonight?" Kiwi asked. Her face looked puffy. Tangles of dark hair spiraled around her head.

"Please don't talk with your mouth full."

Kiwi chewed and swallowed. "Are we going to sleep in the truck?"

"I hope not," Libby said. "But I talked to a lady back there, and this town doesn't have a motel we can afford. We can keep driving, but we might end up in a parking lot again. There's not much out here."

Libby glanced at Kiwi over her slice. "The lady I talked to invited us to crash at her house."

"She did? Without even knowing us?"

Libby shrugged. "She used to be in the Army. She seemed nice, and the bartender vouched for her."

"Would I have to sleep on the couch?"

"Would that be worse than the truck seat?"

"Not possible—if she has a place to pee." Kiwi chewed. "Anybody else live with her?"

"I don't think so."

"What the heck," Kiwi said and shrugged.

When Libby returned to the Sleepy Iguana, Myra was still on her barstool.

"Just so you know," Libby told her, "I'm straight."

"I knew that," Myra said.

They followed Myra's gray Honda from the bar, rolling slowly down a street of small stucco homes. Old cars hunkered in the shadow of carports meant to protect their paint from the sun. Myra pulled beneath one of them and cut her lights. Libby parked the truck behind it and got the suitcase from the truck bed. Kiwi climbed down out of the cab, carrying her pillow and Moxie. There were no yard lights, just a high desert moon.

Myra waited for them on a stamp of lawn by the front door. "This is my daughter, Kiwi," Libby said, her hand on Kiwi's shoulder.

"Hi, kid," Myra said.

Kiwi looked at her. "Hi, lady."

Myra chuckled. "My name's Myra. Welcome to my humble house."

15

The place was small, two bedrooms with a bathroom between them. The extra room was made up neatly with a double bed covered with a spread with a cactus print. A peach-colored lamp sat on an end table. Ten times nicer than the last two places they'd stayed. Libby almost relaxed.

"This is great, Myra. We sure appreciate it."

"No problem. You're welcome to use the bathtub if you want. Extra towels in the cabinet. Let me know if you need something you can't find."

After they'd both had a bath, Libby lay awake beside Kiwi in the soft bed, the smell of apricot shampoo like broken glass in her lungs, sharp with memories of a former life, a time when Kiwi had friends to play with and Deacon came home at night for dinner.

Exactly where had they landed this time? A nameless town in a featureless wasteland. But a place, perhaps, where nobody would come looking.

Chapter 3

Kiwi's Journal

15 October 2008
(That's the way they write dates in the Army.)

THIS MORNING I WALKED to the school we drove past the first night we got here. I've been to six different schools, all in different places. School is one thing you can count on to stay pretty much the same, no matter where you are. The first thing I do in every new town is get enrolled.

Back in San Jose, I was in Mrs. Kettleman's class for most of fifth grade. Of all my teachers, she's my favorite. She had gray-brown hair and glasses and little wrinkles around her mouth. Sometimes those old teachers are the best. Mrs. K liked me, but she liked everybody, really. There was this kid named Jory who was loud and mouthy and acted out half the time. Once when he was being obnoxious, Mrs. K just kept looking at him until he shut up, and then she said, "I still love you, Jory." And she wasn't being sarcastic either.

After that, Jory put his head down on his desk and covered up his face. It was hard to resist Mrs. K, especially when she focused on you.

I used to stay after school sometimes and help Mrs. K clean up the room. Most of the kids rode the bus home, but I walked, so I could stay as late as I wanted. One day when I was helping out, Mrs. K gave me this notebook I'm writing in. It was brand-new, with a lavender cover and tiny pink flowers. She said it was a journal, a book in which to write your thoughts and stuff that happens and how you feel about it. Mrs. K said I was excellent at writing. She taught me how to write conversations between people. It was fun, and the punctuation was easy once I figured out the logic to it. Sometimes I make up conversations just so I can use the quotation marks.

I'm pretty good at math too and science is my favorite. But Mrs. K was the only teacher who ever gave me something special like that. I wish I hadn't had to leave San Jose without telling her. But I had told her on the first day that I was temporary. I've always been temporary, even when Dad was alive. That's part of being an Army brat. As soon as I got comfortable in a new school, we moved again. I always warned my new friends so they wouldn't get too attached.

Mrs. K said a journal would be like a permanent friend for me, one I could talk to and take with me wherever I went. And she was right. That journal was a lot like Moxie. It made me feel less alone. I'll never forget Mrs. Kettleman.

But today was about getting a new school. Luckily, most of them are organized the same. I found the principal's office right inside the front doors like always. Inside was a big lady with curly hair and those teensy reading glasses that fold up into a tube. She had a jack-o'-lantern made out of construction paper sitting on her desk. Paper spiders wiggled from long threads that were stuck to the ceiling with thumbtacks. These people took Halloween seriously. I liked that. Halloween is my favorite holiday.

A plastic sign on the desk said *Mrs. Nelson*. I didn't think she was the principal, but you never knew.

"I need to enroll in your school, please," I said.

The big lady looked over her glasses beyond me as if she was expecting somebody else. Then she looked back at me.

"You have a parent with you?" she said.

"No, ma'am." I stepped closer to her desk so I could check out the jack-o'-lantern. It was made like slats on a window blind that had both ends stapled together and then squashed so the slats curved out round in the middle, like a pumpkin. The eyes and nose and smile were stuck on separately. I bet I could make one of my own.

"How did you get here?" the lady said.

"I walked."

She frowned and her extra chin wiggled. "How old are you?"

I told her I was eleven, and I'd finished fifth grade at my last school so I would need to be in sixth.

She looked at my black leggings, baggy at the knees because I'd slept in them. I had on my mom's Holstein T-shirt over my leggings, with a pink ribbon for a belt. The neck of the shirt was too big but the shirttail covered my butt, so I figured it ought to meet the school's dress code, if there was one. The ribbon almost matched my pink flip-flops. Maybe that would help, I thought.

The lady who might be Mrs. Nelson pushed a button on her telephone and said into the receiver, "Could you come out here for a minute?" She paused, careful not to look at me. "You need to see this for yourself."

It wasn't three seconds before a door behind her opened and another big lady came out. This one wasn't wide, just tall. I wondered if the kids here were big too. I was used to being the smallest person in my class, but this place looked like the Land of the Giants.

The tall lady looked me over. Grown-ups sure know how to make a kid feel uncomfortable. She said, "I'm Mrs. Gardenhire, the principal of this school. May I help you?"

"I'm Kiwi Seager," I said. "Nice to meet you."

I stuck out my hand, and after a pause, she shook it. She could have palmed a basketball with those mitts. Her feet wouldn't fit any glass slippers either.

"I'd like to enroll in your school, please," I said for the second time.

The principal pointed me to some chairs along the wall, and we both took a seat. She looked interested, and kind of interesting. She wore tan pants and a top with flowers, and her hair hung down to her waist in a single braid. She didn't look like any principal I'd ever seen. Her eyelashes were superlong and so pale they were nearly white. It was hard not to keep looking at them, so I didn't try.

I told her I was new in town, and this was the closest school I could find to the place where we're staying. She asked where that was. I said on Universal Street, with a friend, until Mom got a job and we got a place of our own.

"Is that why your mom didn't come with you today? She's looking for work?" she asked.

I thought about that for a second. Then I said, "Sure. We can assume that."

She smiled when I said *assume*. Adults are always impressed with my vocabulary, although if they spent as much time reading as I do, they'd have big vocabularies too.

I told Mrs. Gardenhire I didn't have any paperwork from my last school, but I could tell her the name and where it was, if that helped. Every school I went to always wanted papers from the school before. I'm not sure why.

She said that would be helpful. Her face looked different when she smiled. "Let's go into my office and start some paperwork of our own," she said.

She stood up—and up and up. I felt like an ant following a giraffe.

Her office was crowded with plants, and on the wall, there were pictures drawn by kids. Hers was a friendly office. I hoped the kids at this school were friendly too and that I could stay here for a while. Maybe even through Christmas. If they went this crazy decorating for Halloween, I could only imagine what they did at Christmas.

I took a seat in front of her desk and answered her questions about my last school. She said their school was called Sand Flats Elementary, but I knew that from the sign out front. The town is called Sand Flats too, and the name pretty much describes what it looks like around here.

Mrs. Gardenhire asked whether I had been in school this fall, and I told her yes, for a few weeks. I didn't want her to ask why I left, so I changed the subject. "Do you have a free lunch program? We're a little short on money right now."

I love school lunches—those little boxes of milk and the plates with separate spaces for carrots and a cookie. My stomach growled when I thought about it.

"We do," Mrs. Gardenhire said. "Have your mom fill out this form and sign it, then return it to me." She handed me a sheet of paper with fine print and lots of blanks.

I didn't have a pocket, so I folded the paper in fourths and stuck it into the top of my leggings.

"I'd like to meet your mother," she said. "Could you ask her to come to the school?"

"I can always ask," I said. "When do I start sixth grade?"

"How about tomorrow?"

I had been hoping for that morning, and I must have looked disappointed because she frowned and smiled at the same time. She said she could ask Mrs. Nelson to bring me a lunch from the cafeteria, and I could eat there in the office.

"That would be great," I said. "I'm hungry as a caterpillar." That was a reference to a kids' book called *The Very Hungry Caterpillar*. But I couldn't tell if Mrs. Gardenhire got it.

She had cafeteria duty, so I ate my lunch on the least cluttered corner of Mrs. Nelson's desk in the front office. She'd brought herself lunch too. She read a magazine while she ate, so I got a newspaper from one of the chairs and read it. The cheese sandwich was gummy, just the way I like it.

The office was very quiet, too quiet for my tastes. So I said, "Listen to this. It says here the town's drinking water may be contaminated with prescription drugs. How the heck did medicine get in there?"

Mrs. Nelson blinked at me, and I wondered if I'd pronounced *contaminated* wrong.

"I have no idea," she finally said. "Doesn't the article tell you?"

I read some more, and it did. "It says people flush them down the toilet. Yikes! Does that mean we're reusing toilet water?"

"I don't think so," she said. "That's what water filtration plants do. They treat the water and kill the germs and pour it back into the rivers and lakes. By the time it gets to your faucet, it's clean again."

"Not very, I guess, if it still has drugs in it."

"Good point," she said, and looked at me over those teensy glasses. "You're a good reader, Kiwi."

I said thanks, and then she wanted to know how I got a name like Kiwi.

"Is that a nickname?" she asked.

"Nope," I said. "My mom craved kiwi fruit when she was pregnant. She ate so much of it that I was born kind of green; she says that's why she named me Kiwi."

"You don't say—what did your father think about that?"

"I never asked him. He was killed in Iraq when I was in third grade, so it's too late now."

Her big voice got soft. "I'm sorry to hear that. Losing him must have been rough for you and your mom." She offered me her open bag of potato chips. I stuck my hand in and grabbed a fistful.

"There's a kind of bird called a kiwi," she said.

My eyes snapped open. I'd never heard that before.

"I think it lives in Australia. Somewhere like that," she said.

I couldn't believe I didn't know about a bird with my name!

"I'll have to check that out," I said.

I finished my lunch, and Mrs. Nelson pointed to a trash can behind her desk. I dumped my trash in.

"It was nice having lunch with you," I said. "See you tomorrow."

"It was nice having lunch with you too." Then she laughed, but I have no idea why. Her face was friendly when she smiled, even with those big teeth. I felt her watching me as I went out the door. I liked Mrs. Nelson.

Outside on the playground, kids were hollering and climbing on the monkey bars and stuff. I had to walk right past them and then around to the street I'd come down before. I always pay attention so I can find my way back. I hoped Mom was still where I'd left her.

Sometimes I have a bad dream in which I come home from school and Mom has packed her stuff and gone. The dream started after my dad died and Mom started to move us around even more than when we were in the Army.

The dream got a lot worse *A.R.*

My life is divided into two parts—*B.R.* is Before Rocket, which was before San Jose. And *A.R.* is After Rocket. The part in the middle, With Rocket, was a nightmare of its own.

Mom wasn't in the house when I got back, but her stuff was, so it was okay. Maybe she did go hunt for a job today. The person we are staying with is a woman, which is a lot better than when we bunk in with some guy Mom just met and I don't know at all. That's how we got in trouble before.

The lady's name is Myra, and she used to be in the Army too. Now she works in an office at a warehouse. Mom and I share a bedroom here. The last place, I had to sleep on the couch. When I was little and Dad was alive, I had a bedroom all to myself. We lived on an Army post. If he hadn't been sent to Iraq, we were going to get a dog.

Mom was different after we got the news that he was killed. It's hard to explain. It was like she used to be a picture, and when he died she cracked into a jigsaw puzzle. Every so often, pieces would come loose and fall out.

A.R., she lost a whole big chunk—the chunk where she loved her daughter. But I understand why she can't love me anymore.

I'm hoping if we both live a long time and I never do another bad thing, maybe she can forgive me. For now, I'm trying to keep a low profile. That means I stay out of the way and keep quiet. Unfortunately, I'm not very good at low profile.

My hand is cramping from writing so much at once.

I'm hungry again too, and Mom's still not home yet, or Myra either, for that matter. I think I'll look in the fridge and see what I can find. It wouldn't be the first time I went hungry.

But I always hope the last time will be the last for good.

Love,

Kiwi

Saturday, 18 October

I went two days to my new school this past week, and only one girl talked to me. Her name is Karen. She seems nice, but she ate lunch with her friends and I ate by myself. I hate the first few days in a new school. But it will be okay after a while.

Mom got a job—being a waitress again, which she hates. But she wants to be paid in cash, and apparently that makes it harder to get work. The name of the place is the Sleepy Iguana, the same place we stopped the night we met Myra.

Mom's hours are 7:00 p.m. until 2:00 a.m.

The only time I see her awake is after school.

I'm out of school today because it's Saturday, and I went to get my library card because I'm a bookaholic. I asked Myra where the public library was. Unlucky for me, it's on the other side of town. But lucky for me, it's a very small town. Myra thought maybe I should wait till Mom got up and could go with me, but I drew a map with the directions and told her I'd be fine. I walk places by myself all the time.

I counted six blocks between Myra's house and the library. If we stay here very long, maybe I can figure out a way to get a bicycle.

My trip to the library, however, was almost a waste. I thought a library card was a basic right of any American person. Not in Sand Flats, I guess. They wouldn't give me one without a parent's permission. They gave me a paper for Mom to sign, but they wouldn't even let me log on to their computer without a library card number. Jeez. Finally, a lady at the desk felt sorry for me and gave me a temporary number. Temporary me.

After a bunch of hassle, I got logged on to the internet and typed *kiwi bird* into the search window. Here's what I learned.

The kiwi bird lives only in New Zealand (that's close to Australia) and is about the size of a chicken. And it can't fly! It has little bitty wings, which are basically useless, and no tail. It gets around by walking or running and can outrun a human if it wants to. It comes out mostly at night, so lots of New Zealanders have never seen one except in a zoo.

If you ask me, the kiwi is one weird-looking bird. Imagine a fluffy hedgehog, only the size of a chicken and balanced on two feet (each with three toes) and with a long, skinny beak. I do mean *l-o-n-g*, like an anteater's snout.

I'm not flattered to share my name with this oddball bird. But there's one thing to admire—the kiwi is a survivor. It belongs to an ancient order of birds that are all extinct except for the kiwi. It is also a symbol of New Zealand's army. If my dad had been in the N.Z. army instead of the U.S. army, he'd be called a *kiwi*. That would be wicked cool!

I wrote down a bunch of facts about the kiwi bird and drew some pictures. Maybe I can use them for a report for science class. Mr. Mathis is the science teacher, and I think I'm going to like him.

I did another search on the computer and found a link to a video somebody had made about the kiwi bird. I clicked it but it didn't work, so I got the nice lady again. She had logged me on with some kind of kid code that wouldn't let me see naked pictures or something. I showed her what I wanted to watch and she checked it out first. It turned out to be a cartoon, so she went back to her desk and let me watch. It was a strange cartoon. I had to watch it three times to figure out what was happening.

It opens with this little bird trying to tie a rope to some trees growing on the side of a cliff. He pulled on the rope until the trees stood straight out from the cliff, then he nailed their roots to the ground. When he was done, it was like a forest growing sideways. This didn't make any sense to me until I saw what he did next.

He put on this little cap with a strap on it and earflaps, and he backed up like he was revving his motor. Then he ran right off the edge of the cliff! So he was falling like a zillion miles an hour, straight down and headfirst. But then the picture slo-o-o-wly turned on its side, and it was like he was sailing over the trees he had nailed onto the side of the cliff. He stuck out his stubby wings and flapped them in the breeze. He was *flying*! He went to all that trouble so he could know what it was like to fly.

A little tear came out of his eye, and he blinked it away. It ended with him sailing into this misty fog, but you knew he was actually falling, and eventually he would hit the ground—splat—and die. He gave up his *whole life* to know the thrill of flying, just one time.

I watched it over and over until the library lady came and asked if I was crying. I told her no, but my stomach hurt, and I had to go home.

I couldn't get that little bird out of my mind. I kept hearing the sad music from the cartoon playing in my head.

Love,

Kiwi

Sunday, 19 October

Sometimes when I'm out walking by myself not feeling so good, I play the Traffic Game. I made it up a long time ago, after Mom and I moved off the Army post.

Here are the rules:

> 1.When you come to an intersection, instead of looking both ways for cars, five steps before you get there, you close your eyes and step off the curb.
> 2. Don't open your eyes until you think you're going to trip on the curb on the other side. If cars are coming, they have to stop for you. Or not.

Usually there isn't much traffic and nothing happens. But sometimes I hear a car coming, getting closer and closer, and I wonder if it will see me and stop or knock me up in the air like a doll and break my bones. But I keep my eyes closed unless the car honks. That always scares the bejesus out of me and makes me jump and run. Then my heart pounds so hard I have to sit on the sidewalk to recover.

On the way home from the library yesterday, I was bummed out about the kiwi-bird cartoon, so I decided to play the Traffic Game. The streets were quiet on a Saturday and they hardly had curbs at all. Myra said that's because it seldom rains, so they don't need tall curbs. Anyway, about two blocks from Myra's house, I closed my eyes and walked out into the street. I was humming "Mad World," the song that was in my head from the cartoon.

I heard rap music before I heard the car. The music got louder and closer, and my heart was beating along with the music pumping out of the car. My feet wanted to run, but I wouldn't let them. I kept my eyes shut. The music got louder and louder. Closer and closer. I was starting to picture my body flying through the air and landing in a heap of bloody bones. Just when I thought sure the car would hit me, I heard the brakes screech. I could feel the heat coming out of the engine.

That's when I jumped and landed on my butt on the sidewalk. This big gangsta-rap guy leaned out the window of his old black car. It was a lowrider that sat about three inches off the ground.

He yelled, "You crazy, Sista? Get the (bleep) outa the street!"

I looked up at his dark eyes, close enough to burn a hole right through me. My butt felt like it was broken, but my chest hurt even worse. I gave the guy a big chicken smile and said, "Sorry! Have a nice day!"

He let out a bunch of other bleep words. His car sounded like thunder when he drove off.

I couldn't breathe normally till I got to Myra's house, and my butt's still sore. But that was the best Traffic Game ever!

Afterward I forgot to feel sad for a long time.

Love,

Kiwi

31 October—Halloween 2008

All day at school, kids talked about their costumes and where they were going trick-or-treating. Mom said I couldn't go because Myra's neighborhood isn't safe. I didn't have a costume anyway, and I didn't have anybody to go with. And that all sucks because *I love Halloween*!

I decided to make myself a costume anyway.

I asked Myra if she had any old clothes or sheets I could use. She gave me a rag box, and guess what I found? A Superman T-shirt. It was faded, with holes, but you could still see the big red S on the front. So I decided to be Super Girl!

I put the shirt on and it reached past my knees. The shoulders drooped, and the sleeves came down to my elbows. I asked Myra who in the world had worn that shirt, Shrek's big brother? She said, "Long story" and kind of grinned. Maybe she did use to have a boyfriend!

The Superman shirt went over red leggings, and I wore my regular sneakers for traction. For a cape, I used a shirt of Mom's and tied the sleeves around my neck. I'm not sure if Superman wore a mask, but Super Girl does. I made one out of paper, colored it black, and tied it on with one of my shoestrings.

It wasn't dark yet by the time I finished dressing up, so I went out to the front porch. I stood there with my hands on my hips, watching out over the world for people who needed saving, like children that were bullied or lost or orphans. Then I ran across the porch—it took only two steps—and jumped off the end like I was flying to the rescue! I pictured my cape billowing out behind me, but it just sort of hung on my back and didn't help much.

Myra had bought candy, so when it got dark, I stood at the door and waited to hand it out. She said not many kids usually came door to door on her street, and she was right. Only one kid came by. He was taller than I am and wearing all black for his costume. I asked him who he was supposed to be; he said something like *Barf Aider*. Why would anybody want to aid barf? That made me giggle, and he got mad and left. I didn't mean to hurt his feelings.

The rest of the night, Myra and I watched TV and ate Tootsie Rolls. Halloween had turned out okay after all—despite the marker I had used to color my mask leaving a black outline on my face that I can't get off.

Love,
Kiwi

(The next morning, before school.)

P.S.
Last night I had the bad dream. There was something dark and scary and alive hovering over me. With teeth. Sometimes the *Thing* is inside

28

me instead of outside, and I'm the dark scary thing. That's even worse. I woke up about to pee my pants.

I can't tell Mom about my dreams because she doesn't need the worry. She doesn't like to talk about scary things. Even B.R., she wouldn't talk about Dad dying. Whenever I asked a question about him, it made her cry. And A.R., she sure didn't want to talk about San Jose.

If that big dark *Thing* eats me up someday, my journal will be the only evidence of what happened to me.

Note to self: Do not ever again eat eighteen mini Tootsie Rolls before bedtime.

Chapter 4

Deep End of the Desert

LIBBY PRESSED THE cell phone to her ear and listened to the whirring of Justine's phone, three times, four. She clawed at her hair. Maybe Justine had gone to church or the grocery store. She didn't know much about her former mother-in-law's life. When Deacon was alive, they had visited his parents in Alabama every summer and Christmas. Like Libby, Deacon was an only child. That was the only thing from their upbringing they'd had in common. The Seager family home had high ceilings and floors that creaked when you got up in the night. Libby hadn't known what antebellum meant until then, but she'd liked the friendly old house and Kiwi loved it. Before she could walk, Kiwi had crawled up the tall stairs. She had no fear of falling.

Five rings, six . . .

Libby tried to remember the difference in time zones. Two hours later? Three? Justine lived alone in the big house now, comfortable enough on Social Security and her husband's retirement. Deacon's father hadn't lasted a year after his son was killed; Justine always claimed her husband died of a broken heart. Libby remembered thinking that you don't die of that, at least not suddenly. I'm living proof.

A woman's voice finally answered with a soft, "Hello?"

"Justine, is that you? It's Libby."

"Libby! It's good to hear from you." Justine cleared her throat, and her tone took on more life. "How is Kiwi?"

"She's fine. Says to tell you hi." The first white lie. Kiwi didn't know she was calling; Libby couldn't have her using up minutes on Myra's cell phone. "How have you been?"

"Okay. I'm . . . okay."

Libby heard the pause and wondered if Justine was having health problems. But she didn't ask. "I wanted to let you know we're not in San Jose anymore. I need to give you a new address to send the check." Deacon's government check, the blood money paid to families like hers. When Libby had moved off the Army post, she'd listed Justine's house as her permanent address.

"Let me get a pen that works," Justine said. Libby heard her rummaging. "Why did you leave San Jose? Better job?"

"Not exactly." She turned her back toward the kitchen and lowered her voice. "Listen, Justine, we had some trouble there. If anybody calls or comes around looking for me, anybody, please don't say where I am. Okay?"

"What kind of trouble, Libby?" Justine's voice sounded kind and concerned, like she wanted to help. That's the kind of person she was. She'd always been good to Libby, although they had nothing in common except their love for Deacon. Now all the two of them seemed to do was make each other sad.

"I can't talk about it right now," Libby said. "We're okay, though. Don't worry." She paced the matted carpet of Myra's living room. "Got your pen?"

"Ready."

Libby gave her Myra's address and zip code. "We're staying with a friend for now. I'll try to get a cell phone soon and let you know the number."

There was a pause on Justine's end. "I wish you'd come visit. You know you're welcome to stay with me as long as you want. Plenty of room in this big old house."

Libby hadn't been back to Deacon's childhood home since the funeral. An image of herself in black, an Army honor guard presenting her the flag from Deacon's casket, floated through her mind. The flag was folded into a tight triangle, just like her heart. When they'd placed it on her outstretched hands, she had been shocked by its heaviness. Afterward, she gave the flag to Justine. She couldn't stand to look at it but knew that Justine would treasure the flag and give it a place of honor in her home.

"I know," Libby said, "and I appreciate it." But police always look for fugitives with their relatives. "The trip's expensive, you know? When we get a place of our own, maybe you can come see us."

"Just let me know when."

That wouldn't be happening, Libby thought. Justine hated to fly. Even if Libby got her own place eventually, she couldn't see Justine making the trip to see them by herself.

The melancholy tone crept back into Justine's voice. "I'll bet Kiwi's growing like kudzu." Her only grandchild, and she hadn't seen Kiwi for nearly three years. Libby squeezed her eyes shut. "Did she get a school picture this year?" Justine asked. "I'd sure like to have one."

"I don't think they've taken them yet." Libby shifted the phone to the other side, sweeping her hair away from her face. "Listen, I'd better get off my friend's phone. If you'll send the checks, I'd appreciate it."

"There's one here now that I already had addressed to San Jose. It's a good thing you called today." Justine had been faithful about forwarding the money. And when she did, she always put in a trinket or a letter for Kiwi, sometimes both. That never failed to make Libby feel guilty, although she couldn't say why.

"All right then. Take care of yourself. I'll talk to you soon," Libby said. Another white lie.

"Give Kiwi a hug for me. Please tell her that Grandma loves her."

When Libby hung up, Deacon's face floated behind her eyes, relaxed and smiling, the way he was before his orders came, the way she liked to remember him. With the vision came the familiar ache, heavy and dark. She blew her nose viciously and crammed the tissue into her jeans pocket. No time for regrets; she couldn't be late for work.

She found Myra in the kitchen having her evening coffee. How did the woman sleep at night with all that caffeine? Two cups in the morning and Libby was as jumpy as a racehorse.

"Thanks for letting me use the phone," Libby said. "When my check gets here, I'll pay you some rent."

Myra's face remained as placid as a moon.

"No need," she said. "You can help with groceries if you want. Or not."

Libby nodded. "I will—as soon as the check comes."

The Sleepy Iguana was a dive, no other way to say it, and the pay was pathetic—minimum wage plus tips. But the place was within walking distance of Myra's house and Libby could wear jeans to work. On weekdays, the bar wasn't busy, but Shaun, the bartender who had hired her, had promised that the weekend tips were better.

Libby hoped so. Some places the weekend started on Thursday, but that didn't seem to be the case at the Sleepy Iguana. When her shift started at seven, only three customers slouched at the bar, drinking their dinner. Her section was empty; she felt useless, as if Shaun had hired her out of pity.

Libby pulled the iguana-logo T-shirt over her tank top and knotted the tail beside her hip. She circled through the bar, clearing off the leavings of lunch customers, wiping off the faux-wood tops. Upstairs in a private room, a better class of losers hung out and gambled, and the tips were bigger. But the other waitress, Denise, worked the private room, and Libby stayed downstairs. Denise wore long earrings and short skirts to work, showing off well-defined calves she'd earned by lugging trays of drinks and nachos up the staircase for two years.

Libby picked up a pair of beer mugs and carried them behind the bar. Plunging them into soapy water, she thought about Myra's offer to get her on at the warehouse where she worked. Libby could do filing and inventory or maybe learn to drive a forklift for even better pay. But the company required a background check and a social security number.

She couldn't take the chance. She hadn't told Myra why, and thankfully, Myra didn't ask.

Denise swung down the stairs, an empty tray hanging from one hand. She waved and Libby waved back. Upstairs, a TV blared, but the poker game hadn't started yet. Denise leaned on the bar, flirting with Shaun in a harmless way. She was married to a race-car driver who was trying to break into the big time and probably would be trying forever.

Shaun, the manager as well as the bartender, rode a motorcycle to work. He had a slow, easy smile, but his eyes watched Libby in a way that made her ill at ease. His wasn't a sexual look exactly, more like he was trying to figure her out. That was what made her nervous.

The front door opened, flashing the last rays of daylight across the dusty floor. A man and woman wandered to a table in the back corner. Glad for a customer, Libby gave them a few seconds to get settled and then went over, forcing a smile.

"Hi, folks. What can I get you?"

"Anchor Steam, in a bottle," the guy said. He was porky and partially bald, with the club-shaped nose of a regular drinker. Maybe they would run a big tab.

Libby looked at his companion then—and froze.

The woman had a pinched mouth and short, garish hair that stood out like a bad aura around her face. And her face was the face of Libby's dead mother.

Libby stepped back from the table. At home, in a cedar box, she'd saved a newspaper clip identifying her mother as the driver of a car that had plunged off a mountain road in the lower Cascades. DUI. Yet here was Dayleen in a dusty bar in the desert, light-years away.

Then the woman smiled and the illusion was broken. Her eyes weren't as hard as Dayleen's, and there was no chip on her front tooth. "Whatever lite beer you have on tap," the woman said. Dayleen would have ordered bourbon and Coke.

Libby's heartbeat was still ragged as she stood beside the bar and waited for Shaun to set up the beers. Her eyes lost focus, and she remembered a low-rent flat, a kitchen table with chrome legs and a scarred top. She saw her mother's booze-glazed eyes as she'd lurched to her feet, yelling curses at her daughter, the chair toppling behind her. Libby had yelled back, and now her jaw ached with the memory. That night, part of her had receded like an out-of-body experience. She had seen their ugliness; they were over-the-top actors in a play any normal person would walk out of. And Libby did walk. That had been their last fight, the last time she had seen her mother. Libby had been sixteen.

Shaun's voice came to her through the fog. "You okay?"

She blinked at him and pushed a strand of hair behind her ear. Her face felt damp. "I'm fine." She reached for the drinks he'd set on the bar.

"The Ghost of Nightmares Past," he said, his smile ironic.

The comment surprised her. She gave him a weak smile and wondered how he knew.

She returned to the couple and managed to set down their beers without spilling them or looking at the woman's face. The porky man ordered nachos and another round. Libby brought a clean ashtray and remembered to smile. Two blue-collar guys in their forties came in and sat at a table in front. She heaved a deep breath, glad for the customers. Maybe she would earn some tips tonight after all.

She joined Denise at the service end of the bar, waiting while Shaun filled their orders and Denise sneaked a smoke. "What's the story on Shaun?" Libby asked, keeping her voice low.

Denise shrugged and exhaled a stream of menthol-scented smoke. "He doesn't talk about himself. Lives alone as far as I know. Jimmy talked to him one night and says he's single." She narrowed her eyes at Libby. "You interested?"

"In Shaun? No way. Just curious."

"Right." Denise smiled and stubbed out the cigarette. She turned away and followed two new customers up the stairs.

Just before midnight, the couple at the corner table finally left. They shouldn't have been driving, but that wasn't Libby's problem. She stacked the nacho platter and glasses. When she picked up the tip, she sighed and held it up for Shaun to see. He grinned and shook his head. After eating and drinking for four hours, Porky had left her one dollar.

Libby looked at the crumpled bill: Was this what her life was worth?

Chapter 5

Dreams of Deacon

LIBBY SAT UP IN THE dark with a blue-black headache. She kicked off the top sheet and winced, her scalp strung as tight as high-voltage wire. Each heartbeat throbbed in her eyeballs. Beside her, Kiwi slept with her lips parted and her breath even. Libby envied her sleep. Maybe kids were immune from a guilty conscience. Libby couldn't remember ever being that young.

Over-the-counter sleep aids had stopped working months ago, and in San Jose she'd tried the kind of drugs you don't get at a drugstore. Those knocked her out but made waking up a different hell. Last night, she'd used vodka. The result was a wretched headache and a nightmare that felt like a bullet to the chest.

She eased herself upright on the edge of the bed and closed her eyes. The dream replayed in her head: Deacon was deployed and her car had broken down. She was stranded and couldn't pick up Kiwi from school. It was the kind of problem mothers dealt with every day, but Libby couldn't cope. In the skewed logic of dreams, she had phoned Deacon in Iraq. He was frustrated and angry: What could he do about it from there? Military wives had to be strong, he told her. They had to take charge while their husbands were deployed overseas. Was she neglecting Kiwi? Then the dream shifted, and she was hunting for pieces of his body in a Baghdad slum. Her phone call had distracted him; his Jeep had run over an IED. It was her fault.

Libby ran to the bathroom and retched into the commode. She held her hair out of the water and threw up again, her head alive with pain. When the spasms stopped, she sat back on her heels and wept.

The dream was wrong, dammit. Deacon wouldn't have been angry or accusing. That's not who he was. He would have stayed calm and explained what to do about the car, the way he always did. And she had not talked to him the day he was killed.

At the sink, she splashed water on her face and searched Myra's medicine cabinet for aspirin. She clutched three tablets but couldn't make herself drink water from a bathroom tap, an aversion left over from the slovenly bathrooms of her childhood. She padded into the kitchen, filled a glass of water, and swallowed, feeling the pills and cold water all the way down. Work fast. Please work fast.

The house was eerily silent. She stood at the kitchen window and looked out into the tiny backyard, bleached by moonlight. A rusty shovel stood among desert weeds, as if Myra had once thought of gardening but abandoned the idea mid-dig. A panel of wood fencing sagged inward, exposing a black dog asleep on the neighbor's porch.

Libby felt a sharp longing for damp ocean breezes and the smell of saltwater. Perhaps that was the reason she couldn't seem to leave California. She had come to its tattered edge and stopped.

The dream was wrong about Deacon. But it was only too right about her—she was hopeless.

Libby had been on her own for two years when she met Deacon. At eighteen, her history already included three men who were losers, the first being her father. He'd married her mother because she was pregnant. Most of Libby's childhood memories were of her parents' drinking and fighting; sometimes those fights got physical. When she was ten, her father divorced Dayleen and moved to another state. Libby never saw or heard from him again. Dayleen's downward spiral escalated until Libby left her too.

Libby had spent those first two weeks on the street, scared and hungry, before moving in with a guy her age who had dropped out of school the year before. Brent was a stoner, but at least he was nonviolent. Libby dropped out too. But a guidance counselor tracked her down and threatened foster care unless she saw a shrink and stayed in school. The shrink had a greasy smile and puffy eyes. Libby hated him.

Brent lived like a pig, and Libby suspected he was stealing to pay for his weed. Eventually she moved in with the manager of a coffee shop where she'd been working. Luke was mid-twenties and handsome, with an inflated idea of his own abilities. Soon he decided to head north for imagined opportunities, and Libby tagged along. She had passed her GED by then, and there was nothing to keep her in Oregon. On the way to Washington, Luke stopped for a hitchhiker who gave Libby the creeps. When she objected to giving him a ride, Luke left her at a fast-food place on the outskirts of Fort Lewis. Luke and the hitchhiker moved on.

The restaurant had a help-wanted sign in the window, and Libby applied on the spot. The female manager gave her a job and a ride to the local women's shelter. Weeks turned into months. Libby couldn't afford an apartment on minimum wage, and she didn't have enough education or experience to get a better job. One morning she looked in the stained mirror at the shelter and wondered if she could scrape up enough pills to overdose or at least the courage to jump off the river bridge.

That was her frame of mind when a local redneck showed up on her evening shift and started to give her a hard time because his fries were cold. Never mind that he'd already eaten half of them before he decided to complain. His alcohol-glazed eyes reminded Libby of her father, but she did her best to placate the man because she needed the job. She offered to replace the order. But the customer just kept on yelling, using the f-word, and holding up the line until she finally had had enough. Enough of him, enough of the job, enough of sorry-assed men.

She leaned in. "Mister, why don't you light a match to your bourbon breath and heat up the fries yourself?"

The man's face inflamed, and he reached across the counter and grabbed her wrist, twisting her arm hard. Before either of them knew what was happening, the soldier who was next in line had jerked the guy's arm off Libby, behind his own back, and up between his shoulder blades.

Libby caught her breath, expecting a fight and to get fired. The soldier was two inches shorter than her assailant but solid muscle, with an air of moral superiority that silenced the room. He kept the guy's arm pinned between his shoulder blades, one leg blocking his knee so he couldn't move.

"I'm sure you don't want trouble," the soldier said calmly, "and neither does this young lady who's just trying to do her job here. Cold fries don't give you the right to put your hands on her." Libby saw his grip on the man's arm tighten, just enough to make the man wince.

The unruly customer, aware of the glares from the other patrons and the steel in the soldier's jaw, said grudgingly, "Okay."

"Then why don't you apologize and accept the hot fries she offered?" the soldier said.

"I don't want the damned fries. I don't want nothin' from this place." With that, the man pulled his arm free and made for the door. "I'll never eat here again!"

The customers applauded.

The incident was all over in a matter of seconds.

Plenty of soldiers from Fort Lewis came into the restaurant, and mostly they looked alike to Libby. But this impromptu hero had a smile that sent a thrill down her arms. No man had ever stood up for her. She didn't trust uniforms. Yet here was a clean-cut guy in camo, taking her side without a thing to gain from it.

"Are you okay?" he asked.

She rubbed her wrist where red fingerprints remained. "I'm fine. Thanks."

"My name's Deacon."

She smiled back. "I'm Libby. Your order, soldier, is on the house."

Luckily the manager agreed, so Libby didn't have to deduct the burger and fries from her paycheck.

Deacon stopped by frequently after that. Sometimes he'd already eaten at the mess hall and came just to have coffee and talk with her on her break. Libby was soon infatuated but also suspicious. She couldn't figure out why he liked her; the attraction made no sense. One day she told him that, straight out. He said she should think more of herself. By the time he asked her on a date, she was already in love.

Libby had no frame of reference for a normal marriage. Deacon did not yell. When they argued, he wanted to talk through the problem without placing blame, a skill foreign to Libby. Shouting and slamming doors had been standard weapons in her mother's house, where nothing was ever settled. Gradually, however, she learned to trust that he wouldn't hit her or leave her. With Deacon, love wasn't a competition; they were on the same team. Even when she accidentally became pregnant their first year of marriage, he wasn't angry. He bought cigars for his friends.

Deacon was selected for officer candidate school and decided to make the Army a career. There were good years, before 9/11, before the hijackings that sent planes into Manhattan's Twin Towers, the Pentagon in D.C., and a Pennsylvania pasture. She tried hard to learn how to be a good parent, but motherhood didn't come naturally. Showing affection to her daughter was awkward; she had no model for such behavior. Little wonder that Kiwi worshipped her father, who could make her squeal with joy. Libby tried not to feel left out when Deacon came home and Kiwi jumped into his arms. Libby wanted to do the same.

In the dark of Myra's tiny kitchen, Libby recalled the safety of her husband's arms, and the crescent-shaped scar on his chin, a mark she had loved to kiss. She laid her forehead against the cabinets and ached for him. How could he be gone? Nearly three years, and still his absence was a deep open wound.

From the cupboard over the refrigerator Libby took down Myra's bottle of vodka. Hair of the dog. She poured a good inch in the water glass and swallowed the fire. She'd have to replace the bottle soon, maybe snag one from work. She poured again before putting the bot-tle away.

When Deacon was alive and loved her, she was a better person. Without him, she had reverted to the sorry creature she'd been before they met.

Libby woke to Myra making coffee. She had dozed off on the sofa in the living room, and now daylight knifed between the curtains. A few minutes later, she heard Kiwi get up and thump down the hall to the bathroom, her footsteps hollow on thin carpet. Libby wanted to get up and move to the bedroom, sink into the cool sheets and sleep, but her limbs were filled with sand.

She dozed off again, and the next time she roused, Kiwi and Myra were at the kitchen table. She could hear their low voices, their spoons clinking against cereal bowls. How the two of them found things to talk about never ceased to amaze her.

Libby dragged herself from the sofa and headed to the bathroom. She had a crick in her neck and her head felt like a foreign hemisphere. She washed her face, brushed her teeth and tongue, pulled a brush through her hair, and walked to the kitchen in her mismatched pajamas.

Kiwi glanced up as she came in. Already dressed for school, she took in Libby's sour look and mood, although her expression stayed blank.

"Morning, Mom."

Myra looked up, too, but said nothing. Libby poured a cup of coffee and joined them.

"Do something with that hair before you go," she told Kiwi.

"Would you fix me a ponytail?"

Libby cupped her hand over the coffee mug and felt the warmth. "You can do a ponytail. You don't need me."

"I know, but you do it better."

When she was younger, Kiwi used to complain and twist away when Libby fixed her hair. Now, if Libby was up early enough, Kiwi would beg her to do it and never said a word or even flinched if she pulled too hard. What the hell. She had tried to teach Kiwi to be self-sufficient; maybe she had gone too far.

"Comb the tangles out first," Libby said.

Kiwi drained the last bits of cereal and milk, set her bowl in the sink, and trotted to the bedroom. She's getting tall, Libby thought, but height was relative. Neither Deacon nor Libby had given her tall genes. Kiwi still looked small next to her classmates.

Myra looked at Libby over the rim of her cup. "Rough night?"

"Ummm."

"Vodka will do that."

"So will living." The caffeine in the coffee was beginning to help. Libby only wished it was stronger.

"It's my night to work late," Myra said. "Will Kiwi be okay until I get back? Should be about ten."

Libby would have to leave at 6:45 p.m. for her shift at the bar. More than three hours' difference, but it wasn't Myra's job to babysit. "Sure. She's used to it."

"I don't like her being here alone at night," Myra said.

"Neither do I."

On Libby's last evening off, she and Myra had sat at this very same table having a drink while Kiwi watched TV. No one was more surprised than Libby when, by the second drink, she had told Myra about running away from home at sixteen. Come to find out, Myra's story had been different but had ended the same.

Throughout high school, she had hidden her sexual orientation. On the eve of graduation, emboldened by her standing as class salutatorian, she had sat her parents down and told them she was lesbian. The next night, she crossed the stage wearing a black eye with her cap and gown. While her classmates partied afterward, Myra had loaded her clothes into her used Volkswagen and driven away. She did a tour in the Army, worked her way through business school, and never went home again. Libby wondered if she'd been taking in strays ever since, searching for family.

Myra cleared away her cereal bowl. "They still haven't filled that opening at the warehouse," she said. "It's eight to five, plus one night a week." She picked up her jacket and keys and left without speaking again, locking the kitchen door behind her.

Kiwi returned then with her hairbrush and a pink scrunchie. She flopped down between Libby's feet. With long strokes, Libby began to brush her daughter's hair back from her forehead. In her left hand, she gathered the strands into a soft rope, sable brown and highlighted by the sun.

The ponytail hung in a determined spiral past Kiwi's shoulder blades. When did her hair get so long?

Sufficiently caffeinated, Libby offered to walk Kiwi to school. The fresh air would do her good; she could come back and try to get a little more sleep.

The desert mornings were cool, but the days warmed drastically by afternoon, even a month before Christmas. Western Oregon, where Libby had grown up, would have snow on the mountains by now. She didn't miss the cold, only the smell of it and the memory of silver-blue sparkles of diamond dust on the slopes. A rare pure memory from her childhood.

Kiwi walked beside her quietly, her backpack bumping against her back. At her age, she ought to be hopscotching cracks in the sidewalk, Libby thought. She had expected behavior problems after San Jose, but there had been no tantrums or crying jags. Kiwi didn't complain or argue nearly as much as she used to. And she had become far too serious.

Their steps echoed on the sidewalk.

"Everything going okay at school?"

Kiwi shrugged. "Sure. Why wouldn't it?"

"I don't know. New school, new kids."

"You could come inside this morning and meet Mr. Mathis, my science teacher."

Hopeful little eyes turned upward toward Libby.

Libby gestured at her faded sweat pants and unwashed hair. "I'm not dressed to meet your teachers."

"You look fine," Kiwi said. Then, "Whatever."

A few months ago, she would have haggled relentlessly to get what she wanted. Her quick retreat sent off alarm bells.

"They're going to have an open house for Christmas," Kiwi said. "Maybe you could come then?"

Libby frowned; she had no desire to meet Kiwi's teachers. The idea of dressing up and trying to make a responsible impression was exhausting.

"The check came yesterday," she said, changing the subject. "What would you like for Christmas?"

Kiwi thought about it a few steps. "Could I get my ears pierced? I'm the only girl in my class who doesn't have them."

"It kind of hurts, you know."

"I know." Kiwi shrugged again. She was doing that too much. "Karen told me about getting hers done. She said it wasn't too bad."

Libby hadn't heard of this Karen person before but assumed she was in Kiwi's class. "Okay then. Maybe next Monday when I'm off work. And afterward, we can pick out a couple pairs of cute earrings."

"Sweet!" Kiwi did a little hop, and Libby smiled.

They had reached the corner of the elementary school campus.

"Gotta go," Kiwi said. "Thanks for walking with me."

Libby watched her go, the backpack still bouncing. Kiwi's request for pierced ears made her feel better. That was normal, something little girls always wanted. But as she went to leave, Kiwi turned back with that old-soul look on her face.

"You should get some sleep before work, Mom. You look tired."

Black specks crawled across Libby's vision. She saw a weekend morning, a family of three planning a picnic and trip to the zoo. A little girl with wild hair and chubby knees bouncing in her chair, eyes full of morning sun: "If we're going to do everything, we'd better hurry up!"

For a disembodied moment, Libby did not recognize the lanky girl standing on the sidewalk, looking back at her with troubled eyes. Who was this child?

Chapter 6

Kiwi's Journal

3 November 2008

MR. MATHIS IS NOT AS old as most teachers. He's always making jokes, and some of the kids don't get them, but I do. When I laugh, he winks at me. I like science, so we get along great.

Mr. Mathis also discusses serious matters with us, which I also like. The other day we were talking in class about the word *hate*. Mr. Mathis said *hate* is a four-letter word. He meant a bad word like *shit* or *bitch*, although that last one is actually five letters but sounds even worse, if you ask me.

Kids at our school are always saying they *hate* math or they *hate* some other kid. But Mr. Mathis said *hate* is one of the meanest of the bad words, and he won't allow it in his classroom. He said it's not right to hate other people, no matter how different they are from you. He said hate is one of the main causes of crime and wars.

I thought about that quite a while. I *hated* Rocket. Who wouldn't? He was mean and awful. But if I hadn't given in to hate, maybe what happened wouldn't have happened, and I wouldn't now be doomed to hell. But then I thought—if it didn't happen, we'd still be living in his apartment in San Jose. Hell can't be much worse than that, just hotter.

I thought about my dad too. As far as I know, he never hated anyone or anything. Maybe Brussels sprouts, but that shouldn't count against anybody. He'll be in heaven for sure, so I'll never get to see him again. Dad got killed in a country halfway around the world, where people kept setting off bombs for no good reason. He was blown to bits—we weren't even allowed to see him when they shipped him home. They gathered up his parts and closed him up in a casket. But you don't need your body in heaven, just your soul.

I have a picture of us together that was taken right before he left. He's in his uniform and that nerdy hat the Army makes you wear, and he's smiling like he has no idea he's going to get killed in just a few months.

I asked Mr. Mathis if hate caused the war in Iraq. He said it was more complicated than that, but it started with hate. So I'm not going to use that word anymore. Period. But I *strongly dislike* the people who killed my dad.

Love,
Kiwi

7 November

When Mom and I left San Jose, I decided to write down everything that happened from then on in my journal. That way if I died suddenly by surprise, there would be a record of my life. If my dad had kept a journal, I could read it now and find out what kind of kid he was, and what scared him or worried him. I could find out what he did every day in Iraq and what it was like over there.

I keep my journal in my backpack or hidden someplace. Nobody else gets to read it, ever. Mom doesn't ask or bug me to see it either—for one, she promised not to, but also, she has something she keeps private too. Hers is a little cedar box. On top, in black cursive writing, it says Royal Gorge. Daddy got it for her when they were on their honeymoon.

So it's older than I am. The box has a little gold lock, and the key is on a charm bracelet that Mom wears all the time, even when she's sleeping. Once I asked Mom what she kept in the Royal Gorge box, and she said memories.

Thanksgiving is almost here, so at school this week, my language arts teacher had us write about home and what it means to us. When I think of home, I think of my Grandma Seager's house in Alabama. It's the exact opposite of temporary. Her house was built before the Civil War, for crying out loud. I remember a wooden staircase that went up forever. And a big front porch with a swing. Not a kid swing, but the kind old people sit on.

My grandpa died when I was in fourth grade, and I didn't even know it until he was already buried. I can't remember his face anymore, but I remember he smelled good and had little soft hairs that stuck out at the neck of his plaid shirt. I think he laughed a lot, but I might have made up that part.

One summer when I was little, I was sitting on the porch swing with my grandma. Mom and Dad and Grandpa were there too. As it started to get dark, lightning bugs floated up from the grass. It was like watching for stars to come out. There were just a few of them at first, then more and more until the whole yard was twinkling tiny lights. Grandpa kept slapping his arms; he said what we thought were lightning bugs were really mosquitoes looking for us with flashlights.

I wonder if Mom has that memory in her Royal Gorge box.

Love,

Kiwi

10 November
(Note: Colons are my favorite punctuation. We studied them this week in language arts.)

One thing about knowing you're going to hell when you die: Nothing else can scare you much. I'm not afraid of monster movies anymore, or spiders, snakes, or scorpions. Or tarantulas, which supposedly live here in the desert, although I've never seen one. I brought home a whole armful of library books about insects and arachnids this week.

I'd like to see a tarantula, actually. Not in a cage, but outside walking along on all those hairy legs. I've seen them on TV and once in a terrarium at my old school: but never in the wild. Once I kept a grass spider in a big jar for two weeks. The spider was a female, I'm pretty sure, because she was so big. In spiderdom, the girls are usually bigger. She was beautiful, too, with brown and yellow stripes down her back like Charlotte in *Charlotte's Web*. I wanted to watch her lay eggs, and in the fall, see the teensy spiderlings hatch out. But when I told Mom that sometimes the adult spiders eat their own young, she made me turn the spider loose outside. Actually she wanted me to step on her, but we compromised.

I'm not eager to meet a scorpion outdoors on its own. When we had our video phone call with Dad from Iraq, he said he'd seen a black scorpion that was six inches long. He said the scorpions come out at night, so they're hard to see. No trips to the bathroom in bare feet in Iraq, that's for sure. Unfortunately, I cried all through the video chat, so I couldn't ask any questions.

If I grow up, I'd like to have a job like that girl on the animal channel, the one whose dad was killed by a stingray. She gets to be on TV and talk about animals and handle all kinds of reptiles and insects. She doesn't seem afraid of anything, but she'll probably get bitten by something and die young like me. Only I'll bet she's never done anything bad enough that she'll have to go to hell. I kind of wish she would: then I'd have at least one friend down there.

I figure I will die way short of the 80.4 years that's the national life expectancy for women. I looked that up on the internet at the library. My goal is to see that Mom gets settled before I go, so maybe she can reach the national average. She's had a pretty crappy life, some of which is my fault and some of which is not. My last wish is to make her love me again before I go off to eternal damnation. I think that would be good for both of us.

But I don't know if she ever could again.

My dad used to tell me not to make excuses when I did something wrong, but I would like to say that there are worse people than me in the world. I did something terrible, but I'm not actually mean, like a certain person I used to know: who is the same one I did something terrible to in San Jose. I don't like hurting people, and except for the one time, I've tried not to. I'm hoping my good intentions earn some bonus points with God. Maybe he'll let me out of hell after, like, 250 years.

Sometimes at night I think about what hell's going to be like. I'm not sure I believe the fire-and-torture stuff. I can't picture God being that cruel. The priest at the church on post said God loves us even when we sin. It doesn't seem logical that a God who loves us and can forgive us anything if we ask him would also torture people with fire, especially little kids. Either:

(a) he doesn't love us all that much

or

(b) hell has been greatly exaggerated.

But who knows? Someday maybe I'll ask God to forgive me and see what happens. Father Bastoni said you have to be truly sorry for what you did. And I'm not. I think eventually I will be, but not yet. I still remember too much about Rocket.

For me, the scariest thing about hell isn't the fire, it's the possibility I'll bump into him, into Rocket. What if he spends eternity chasing me around, trying to get even? There ought to be separate compartments in hell so the evil kids don't have to hang around the evil grown-ups. Then again, there probably aren't many kids in hell. Most people don't do really bad stuff until later in life. I'm a prodigy.

If I see Rocket in hell, I wonder if he'd still have that hole in his neck. If it was heaven, he'd be all healed up, but I doubt if anything heals up in hell.

Stop! That's enough thinking about hell.

Here's my big good news: I got a job!

This town has a weekly newspaper that comes out on Fridays. And kids deliver the papers door to door after school. So I signed up to be a paper girl. Once again, it would sure help to have a bike. But for now, I walk my route. The newspapers aren't very heavy, and they gave me a big canvas bag to carry them. I still can't carry them all at once. So I make two trips. And I have to fold the papers first.

The papers were waiting for me on Myra's porch when I got home from school today. Mom was out looking for a place of our own; she says the town is short on apartments, and we can't afford the rent for a house. I kind of hope we don't move, because I like Myra.

I rolled my papers, put a rubber band around each one, and then loaded them into the bag. When I finished, my hands were all black. I washed up and then slung the bag over my shoulder and took off. My route is the eight blocks around Myra's house.

Mom doesn't like me walking through this area by myself, but Myra and I talked her into it. Myra asked her neighbor down the block to keep an eye on me, so I can run to that house if somebody starts to bother me. The neighbor's name is Mrs. Joy Wolfing. Myra introduced us and Mrs. Wolfing said I could call her Joy. She's young and big. I think maybe she's pregnant, but it's hard to tell. And I wouldn't want to ask because she might be just fat.

So today was the first time I did the route on my own. The paper is free and every house gets one. I toss it by their front doors. That's a lot of throwing, and tonight my throwing arm is sore. I wish I had a dog to go with me: He could trot along and sniff all the bushes and keep any unfriendly dogs away.

At the end of the month, I'm supposed to get ten dollars for every Friday that I delivered papers. I should get twenty dollars at the end of November, and I'm going to use it to buy something for Mom and Myra for Christmas. After that, I'll save up for a bike.

I'm beginning to get used to Sand Flats. I hope we stay for a while.
Kiwi

17 November

Myra has a whole box of cool CDs, and after school today, I was digging through them, just looking to see what kind of music she had. Myra didn't seem to care, but I forgot to ask permission and Mom went off on me. I think she's afraid that if I get on Myra's nerves, she'll kick us out.

It wasn't fair for her to yell at me in front of Myra. I didn't mean to do anything wrong. But then again, I never do: It just happens. I was embarrassed, but I didn't cry. After Mom went to work, however, I was so jumpy I tipped over my milk. Myra helped me mop it up and told me not to worry about a little spill. She's a little weird but nice through and through.

Myra had to go out tonight, so I'm by myself. I've been staying home alone for a couple of years, so no big deal. I'd finished all my library books, so I turned on a reality TV show. Reality shows are silly, but sometimes I like to see other families that are as screwed up as mine. I like crime shows too, but not when I'm alone in the house. Tonight all the TV shows that were on were boring, so I turned the television off. My stomach still hurt from being yelled at.

The house got real quiet, and then I heard crackling sounds from the roof like somebody was walking around up there. Then the faucet in the kitchen started to drip, but off and on with no warning, so I couldn't get used to it. I heard a train way off somewhere and a dog barking. I wondered if that gangsta guy in the lowrider had a dog, and if he lived close. I tried not to think about him too much.

Mom had told me to take a bath before bedtime. Myra's house is old, and she doesn't have a shower. But her house is also the cleanest place we've stayed for a long time, so I don't mind getting in the tub. There's a radio in there, too, on a shelf above the bathtub, so you can listen to music while you soak. I turned my favorite country station on loud enough that I couldn't hear the creaking roof or the dang faucet.

Myra had some bubble bath on the shelf, and I was pretty sure she wouldn't have cared if I used some. But I didn't want to get in trouble again. So I resisted. I locked the door, ran the tub half full, and got in. A girl was singing through her nose about some guy who'd cheated on her and how she wished he'd go to hell. If he did, I'd see him there.

I scooted way down in the water and then wished I had checked to see if the outside doors were locked. There are two, the front door and one out of the kitchen that goes to the carport. Myra had probably locked up when she left. Or so I hoped. I laid my head back and floated my hair in the water. I looked like brown kelp. Once I saw a sea otter floating on its back in a kelp bed. The otter was so cute I wanted to pick it up and hug it. But if I had, it would probably have bitten me. If there's one thing I've learned, it's that you can't trust what happens next.

Myra's bathroom ceiling is brownish-white with thousands of little bumps, like ceiling warts. The front legs of the radio barely fit on the shelf. The cord drooped behind me near a plug-in by the sink. It looked kind of dangerous. If somebody were to knock the shelf when she got in the tub or catch something on the cord and the radio fell in, wouldn't she be electrocuted?

I wondered how bad electricity zipping through your body might feel. Would sparks fly out or the water turn all jittery like a hot tub? Maybe you'd turn black and ashy like when a cartoon character gets struck by lightning on TV.

I could take one hand out of the water and just reach the cord. So I did. I lay there soaking and feeling sorry for myself, holding the smooth brown cord in my fingertips. A new singer came on the radio, with the kind of deep and lonesome voice that makes your stomach feel empty. I pictured Mom's face when I got in trouble, all red and angry and disappointed in me. It was horrible. But when I'm not in trouble, her eyes look empty, like she doesn't see me at all. I don't know which is worse.

I gave the cord a little tug, but the radio didn't move. So I wound the cord through my fingers, and tugged a little harder.

The radio wiggled and one leg scooted off the edge . . . *thunk*. That thunk made my heart feel skittish, and I thought of those wild horses we had seen beside the highway. So pretty and nervous and all the time needing to run—just like Mom. But she can't run free because of me. Then I thought about Dad and how I wished he could come back to us.

My throat felt as if I'd swallowed a whole potato. My arm jerked, and the radio teetered on the edge of the shelf. My ears started to ring and I found it hard to breathe.

Then I heard a noise. I thought it was in the house.

Maybe the front door? I untangled my fingers from the cord—very carefully—and sat up in the tub.

"Anybody there?" I yelled.

Nobody answered. I waited and waited, but I didn't hear the noise again. I decided to get out of the tub and get dressed. I had goose bumps all over and my skin was shriveled like a raisin.

After I dried off and found something to sleep in, I made sure both outside doors were locked. They were, and I gave a quick thank-you to Myra even though she wasn't home. Now I'm on the couch writing about my night home alone. The sofa cushions smell like somebody who doesn't live here anymore. It's not a bad smell, but kind of moldy and old. My hair's still damp, and I'm wrapped up in my blanket. I found a *SpongeBob* rerun on TV. I've seen them all a gazillion times and know the dialogue by heart. Old Square Pants is my best friend.

I think I'll sleep here on the couch tonight so I'll be sure to know when Mom comes home.

Love,
Kiwi

25 November

I've been thinking a lot about my dad. Here's what I remember about him: He was medium tall and had thick shoulders. His hair was short like black whiskers all over his head, but it felt soft. Mom says I got my curly hair from him, but his hair was too short to curl. Most of the time, he wore his camo uniform and boots, except on weekends, when he always wore shorts—even if it was cold outside.

The face is the most important part of a person, and you'd think that's the part you'd remember best. But when I picture my dad in my mind I can see his body just fine, but his face is a blur. The only way I can recall him is by looking at pictures. I *strongly dislike* that I can't imagine his face.

Yesterday was Mom's birthday. Dad and I used to make the best birthday surprises for her. But I came home to a note that said Mom was meeting Myra for a beer after Myra got off work. It was Mom's day off, and the note said they'd be home by dinnertime. I didn't have a present for her yet. So I decided to fix a surprise birthday dinner. I thought Dad would like that.

Myra doesn't cook much, but I searched the kitchen and found a box of macaroni and cheese and a can of peas. A main course and a vegetable! I also found a brownie mix that could substitute for a birthday cake. Mom loves chocolate. Who doesn't?

Myra has a gas stove. I had never used one of those before, so I thought it wise to test it out. I turned a knob and whoosh! The burner lit up with fire. I turned it off quick. I figured the oven must work the same way, so I turned the oven dial to 350 like the brownie box said. I didn't see any flames, but I figured the fire was kept underneath the oven someplace. I dumped the brownie mix into a bowl and stirred in one egg and a cup and a half of milk. The batter was dark brown and tasted awesome. This birthday dinner was going to be wicked good. Mom and Myra would be so surprised!

That's when I caught whiff of a funny smell coming from the oven. I figured something had spilled in there the last time and was burning off. If Myra never used it, chances are she never cleaned it either.

I couldn't find a baking pan, but I did find a skillet without a plastic handle. I couldn't find any of that spray stuff to keep the batter from sticking to the pan. But I'd seen Mom rub a pan with margarine, so I did that. I poured the batter in the skillet and slid the skillet into the oven. The oven didn't seem very hot, and it smelled like a dead mouse. I figured it would heat up eventually.

I moved on to the mac and cheese. The directions said to boil a pan of water. This time I turned the front burner knob very slowly, set the pan on the burner, and assembled my ingredients: milk, margarine, macaroni, and the cheese gunk that came in the box. Do you know how long it takes a pan of water to boil? Forever!

I waited and waited, and finally decided to check on the brownies. The only smell coming from the oven was that original funky odor. The oven light was out, so I opened the door to see inside.

Whoosh! A big ball of fire flashed right in my face!

I fell back on my butt. I couldn't see anything—I'd gone blind! My eyes filled up with tears and my ears were ringing. Something smelled burned. I gagged. My heart was hammering so hard in my chest that I couldn't breathe. It took a bit, but my ears finally stopped ringing. The house fell quiet. I could hear the *sssssssssss* of the water boiling on top of the stove.

I batted my eyes. I wasn't blind after all! I could see chocolate batter splattered inside the oven. And on the floor and on me. My face felt kind of crunchy, and when I put my hand up to my forehead—my bangs were gone! Nothing left but little stubby hairs in front, like my dad's. I couldn't feel my eyelashes, either.

Luckily, nothing else had caught fire. But my mom's birthday surprise was ruined. I wiped brownie batter off my chin. It still tasted good.

I could now see flames coming through two holes in the bottom of the oven. I guess the explosion ignited the burner. I turned the oven off and the flames went out. I was trying to wipe up all the brownie batter splatter when Mom and Myra got home.

Mom took one look and started to yell at me. That continued for what felt like hours. She seemed both scared and mad; I was just scared. And toasted. Myra stayed out of it and went to her room, but I could swear she looked as if she was trying not to laugh. I was glad she didn't seem upset about the mess I'd made of her kitchen.

My cleanup efforts were going poorly, so Mom eventually pitched in. Every so often, she'd yell some more. When we finally went to bed, she turned her back and wouldn't talk to me.

I whispered *Happy birthday*, but I don't know if she heard me.

The next day, Myra said we didn't have to move out, but Mom said, yeah, we better, before I burned down her house. Today is Saturday, and she's gone apartment shopping again. I wanted to go with her but didn't dare ask. Maybe she thought I'd scare the landlords.

I have a bright red face and my eyes look naked, like a fish's. Can't wait to go to school on Monday and have everybody make fun of me.

I gave Mom a surprise for her birthday, all right. One more reason for her to wish I wasn't her kid.

Love:

Kiwi the Royal Screwup

Chapter 7

Libby and the Bartender

AFTER KIWI'S ACCIDENT in Myra's kitchen, Libby intensified her search for an apartment. There wasn't much to choose from in the small town. The places she could afford were run-down and didn't feel safe. Libby mentioned this to Denise one night standing at the bar while Shaun loaded a tray with nachos and beer.

"What's wrong with staying at Myra's?" Denise asked.

"Nothing, but I can't mooch off her forever." She didn't mention Kiwi nearly burning Myra's house down. Or that if she stayed there much longer, some evening when they were drinking and confiding, she might tell Myra about San Jose.

That couldn't happen.

"Not much demand for housing around here," Denise said with a shrug. "Nobody moves to Sand Flats on purpose."

She ended the remark with a look that asked *Why did you?* Even if Libby had felt obliged to respond, which she didn't, she had no good answer for that question.

Denise picked up the tray of beer and nachos and headed up the stairs, toned calves flexing below her miniskirt. Laughter and the click of plastic chips drifted down in her wake; the Thursday night poker game was starting. Libby wondered if Danny Wyman would show up. He usually did on poker night.

Libby had met Danny one evening when Denise was sick and Libby was handling both stations. After that, Danny started to hang around downstairs, flirting with her between beers. He was older than Libby, with crooked teeth and a chronic stubble. But he gave her compliments and good tips until she finally agreed to see a movie with him on her night off. They were the only two patrons in the single-screen theater, watching a second-run film most people could get on satellite TV. When Danny kissed her good night, a brief peck with no heat in it, he smelled of stale popcorn. And yet somehow she had agreed to go out with him again.

Libby sighed. At eight o'clock, the only drinker downstairs was sitting at the bar, which made him Shaun's customer, not hers. The man sipped beer with his eyes fixed on the TV screen mounted above the back bar, watching rich football players make a living. She leaned against the bar and wished for a cold beer herself, but of course she couldn't drink while she was on the clock. After the last hangover, she'd sworn off the hard stuff. Still, a few beers now and then were essential.

She glanced at the door, wishing for customers to come in and make her shift pass faster. Shaun came by, swirling a towel across the bar top. His ponytail was wavy like Kiwi's and the color of copper under the bar lights. Libby believed such long eyelashes were wasted on a man. She was less nervous around Shaun than she used to be, but his knowing eyes still put her on guard.

"I heard you tell Denise you're looking for a place to stay." He kept his voice low so the customer wouldn't hear.

"Yeah, I've imposed on Myra too long."

"You could have the apartment in back if you want."

She looked at him blankly. "What apartment?"

"Behind the kitchen."

He nodded toward the back of the building. "There's one bedroom, a living area, and a bath, and it's furnished, sort of. You'd have access to the bar's kitchen through a private door."

Libby knew the building had some extra space in back but had thought it was storage. What exactly did he have in mind?

"Where do you live?" she said.

"Somewhere else. I'm not asking you to move in with me."

"I didn't think—"

"Sure you did. You're suspicious and cautious, and that's okay." He shrugged. "The previous owner lived back there, but it's been vacant more than a year. You'd want to clean it up."

"So you own the building now?"

"Bought it a few months ago."

Libby bet even Denise didn't know Shaun was now the owner. The place must be more profitable than she'd thought. Or maybe he was just looking for roots. Some men were like that, not that she'd ever known one, including Deacon. Army men were always on the move.

She tried to imagine herself and Kiwi in an apartment attached to the lounge. Not ideal for a little girl, but at least Kiwi would be right next door while Libby was working. She could slip in and check on her, make sure she went to bed on time.

Shaun took a key from the cash register and placed it on the bar. "Go take a look. The entrance is around back."

Libby met and held his gaze for a moment. She tried to picture living in Shaun's apartment while working in Shaun's bar. Was that a good idea? She was already feeling a certain heat when he was around.

She shrugged. "No harm in looking."

She went out the front and around back to an unmarked door on the sundown side. There was a porch light beside the door but no porch, only a small square of concrete blocks at the entrance. The light wasn't on, and the door was shaded from parking-lot lights. In the darkness, she fumbled the key into the lock. When she pushed the door open, a dry smell greeted her, the scent of rooms shut up too long in a desert climate.

Her hand found two light switches inside the door; she flipped them both. The porch light came on, along with a lamp in a corner of the small living room. The place was furnished like a cheap motel. Brown vinyl couch and chair, blond end tables with matching lamps. In one corner, a table for two, obviously salvaged from the bar, served as the only eating area. Flat, tan carpeting, looking reasonably clean, covered the floor. A double window looked out on the weedy vacant lot behind the bar. There was no ground-floor window facing the side parking lot, a good thing. No headlights flashing through the curtains all night.

She climbed a flight of bare wood stairs. On the landing, a single window overlooked the parking lot. She took four more stairs and stepped into a bedroom with a double bed and a lamp table tucked into the corner beside it. On the opposite wall were two doors, one to a closet and the other to the bathroom. A corroded showerhead hung above the dusty tub, but it would clean up okay. She'd definitely stayed in worse places.

Back downstairs, she found a dorm-sized refrigerator beneath a deep bookshelf at the back of the living room. The fridge smelled musty, but when she turned a knob, the motor kicked on. Close to the bookshelf, she found a door that was locked with a dead bolt from her side. She slid the bolt and opened the door to the bar kitchen. The space was large, with stainless-steel appliances and countertops. It smelled like hamburger grease from the blackened grill, and the concrete floor had a drain in the center.

Libby could hear the TV from the bar on the other side of the swinging door. She had never seen the bar's kitchen before. That was Shaun's domain, where he fried burgers and nuked nachos, the extent of the menu. She could cook here for her and Kiwi. She noticed there was no access to the dead bolt from the kitchen side, so no one could come into the apartment through that door unless she let them.

The scent of grease took Libby back to a kitchen in San Jose, on an afternoon when she should have been working, and Rocket should have been somewhere else. Before meeting Rocket, she had smoked a little weed as a teenager but had never done anything stronger unless you counted a few beers. Rocket had taught her to do them at the same time. He told her the weed would prevent a hangover, the first of his many lies. But for a few hours that day, sitting in his kitchen while Kiwi was safely at school, Libby forgot to think of what she'd lost. Forgot to be a war widow. Forgot to be responsible for a child. She had felt so good that when he offered her, smiling, a small white pill—laughing with her because it was *so tiny!*—she swallowed it without even asking what it was. Soon she was so high that when Kiwi came home from school that afternoon, Libby had greeted her with unusual enthusiasm, not even registering the terror in her daughter's eyes.

The flashback left her sweating. Libby knew quite well that she was responsible for what Kiwi had done a few weeks later. On that midnight drive along the coast highway, Libby had sworn to start over, to make a decent life for Kiwi if only they could escape.

A crummy apartment behind a bar wasn't what she wanted for them. But maybe it was a start. She began to picture the possibilities.

She returned to the apartment and bolted the kitchen door. Upstairs again, she checked the closet space. The bed was not made up, but there were sheets and towels and a bedspread on the closet shelves. No pillows. The mattress was too soft but unstained, and the paint on the walls looked clean. The place was ten times better than anything she had found within her price range in town. And they would have no neighbors, a definite plus. Neighbors were generally a pain in the ass.

The location was farther from Kiwi's school than she would have liked. Libby would have to get up each morning and drive her. But if she got off at 2:00 a.m. and slept until 6:00, she could manage that, and then return home for a couple more hours. Or maybe there was a school bus. Libby took one last look at the bathroom, turned out the lights, and locked the apartment door as she left. The only question remaining was how much Shaun wanted for rent—and whether there were strings attached.

Two customers were in her area when she returned. Shaun had already served them drinks. She returned the key to him and went to take their order for burgers and nachos.

"Our specialty," she said, and they smiled.

When she turned in their order to Shaun, he said, "So what did you think?"

"Not bad," she said, trying not to sound eager. "What's the rent?"

"Whatever you can afford," he said easily, drawing another beer for the lone football fan. "It's not bringing in anything now."

"Two hundred a month? You know my wages."

He laughed and pushed through the swinging doors to start the burgers. She expected him to counteroffer and was prepared to go four hundred if she had to. He knew about Deacon and probably realized she'd be getting a regular check.

But when he came back, he said, "Two hundred a month and one more night's work. I'll teach you to tend bar and flip burgers so I can have Sunday evening off sometimes."

Sunday was one of only two nights she got to be home with Kiwi.

"Why don't you close the bar on Sunday?" Libby asked. "Can't be much business."

"We have some regulars who stop in to brace themselves for a new week. The upstairs is closed, so Denise works the floor. It wouldn't be every Sunday, just once or twice a month." He headed back toward the kitchen to tend the grill. "Think it over."

Two hundred a month was a steal, and they both knew it. He was doing her a favor, and she wondered why. Suspicious again, she wondered what he would do on his Sundays off. Ride his Harley in the desert? Maybe there was a woman in his life.

A little later, she pulled him aside. "Okay, it's a deal. I'd like to move in after the holidays, if that's okay." She couldn't face another move just before Christmas, a new set of unfamiliar rooms. This would be the third year without Deacon, each one as bad as the last. The holidays were a hard time for Kiwi too. She and Myra had already put up a tree of sorts.

"That'll work," Shaun said. "Let me know if something in the place needs fixing." He set the burger baskets and nachos on the bar. "One other thing." His eyes flickered up to her face and held. "Danny Wyman is not a guy you should go out with."

Libby took the baskets and a step back, frowning. "Being my landlord doesn't give you the right to choose my friends."

"I'm not trying to choose them. I'm trying to be a friend."

He turned away without meeting her eyes, but the warning was clear. Did he know something about Danny that she didn't? Regardless, whom she dated was none of his damned business. But she didn't want to make an issue of it and lose the apartment.

She delivered the nachos and burgers and watched two more couples come in and take a booth in her section. After that, several workers from a highway construction crew came in. She stayed busy the rest of the night and made good tips. But the place was nearly empty again when the upstairs poker game broke up about midnight. Danny Wyman lumbered down the stairs with five other guys. He must have come in while she was looking at the apartment.

One of the men, the night's obvious winner, ordered a last round for the group. Danny, however, didn't join them. His face looked stormy as he headed for the door. Maybe he lost big, Libby thought. Still, she expected a wink or a wave, some kind of acknowledgment. But Danny left without even a glance in her direction. Looked like Shaun's warning was irrelevant.

Funny, Shaun thought Danny was bad for her, but he had it backwards. What she hadn't told Shaun and would never tell him was that for her, Danny Wyman was a safe option. She felt no attraction to him, no desire to please him or make him happy. She didn't give a flying fig what Danny Wyman thought of her. Unlike Shaun, whose quiet darkness drew her in despite her knowing better.

Chapter 8

Kiwi's Journal

25 December 2008

EVERY CHRISTMAS REMINDS me of the year Mom and I came back from my dad's funeral in Alabama. It's a long, long car trip from Alabama to Washington, especially when nobody is talking.

Christmas Day we were by ourselves in our duplex on the Army base. The next day, we would have to pack all our stuff so we could move, but on Christmas, we didn't do anything. Mom stayed in her bedroom and pretended to watch movies, but I knew that most of the time she was crying.

I spent the day in my room looking out the window. The sky was gray and cold, and our street was mostly empty, because our friends had either gone home for the holidays or already moved away. In the Army, that happened a lot.

I had two big boxes in my room that I was supposed to use to pack. I climbed into one of them and curled up with Moxie and my blanket. It was kind of like being in a cave. My dad got Moxie for me before he left. I stuffed my nose into Moxie's fur and found a little bit of Daddy's smell. We stayed in the box until I finally fell asleep. Ever since, Christmas Day makes me sad.

This year, though, we gave Christmas a good try. Myra put up a fake saguaro cactus. You pronounce it *c-war-o*, not *cigar-o*, though it did kind of look like a big green cigar with arms. Saguaros don't grow in this part of the desert, but Myra likes them anyway. I helped her decorate it like a Christmas tree. She hung a string of red lights that look like chili peppers, along with some desert flower and bird ornaments. We hung them on the fake spines of the cactus. It wasn't very Christmasy, but it was unusual, I'll say that.

We exchanged presents too. At the Walmart store in Creosote City last week, I found a little silver angel for Mom's charm bracelet. I told her the charm was her guardian angel. She smiled like, yeah, right. Maybe it will remind her of the little girl she loved before I *fell from grace* (that's what Father Bastoni calls it when somebody sins). For my Christmas present, as Mom had promised, I got my ears pierced. The piercing part didn't hurt as much as I thought it would. Getting tears in your eyes doesn't count as actually crying. I get tears in my eyes, but I hardly ever cry.

That was a week ago, and now I have tiny gold studs in my ears. I have to clean the holes with alcohol every day so I don't get an infection. Mom also got me a pink T-shirt and a pair of earrings with pink rhinestones and real silver backs. She said I couldn't wear the earrings until my ears heal completely.

I got Myra a new rubber spatula for Christmas to replace the one I ruined the night I tried to make birthday brownies and blew up the kitchen. I didn't have any money left for Christmas paper, so I wrapped my gifts in leftover newspaper. Myra got a big laugh when she opened hers. She gave me a hug with one arm, like she didn't know how to do a real one. She called me a good kid and said the spatula was the nicest one she'd ever owned.

Mom said we're moving out of Myra's in January. I don't see why. Myra seems to like us, and in a new place, I'll be by myself even more than I am now. But at least I won't have to change schools.

Myra got me two books for Christmas. They were from the used bookstore, but they're in excellent condition. One's the Boxcar Kids series that I read back in third grade, but I didn't let on. She knew I liked to read, and it was nice of her to think of getting me a book. I made sure she saw me reading it. The other book was exactly what I needed—a paperback dictionary! I forgot my old one when we left San Jose so fast. Now I could check the spelling of words I use in my journal or in reports for school. My New Year's resolution is going to be to use my dictionary to learn one new word a week.

With the presents done, we sat down for a dinner of roasted chicken from the grocery store. So far, the day had been one of my best Christmases yet, but things always change, don't they?

After we cleaned up after dinner, Mom said she had to go to work. She put on her best jeans and a cute top and earrings, and she fixed her hair better than usual. Then she left. I'm not a moron. Hardly anything is open on Christmas, and I bet the Sleepy Iguana wasn't either. She was going on a date.

When my mom and dad got together, it must have been Dad's idea. On her own, my mom only picks bad dudes, the worst losers in male history. It's like she thinks the only men who'd be interested in her are the creeps and weirdos. One time I got mad and told her that. So now she tries to hide it from me when she meets a new one.

As soon as the door shut behind her, my stomach began to feel like I'd swallowed a big juniper stump that somebody had set on fire. I asked Myra, "Where do you think she's going?"

"She said she had to work," Myra said, but she wouldn't look at me. I could tell she didn't believe what she was saying either. I went to our bedroom, closed the door, and started to write in my journal.

On the post where we used to live, I saw a play one time about a bunch of orphan boys set in a place a long time ago. Tonight I feel like that Oliver Twist—so lonesome you wonder why you don't die from it.

I was writing in bed when I had a feeling that I wasn't alone. I looked up, and there was this guy sitting on the floor in the corner of the room. Now that's weird. Even on Christmas. Did I mention that he did not have a long white beard or a red suit or reindeer and sleigh for that matter? Instead, he was in camo pants, like Dad used to wear, and a plain T-shirt the color of sand. He was leaning against the wall as if he was perfectly at home. It was weird, but I wasn't scared.

So I said, "Who are you?"

"My buddies call me Bones," he said.

I might not have been scared of him, but I also didn't know if I was supposed to be his buddy or not. He looked young like a soldier, with his hair cut high and tight. But his eyes looked old. It was odd, but I felt like I already knew him. And could trust him. So I told him my name.

He crossed his ankles in front of him and his toes wiggled inside his olive green socks. It reminded me of how my dad always took his boots off in the house.

"Another Christmas down the rabbit hole," he said.

"That's the solid truth." I rolled over on my side to get a better look at him. "Christmas is overrated."

He kind of frowned, as if he was considering what I'd said. "I guess if you had a big family that got together and cousins to play with, Christmas would probably be a lot of fun," he said.

"That only happens in stories and on TV," I said.

"Maybe so."

He didn't say anything more, so I figured any further conversation was up to me. But where to begin? What do you talk about with somebody who just up and appeared in your room?

"In science class, we've been studying hibernation," I told him. "One Christmas I holed up in a box and tried to sleep through the winter."

"I always liked science," he said. "Hibernation is interesting."

"Everybody knows bears hibernate," I said, "but some reptiles do, too, and then it's called *brumation*. They don't actually sleep. Their metabolism just slows way down so they don't have to eat for a long time."

"Cool. What reptiles?"

"The red-eared turtle, for one. It lives around ponds, not in the desert. When the weather gets cold and the days get short, those turtles can squish down under the mud and not eat for weeks at a time."

"How do they breathe under the mud?"

"That's a good question," I said. "I'll have to ask Mr. Mathis."

He looked worried. "It seems like they would smother under the mud. Or suck water into their nose holes and drown. I would hate to drown."

"Me, too. That would be one of the worst ways to go," I said. "You'd be awake long enough to know you were dying, and I'll bet your lungs would hurt—or explode."

"Burning alive would be even worse," he said.

"Definitely hotter." That made me think of hell. "What do you think would be the worst way to die: drowning, burning up, or being murdered?"

"Depends on how you were murdered," he said. "If somebody shot you in your sleep, you'd never know it."

I was glad to hear that. And pleased to find Bones to be such a good conversationalist once he got started. I asked casual like, "What if you were blown up all of a sudden, and you didn't know it was coming? Like a roadside bomb."

"You'd never know what hit you." He nodded like he knew. "Going out fast has its advantages."

Talking with Bones had calmed the fire in my stomach some, and I was finding it easier to breathe. "I'm feeling better," I told him.

"That's good," he said. "I don't like you to feel bad."

I turned over to write our conversation down, and when I turned back, Bones was gone. I hope he'll come back again. But maybe he shows up only on Christmas.

I fell asleep after that, and now it's morning. I'm sitting on the floor so I can finish writing this. Mom is asleep in our bed. Her breathing sounds like a baby harmonica. I didn't hear her come home, but I'm sure glad she did. When she leaves like that, I always worry maybe she won't.

Something smells good. I think Myra is cooking bacon. Gotta go. I'm hungry as a caterpillar.

Kiwi

2 January 2009
(A New Year and #5 on the Top Ten Worst Days of My Life.)

I'm writing this in the closet at Myra's house because I feel like being in a small tight space where nobody can see me. Luckily, there's a light in here, so I can still see to write.

Here are my Top Ten Worst Days so far. I only have five or maybe six, so there's plenty of room left for more crappy days if I get older.

> #1: The day I found out my dad got blown up by a bomb. This one's the obvious worst. It messed me up for a long time. Mom, too.

> #2: The Last Day in San Jose. This one is the reason I'm going to hell and my mom can't love me anymore.

> #3: The day of my dad's funeral.

> #4: The first Christmas after he was gone. Mom changed after that, and I guess I did too.

Actually, today is probably tied for #5. The original #5 was in third grade when I peed my pants at school. That was the week after we learned Dad was killed but before they brought his body back for the funeral. I hadn't felt like going back to school, but Mom thought I'd be better off if things got back to normal. How can you be normal after something like losing your dad?

I wasn't even talking at the time. It's hard to explain, but it was like my voice had somehow gotten locked in my chest. At first, Mom thought I was doing it on purpose, but the Army doctor told her not to bug me about it and that my voice would come back eventually.

And after about a month, it did. But on that first day back at school, I couldn't even ask to use the restroom. And then it was too late to ask, and I was sitting in a puddle in my seat. I cried, I was so humiliated, but I was only eight. The older you get, I've found, the more capacity you have to be humiliated. Today was humiliating and also stupid. For a smart kid, I do some really dumb things.

This time it began with this kid at school who likes to pick on me. My friend Karen said that means he likes me, but that's torn up, because the stuff he does is mean. He's always giving me the stink eye. He makes fun of my clothes and tries to get his friends to laugh at me. Once he tried to trip me in the lunchroom; another time, he stole a cookie off my tray. But he's real sneaky, so the teacher never sees him. His name is Damick, but I call him Dammit.

Karen, Jasmine, and I were hanging out on the playground at recess, and Dammit came running toward us. He was holding an old dirty paper cup, and when he went by he slung the icky brown liquid in it on me. I was just standing there, not bothering him at all! The gunk went all over my miniskirt and leggings. I don't know what it was, but it looked like diarrhea and smelled gross. I thought I was going to puke, partly because of the smell and partly because I was so mad at Dammit.

I know I promised never to use the word *hate*, but right then I hated that boy. I felt like the Incredible Hulk. I felt like my hair was on fire, but it wasn't. I was just so mad that my head got really, really hot.

Karen said she would take me to the office, and Mrs. Nelson would find me some clean clothes. But old Dammit and his buddies were still pointing fingers and laughing at me. I took off running. Karen said I was screaming, but I don't remember that.

When he saw me coming, Dammit's eyes got real big and he stopped laughing. But he waited too long to run. I tackled him like a football linebacker. We both went down hard, but I was on top, and I started to beat on him with both fists. I don't think I could have stopped even if I'd wanted to. It took me a minute to realize he wasn't fighting back. He'd curled up like a little sissy and started to whimper. I could tell he was cooked. I leaned over and growled right in his face: "You'd better leave me alone, Dammit. I once killed a man."

See what I mean? Stupid, stupid, stupid! As soon as I said it, I wanted to bite my lips off and take the words back.

A teacher grabbed the back of my shirt and pulled me off him. She picked up Dammit by the collar, too, and dragged us to the office. We both were suspended for fighting. His mom came and got him, but nobody answered the phone at Myra's house, so I had to sit in the office the rest of the afternoon in my stinky clothes. Mrs. Nelson looked so disappointed in me.

When the last bell rang, Karen stopped by to see what happened to me. She told me when I was leaning over Dammit, my face looked really scary. She doesn't like him either, however, so she was okay that I'd beaten him up. Karen is a true friend.

Mrs. Nelson called my mom again and this time woke her up. She told Mom she had to come down to the school and talk to the principal before I could go home. When Mom got there, her face looked like a sheet of white paper. She didn't smile at me or chew me out or anything. She just went straight into the principal's office and shut the door. I sat outside and worried about what was being said about me.

On the way home, I told Mom my side of what had happened. She grounded me for three weeks, but she didn't seem as mad as I thought she'd be. She said I could still throw my paper route because I'd need the money for a new skirt and leggings. We threw the smelly ones in the garbage.

I wonder what Dad would think about all this. I know he wouldn't have put up with some kid picking on him, but would he have attacked a bully? I'm not sure. I just hope nobody else heard what I told Damick.

Bones is sitting in the closet with me. He comes around pretty often ever since Christmas. I can tell him anything. He is a good listener.

I asked him what he thought Dad would say about me getting in a fight at school.

He said he didn't know, but he also said in his opinion, there are too many jerks in the world, and if you stop to beat up all of them, you'll never have time for anything fun. He probably has a point.

He also said my closet smells like old shoes.

Your friend:

Kiwi the Delinquent

The Spiderling

Sure enough, Damick ratted me out. On my first day back at school after being suspended, the school counselor sent for me. I had to leave social studies with all the kids looking at me as if I was a freak. The counselor's office was right next door to the principal's.

I knew who Miss Greyson was, but I'd never actually talked to her before. She had hair the color of a cardboard box and wore no makeup. Her smile was friendly enough, but she didn't smile often or for long. She sat me down and got right to the point.

"Kiwi, did you tell Damick that you were going to kill him?"

"No! That's not what I said! He's trying to get me in trouble again."

"Okay, what did you say to him?"

"I just wanted to scare him so he'd quit being mean to me."

"What exactly did you say?"

I looked down at my flip-flops. I was wearing pink socks with them to hide a big scab on my foot where I'd scraped it on the playground. I have another scab on my elbow, but I couldn't cover that one up. Miss Greyson was still staring at me, and finally, she said my name again.

"Kiwi . . .?"

I figured some other kid had overheard what I'd said so I'd might as well tell her.

"I told him I'd killed a man," I said. My heart was shaking my chest, wham, wham, wham.

But then she said: "So you told a fib?"

When you have to lie, you should never hesitate. But I always get a case of the guilties. So I did what Mom says politicians do when somebody asks them a question: They answer something else.

"He picks on me all the time. I got tired of it and went a bit crazy."

She frowned. "What do you mean, he picks on you?"

She seemed truly interested, so I told her all the stuff Damick had done to me since the first of school. It was a long list, but as I reeled it off, most of it sounded kind of silly. I thought Miss Greyson might laugh, but instead, she frowned.

"Did you tell your homeroom teacher about this?" she said.

"No," I said, "nobody likes a snitch."

"There are times when you should tell your teacher or another adult what's going on," she said. "This is one of those times. What he's doing is bullying, and it's wrong."

"It sure is," I said.

She looked at me and her eyes narrowed. I looked back without flinching. I couldn't tell what she was thinking. Finally she said, "Kiwi, is something else bothering you? Something besides Damick?"

How could I answer that?

That list would be longer than my Top Ten Worst Days. So I said, "No, other than him, I like school."

I could tell she wasn't convinced. She kept leaving these big, long pauses after anything I said, as if she was waiting for more. At one point, right before I almost yelled *Say something*! she finally did.

"What about at home? Are you and your mom doing okay?"

"Sure," I said. "She has a new job, and we're getting our own place soon. Right now we live with Myra. She's a friend."

"That's good," she said. "What's Myra's last name?"

That stopped me cold. I didn't know Myra's last name.

Luckily, the bell rang right then. Miss Greyson said I should go back to my classroom, but if Damick bothered me again to let her know. Yeah, that was gonna happen.

On the way home that day, I played the Traffic Game, walking slow across all the streets I crossed with my eyes closed. But there's hardly any traffic in this town even on a weekday, and I didn't even get a good scare.

I told Bones about the Traffic Game tonight, and he didn't get it.

"What if a car hits you?" he said.

"That's the point," I told him. "Maybe it will. Maybe it won't. But if it does—I'll die real fast like a bomb going off."

He shook his head.

"If I had to go to hell when I died, I wouldn't be in any hurry to get there," he said.

Once again, Bones had a good point.

"I guess that's why when a car comes, I always jump out of the way," I said.

"Keep jumping," said Bones.

Love:

Kiwi the Redeemed (new word of the week)

Chapter 9

New Digs

KIWI WAS OUT OF SCHOOL for the January parent-teacher conferences, and Libby didn't have to be at the school until two o'clock that afternoon, so she took Kiwi along that morning to help clean their new apartment. Libby dreaded the meeting with Mrs. Gomez but had tried to seem cheerful about it when Kiwi told her. Kiwi was worried too, Libby could tell. Since she'd gotten in trouble at school, Kiwi wasn't nearly so eager to have Libby meet her teachers.

Libby parked the pickup outside the Sleepy Iguana at about 10:00 a.m. No other cars were in the lot, not even Shaun's motorcycle. They unloaded the cleaning supplies and walked around back. Kiwi hadn't seen the apartment yet. Libby handed her the key to unlock the door. Kiwi pushed it open and looked the place over without comment.

"What do you think?" Libby asked.

Kiwi shrugged. "I'll clean the bathtub first." She twisted her ponytail into a knot, and then Libby handed her the cleanser and rubber gloves.

Libby watched her lean over the tub and start to scrub, hair bouncing like a rabbit's tail. Kiwi was being extra agreeable today. Libby wondered if she had the impending teacher conference to thank for that.

She turned her attention to the bathroom floor and then the toilet, while Kiwi went over the apartment with a dustcloth. Cleaning together was such an ordinary mother-daughter thing that Libby began to feel something she almost didn't recognize—hopeful.

She began to hum a song from the movie *Juno* as she worked, and to her surprise, Kiwi chimed in. Kiwi'd been too young to see the movie, but somehow, she knew the words to the song. Mother and daughter sang together, getting louder when Libby turned on the vacuum cleaner she'd borrowed from Myra.

When they were finished, Libby surveyed their work. "It'll look better when we bring our stuff in."

Kiwi eyed the brown sofa with a frown. "Will I sleep with you or on the couch?"

"Which would you rather?"

Kiwi looked at her. "I like sleeping with you."

Libby sighed. The girl was a windmill in the bed, all legs and thrashing arms, but Libby didn't want to ruin the connection she'd felt with her daughter. "Okay. We've been doing pretty well that way at Myra's."

Kiwi grinned and bounced on her toes. Then her face changed to panic. "What time is it?"

Libby didn't know. She'd left her watch at home, although she was wearing the charm bracelet with its tiny key and the angel Kiwi had given her for Christmas. "It's no later than noon. I have time to go back and shower before the conference."

"Are you sure?" Kiwi's eyes darted around the apartment but found no clock.

"Chill out," Libby said. "I'll peek into the bar and check the time." She went to the door that led to the bar kitchen and retracted the dead bolt. Kiwi was right behind her.

"Kids aren't allowed in a bar," Libby said.

"But it's not open now, is it?" Kiwi said.

"No. It doesn't open till afternoon."

"I want to see where you work. Please?"

Relenting, Libby let Kiwi follow her into the kitchen, where a grease-filmed wall clock read five minutes to noon.

Once Kiwi was satisfied about the time, she became curious. "This is the kitchen. Where's the rest?"

Libby led her through the swinging door. They emerged behind the long bar, and Kiwi's eyes widened at the rows of bottles and glasses hanging in racks. The half-light hid the dust that collected on the wine and martini glasses, which were rarely used.

Kiwi walked out into the shadowy main room and turned a slow circle, taking it in. "Wow!" she said. "This is a real bar."

"Yeah, it's real, all right." Libby felt a twinge of guilt. Had Kiwi not realized her mother worked in a bar? With Kiwi here, she saw the place with different eyes. Fortunately the lights were off, hiding corners that were no doubt choked with cobwebs. For a moment, she felt an impulse to clean the bar the way they had the apartment, but then the urge passed.

"What's up those stairs?" Kiwi asked.

"The poker room."

"Can I see it?"

"No. Come on, let's go get some lunch."

Kiwi turned reluctantly, trailing her hand over a cocktail table. "Are there dancers?" she asked.

"No. Nothing like that. It's just a burgers-and-beer crowd."

"Who's the boss person?"

"His name is Shaun. I've mentioned him, remember? He owns the bar and the apartment too. He'll be our landlord."

"Do you like him?" Kiwi's eyes said that the question was more than a passing thought.

Libby shrugged, keeping her face neutral. "He's okay. He gave me a good deal on the rent."

Kiwi came around the end of the bar to where Libby waited.

"I liked it at Myra's," she said, her voice low.

"Please don't start. We've been through that at least three times."

Libby led the way back through the kitchen and bolted the door behind them. They gathered their things and stepped outside. Libby paused with one hand on the doorknob, a bucket of cleaning supplies in the other, for one more look at the apartment.

Suddenly Kiwi grabbed her around the waist in a fierce hug. The breath went out of Libby, and her body stiffened.

"I love you, Mom. I wish we had Daddy again."

In an instant, Kiwi let go and trotted toward the truck, but not before tears filled the eyes of both of them.

Mrs. Gomez, Kiwi's homeroom teacher, was plump and looked to be about forty. Her classroom was decorated with piñatas. A papier-mâché donkey and chicken dangled by their necks from the classroom ceiling. Mrs. Gomez's hair was cut in short, fluffy layers, and her dark eyes reflected her smile. She came from behind her cluttered desk and sat in a student seat close to Libby.

Libby squirmed. She'd never felt comfortable in classrooms.

"Kiwi is so bright and curious," the teacher said, "as I'm sure you know. She's a delight to have in class."

Libby blinked. "That's good to hear."

"That trouble on the playground, though. I wish she had talked to me about it when Damick started to bother her. We might have avoided their . . . confrontation."

"I'm not so sure," Libby said. "Some bullies won't quit until you thrash them."

Mrs. Gomez wrinkled her nose. "It's not good for girls to be fighting."

Libby thought Mrs. Gomez had led a sheltered life.

"Karen's mother doesn't want her to be friends with Kiwi anymore, and that's a shame," the teacher said.

Libby's stomach pinched. "Kiwi didn't mention that."

"No, she probably wouldn't. Karen still plays with her sometimes."

This was not what Libby had expected from a parent-teacher conference. She cleared her throat. "What about her grades? Is she doing her homework?"

"Oh, yes. I can't speak for her science and math teachers, but she'll have an A in language arts and in social studies." She smiled again. "You work outside the home, don't you, Mrs. Seager?"

"Yes. And my hours aren't great." She wondered if Kiwi had told her homeroom teacher where Libby worked.

Mrs. Gomez handed her a flyer. "You might want to consider our summer program for Kiwi. We offer enrichment classes, including beginning Spanish. With her vocabulary and talent for writing, I bet she'd pick up another language quick as lightning." She smiled as if they were sharing a confidence. "It would give her something to do while you're at work and keep that active young mind occupied."

Libby's eyes glazed over as she read. She couldn't see the words for the disapproval she heard behind the teacher's voice. Mrs. Gomez thought Kiwi spent too much time alone. That was true, of course, but Libby resented her noticing . . . and the judgment. Had Mrs. Gomez ever been a single mom?

"Sounds like a good idea," Libby said. "We'll talk it over." Summer vacation was months away; they might be somewhere else by then. She folded the paper in half and wished she had somewhere to put it. The other mothers probably carried handbags. "Is there anything else?"

"Not unless you have something you'd like to discuss." The teacher's eyes were a question.

"No. I'm good. Glad Kiwi's keeping her grades up." She extracted herself from the child-sized desk and forced a smile. "Please let me know if anything changes."

"Do I have a phone number for you?"

"Ummm . . . actually we're moving to a new place tomorrow. I'm going to get a cell phone and I'll send the number with Kiwi."

"Please do," said Mrs. Gomez. She stood and offered her hand. Libby clasped the round fingers briefly and tried not to rush from the room.

She was barely in the hallway before she bumped into Kiwi and a skinny man with sandy hair and glasses.

"Mom! This is Mr. Mathis, my science teacher!" Kiwi smiled as if she were showing off a new puppy.

The teacher was about Libby's age and had a slightly shaggy mustache. He grinned and stuck out his hand. "Hi. Ian Mathis."

"Libby Seager." She backed up a step, flustered. "Do I have another conference I didn't know about?"

The man laughed. "No, one of my parents was a no-show, and Kiwi wanted me to meet you. She's my prize science student, you know." He winked at Kiwi and her face lit up.

"Cool." Libby forced a smile. "She showed me the astronomy project she's doing for your class."

"Not astronomy, Mom," Kiwi corrected. "Solar energy."

"We'll enter it in the district science fair," Mr. Mathis said.

There was an awkward moment of more smiling. "Cool," Libby said again, feeling like an idiot. A teenaged one, at that, uneducated and underdressed.

She put her hand on Kiwi's shoulder and turned her toward the exit. "It was nice to meet you, Mr. Mathis. Kiwi really likes your class."

"I'm glad to meet you too." He made a motion like a little salute. "See you tomorrow, Miss K!" He held up his hand and Kiwi high-fived it. Then he turned back down the hallway.

"Isn't he cute?" Kiwi whispered, too loudly.

"Shhh," Libby said, hustling her along. "I don't know about cute, but he seems very nice and he sure likes you!"

"He'd like you, too, if you knew him."

"*Kee-wee*," she said, her tone a warning. "I'm not going to date one of your teachers."

"What would be wrong with that? He's single, and Mr. Mathis is a *good* guy."

Libby got the point. Kiwi thought the men she had dated were bad guys. Maybe she was right. But Libby was intimidated by the good ones; she was too fallible, had made too many mistakes. She had married a good guy and look what had happened.

"You do not get to choose who I go out with," Libby said. And because she recalled telling Shaun the same thing recently, her voice sounded rougher than she'd intended.

Kiwi's face reddened. "Well, *somebody* needs to!"

Before Libby could smack her smart mouth, Kiwi broke away and ran down the hall. She slammed the crash bar on the exit and disappeared into a flash of sunlight.

Libby stood still, her chest flooding with heat.

"What the f—," but she couldn't say the needed word inside a school.

She watched the sliver of light where her daughter had vanished. The smell of floor wax and kid sweat stung her nose. Her fists clenched, but in a way, she felt heartened. Kiwi's noisy exit was the first sign of defiance she had seen from her daughter since San Jose. To Libby, the rebellious behavior seemed more normal than not.

They didn't talk on the way to Myra's house. Kiwi laid her head back on the seat and looked out the side window instead. Libby regretted the loss of their brief camaraderie that morning. She had decided to ignore her daughter's outburst, but she couldn't think of anything lighthearted to say to get them back to where they had been just hours before.

Kiwi's newspapers were waiting on the porch, so her attention shifted to that. Libby went indoors but watched through the window. The paper route had been a good thing, something Kiwi was responsible for that she could call her own. When all the papers were folded, Kiwi started off down the block with the ink-smeared canvas bag over her shoulder, still without a word.

Libby knew this silence was not because she wouldn't date Mr. Mathis. When Kiwi hugged her at their new apartment, why couldn't she have told Kiwi she loved her, too, that she was sorry for not giving her the stability she needed? Instead, her voice had locked in her chest like Kiwi's did in those first weeks after they had lost Deacon.

Libby let the curtain fall and went to the kitchen to make dinner. The hum of the refrigerator sounded hollow and lonely. She settled on macaroni and cheese with chopped weenies, Kiwi's favorite.

Maybe it was wrong not to talk about Rocket. But what they had left behind in San Jose was too awful and still too fresh in her mind. She had no words to comfort her daughter, no wisdom to offer. How was a parent supposed to respond to that kind of violence?

If Libby had anyone she could talk to, they would no doubt have recommended professional counseling. But then, Libby didn't trust head doctors. The one she had seen as a teenager was more screwed up than she was and had suggested sex—with him—as a way to bolster her self-esteem. And what if Kiwi had told the shrink about San Jose? Wouldn't he be required to report it to police? All she and Kiwi had was each other. She couldn't risk losing her daughter too.

The pasta was boiling when Kiwi came back from her route. Again, without a word, she retrieved her journal and headed back outside.

"Dinner in fifteen minutes," Libby called, but Kiwi didn't answer.

At 5:45 p.m., like clockwork, Myra arrived home from work. She kicked her shoes toward the living room and made her daily gin and tonic. Libby admired Myra for having only one. Except for a two-year relationship, Myra had lived alone all her life, with nothing to look forward to, as far as Libby could see. In her place, Libby might well have become a hopeless alcoholic.

Myra plopped the mail on the kitchen table.

"You got something," Myra said.

Libby wiped her hands and picked up the padded envelope. It was from her mother-in-law in Alabama. Knowing it would contain the check and a little gift for Kiwi, as usual, Libby slit the envelope with a paring knife, pulled out a white envelope from family services, and dumped the rest of the contents onto the table. Her breath stopped short.

Deacon's dog tags lay on the table like a tumbled skeleton.

After three years, someone had found her husband's ID necklace and sent it home. A note from Justine confirmed this.

"I thought Kiwi might want to have it," Justine had added.

Libby was still holding the note, unable to move, when Kiwi walked into the kitchen. Kiwi's eyes went right to the dog tags. She picked up the chain and read the tags, the larger one and the small one attached by a short, separate chain—the toe tag.

Libby knew what they said:

Seager, Deacon L.
458-52-5555.
O positive.
Roman Catholic.

Kiwi slipped the necklace over her head. The tags hung to her waist; she looked down at them, pressing them against her stomach.

That's when Libby saw the bloody slice that striped Kiwi's arm from elbow to wrist.

Chapter 10

Kiwi's Journal

16 January 2009

TODAY I WENT TO THE emergency room. It's the second time I've been to one. The first time I went to the ER, I was four years old and accidentally sucked a little red bead up my nose. The doctor made me sneeze and it came flying out. I remember watching the bead roll across the floor and the doctor laughing.

This time I got thirteen stitches in my arm. Luckily, in my left arm, so I can still write. They X-rayed it first, to see if it was broken. I made a fuss when the nurse tried to take off my dad's dog tags. She said metal would mess up the picture, but they only needed a picture of my arm, for Pete's sake, not my neck! Finally she agreed to just move the chain out of the way. X-rays don't hurt, but you have to hold absolutely still for them. I wiggled on accident and they had to do it again.

I had to get a tetanus shot too. That was the worst part. Tetanus, or as I prefer to call it, lockjaw, is a disease you can get from stepping on a rusty nail or getting scratched by rusty metal if you don't get the shot. I had the lady doctor spell *tetanus* and write it down for me. I'm going to look it up on the internet at the library to see if it can really kill you like they say it can.

Before the doctor did my stitches, she deadened my arm with some kind of spray that also kills germs. My arm turned yucky yellow and I couldn't feel anything, so it was like she was sewing up somebody else. She was impressed that I could watch. Mom had to leave the room. I didn't watch the shot, though. Shots creep me out.

I landed in the hospital after falling out of the tree in Myra's back-yard. She has only one tree, but it's nice and big. I was sitting up there thinking about stuff after arguing with Mom, and I started to have trouble breathing. This happens a lot when I remember certain things and think about them too long. My chest felt like it was in a seat belt that kept getting tighter and tighter until it squeezed out all my air.

To get my mind off things, I decided to see if I could walk a tree branch with my eyes closed—like the Traffic Game but for monkeys. But I don't exactly have monkey feet, and I had to keep my flip-flops on because the tree bark was scratchy. I made it three steps before I fell.

I didn't see the shovel in the weeds until I landed on it. It hurt when it scraped my arm, and I know this sounds weird, but it also felt good. I watched the blood come out in a chain of little beads that were brilliant red against my skin—fascinating and kind of pretty. When I looked at the cut, my chest loosened up so I could breathe.

I had found the shard of glass on my paper route, and I dug it out of my pocket. The glass was clear green and shaped like an arrowhead. With the sharp point I made the cut on my arm longer. And deeper.

Pain is like a penance for being a bad kid. That's one of the steps we learned about in catechism class: contrition, penance, and absolution. I didn't get far enough in the classes to go to confession, but back then, I didn't have much to confess anyway. I could give the priest an earful now.

When the cut started to bleed quite a bit, I did feel kind of sick and thought maybe I should go inside. When I told Mom I had fallen out of the tree, she was mad at me, as usual. Then we went to the hospital.

✽

The Spiderling

Mom has gone to work now, and I'm at Myra's. I guess it won't be home much longer. Tomorrow we're moving into the apartment behind the bar. Real classy. I know whoever lived there before was a smoker; the walls smell like a dirty ashtray. Myra's is the only place we've lived since Dad died that didn't smell funny.

So once again, I'm going to be temporary. I'm not going to say good-bye to Myra when we leave because I'm pretty sure I'd get tears in my eyes, like a big baby.

Bones is keeping me company tonight. I hope he can still come around when we move to our new apartment. Karen has been acting funny at school, and Bones may soon be the only friend I've got. Not counting Sponge Bob, who talks a lot but never listens.

Bones noticed my dog tags right away. "Your dad's?" he asked.

"Yup. When he got blown up, they couldn't find them."

"I had dog tags once, but I lost them," Bones said.

"I'm never going to lose these," I told him. "I'm going to wear them 100 percent of the time."

"Cool," he said. He said that a lot.

"These tags actually hung around my dad's neck. They might still have his DNA on them. Like sweat and skin cells. Maybe even some microscopic blood." I wished I hadn't thought about my dad's blood because my stomach now felt queasy. The smell of the yellow antiseptic on my arm didn't help.

"Where do you think his dog tags have been all this time?" I asked Bones.

"Maybe one of his buddies picked them up and kept them because they were friends, then finally decided he should send them to the family."

"Yeah. I bet that's what happened. My dad had good friends in the Army."

My left arm was starting to hurt a lot, so I propped it up on a pillow. Bones looked at my stitches and nodded as if he approved.

"So why did you jump out of the tree?" he said.

I told him I didn't jump, I fell.

He shook his head. He didn't buy it. "You knew you would fall. You meant to. And then you cut your arm."

He had me there. I explained how I felt better after my arm got cut open, and he looked worried. "I don't like it when you hurt yourself."

I appreciated that. Bones is a good friend.

"So you won't do it anymore?" he said.

I sighed. "I can't promise. Sometimes my chest gets so tight, I feel like I might suffocate. You don't want me to suffocate, do you?"

"Absolutely not."

"Okay, then."

But I promised to do the best I could, and he said that was all any-body could do. Bones never gets upset. Not even with me. When he's here, my chest feels fine. I can tell him anything and he still likes me. I haven't had anybody to talk to like that since Mrs. Kettleman back in San Jose, and that was before I shot Rocket. Even with Myra, I have to keep secrets.

"I hope you'll still visit me at the Sleepy Iguana Resort," I told Bones, but I was starting to yawn and Bones had disappeared. Maybe someday I'll tell him about Rocket. But not yet.

Later,
Kiwi Zipper-Arm

22 January

We've been in our new place five days. I like knowing Mom is right next door when she's working, but I miss having Myra around in the evenings. Between homework and chores, I haven't had time to write in my journal. Most of the stuff that has happened since I last did was boring, but two exciting things did happen.

Number Two Exciting Thing: I demonstrated my solar-power proj-ect in Mr. Mathis's class, and he said it was *excellent*. I got an A+! He's going to enter it in the sixth-grade division of the district science fair. Only two kids from our school get to enter. He says mine has a good chance to win a ribbon. The science fair is held in Creosote City in a big exhibit building called a coliseum (new word of the week).

Number One Exciting Thing: I found a peephole in our apartment!

Last Sunday, we loaded our four boxes and one suitcase into the truck. We haven't owned furniture in ages, so moving was easy. But we forgot to clean out the drawers and shelves at the new place, so Mom assigned me housekeeping chores while she was at work. Chores are usually boring, but this time I didn't mind. Whenever I'm alone in a new place, it's not as lonesome if I have something to do.

I cleaned out drawers and unpacked the boxes and hung up all our clothes. I cleaned our minifridge, too, because who knew what might have been in there before. Somebody might have stored drugs or body parts. After I finished that job, I put some furniture polish on a rag and wiped down anything made of wood. The lemon oil made the place smell a lot better.

In our bedroom upstairs, there was a picture on the wall of a cowboy and his horse herding cows. The frame was wood, so I took it down to dust and oil it. And guess what? There was a peephole in the wall behind it! The peephole looked just like the ones in motel doors or the movies. Mom had told me our bedroom was next to the poker room above the bar. At night I had heard men talking over there and sometimes laughing. Maybe now I could see what they were doing. I stood on the suitcase and peeked through. I was kind of afraid of what I might see, and my heart was really thumping.

But all I could see was some guys drinking beer. I watched anyway because that beat TV reruns. We get about three stations on our crummy TV. After a few nights I got bored with that view and started to think that if there was a peephole upstairs, maybe there was one that looked into the main room of the bar downstairs. That's where Mom works, so that would be more interesting.

I searched every square inch of the wall in the living room between us and the bar. That wall had bookshelves built in and cabinets below that. No peephole. But I did find a box of tools in a cabinet beside the fridge. I hadn't cleaned out those shelves because we didn't have anything to put in them.

The toolbox had a hammer and pliers and a little saw and a bunch of screwdrivers and wrenches. And something I'd never seen before—a tool with a drill on one end, a big U-shaped handle in the middle, and a round knob on the other end. I played around and figured out how to drill holes with it. You didn't even have to plug it in.

I decided not to show Mom the drill. Some things she just didn't need to know.

The next day after school, I took the tools out back and practiced drilling holes in an old board and the side of the building. I had an idea that I could drill a hole through the back of the shelves in the apartment and make my own peephole into the Sleepy Iguana.

That evening, I listened to the wall, which was not easy because of the shelves. I had to stand on a chair. The wall had dark wood paneling, and I thought a hole back there would barely show. I picked a place about eyeball high and started to drill. To use this tool, you put the point of the drill thingy on the spot, hold the knob real tight, and with the other hand you turn the U-thingy around and around like you're stirring. I hoped the hole didn't come out the other side where the bottles and glasses were in the bar. Something might fall off and break, and I'd get caught.

It was slow going anyway, and when the shavings came out they were nearly white. This hole was going to shine like a star! But I decided I'd worry about that later.

I worked at it a long time before I figured out that I had hit one of those thick boards they put in walls to hold them up. I've seen houses being built, and I knew there were spaces between those boards. So I moved over about six inches and tried again. Then I realized I was drilling right above the minifridge, and there might be electrical lines in the wall.

That could be shocking! So I moved over farther and started again.

I made four holes before one of them shot right through the paneling. Success! I put my eye up to the new peephole—and saw nothing but black. Obviously, there was a second wall on the bar side. And my drill thingy wasn't long enough to go all the way through. After all that work! Mr. Mathis says necessity is the mother of invention. If you need something you don't have, invent something that will work.

So I went back to the toolbox. A longer screwdriver proved perfect. It had a pointed end and little grooves in the tip almost like the drill. I pushed it through the hole and into the second wall and started to turn the handle. I could hear music playing over in the bar, so I figured they couldn't hear a thing. I pushed and pushed and turned and turned and then zip! The screwdriver went through.

I put my eye up to the hole and held my breath. Here's what I saw: Nothing. There was a faint light. Then all of a sudden something moved past, and I realized I had just seen my mom's shirt! The hole was about shoulder high on her. She was waiting on tables in her Sleepy Iguana T-shirt. My peephole worked!

I watched a long time and saw Mom pass by again. After a while, I could make out empty tables and chairs, but that was about all. I could hear some of what people said, too, when I put my ear to the hole. Once I saw that Shaun guy and I think he was talking to Mom. He has a real low voice, and I couldn't make out what he was saying, but her laugh was like an alarm going off in my head.

I got down quick. I had to figure out how to cover up four holes in the back of the shelves before she came over to check on whether I'd gone to bed. She did that most nights.

I found the book Myra had given me for Christmas and the one I brought from San Jose and stood them up in front of two holes, face out. Then I made two washcloth roses and stuck them in two drinking glasses. I set those in front of every other hole—book, rose, book, rose. The washcloths are peach and look pretty against the dark wood. Mostly it looks like somebody who wasn't very good at it tried to decorate the house.

Tomorrow after I throw my paper route, I'll stick the screwdriver back through the wall and see if I can make the hole bigger. It gives me something to do that isn't dangerous. Unless our landlord discovers it. But he's the main reason I need to keep an eye on Mom.

Later,
Kiwi the Spy

Chapter 11

Bartender Lessons

LIBBY WAS WIPING TABLES when the upstairs poker game broke up at midnight. The players lumbered down the stairs and went home, and the bar was empty. Even Louie, a sixty-something regular who often stayed until closing, had called it an early night. Shaun let Denise go home. He probably would have let Libby go, too, if she'd asked. But the hourly wage was worth staying for, and the truth was that she liked being there alone with him. Since she'd left Myra's, she had no one to talk to except what passed for conversation in the bar. She and Denise were friendly, but too different to be friends. Libby had come to enjoy Shaun's company.

Shaun was cleaning up the back bar when she brought the last of the beer mugs to the sink. "This might be a good time for bartender lessons," he said. "You up for it?"

The idea made her nervous, but learning to bartend was part of her rental arrangement. "Sure," she said.

For the next hour, he took her through reloading empty kegs, clearing the taps, and mixing margaritas from scratch. The bar did not serve blended drinks. He said it like a point of pride, which made her smile.

He showed her how to make his popular nachos and the steps for cleaning the grill. Working next to him, Libby felt his body heat like a magnetic field. Fool, she told herself. Why did she crave that maleness? With the exception of Deacon, men had always brought more grief than pleasure.

The only part of tending bar that worried her was the cash register. "I've never been comfortable handling other people's money," she said. "I'm always afraid I'll make a mistake."

He shrugged it off. "If I'm not worried about it, you shouldn't be either. This isn't exactly high finance. Just put copies of all the tickets in the drawer with the cash when you lock it up. I'll balance it out the next day. The bar closes at midnight on Sundays, and Denise will help you clean up. That's about it," he said. "Smile at the customers and you'll be fine. Ready to try it this Sunday?"

She didn't feel ready but appreciated his confidence in her. She took a deep breath. "Okay."

"Good. Then let's shut the place down and go home."

They finished cleaning up, and he locked the door. They walked around the side of the building. His Harley-Davidson was parked not far from the door to her apartment.

The desert night was cool and still, a sickle moon hanging in the starry sky. Up on the interstate, headlights arrowed through the dark. The lazy swoosh of traffic sounded almost like waves against a beach. Homesickness for the ocean washed over her.

Shaun stopped beside the chromed-up cycle and crouched to adjust something in the saddlebag. Libby stopped too. "I'll bet that thing can tear a hole in the wind."

"You like bikes?"

"Yeah. No. I've never been on one. But I like speed."

"We'll have to go for a ride sometime."

She imagined straddling the seat behind him and streaking down a narrow blue road, lizards skittering away beneath the creosote bushes.

"Ever ride it down Highway 1 along the coast?" she asked.

He smiled. "From Oregon all the way south to Morro Bay. Back when I had more money than sense."

"You had money?" She was glad when he laughed.

"Actually, I did." He stood, knees crackling, and patted the handlebars. "Harley here is about all that's left of those days." He swung aboard the bike and inserted the key, but still Libby lingered.

She knew she ought to go inside. But she wasn't ready to turn loose of the moment, the intimacy of being there together in the desert night. She shifted from one foot to the other, stalling.

He looked up at the sky. "On a clear night like this," he said, "I would stop on a bluff above the ocean along Big Sur. Maybe one or two in the morning. Get off the bike and stand on the rim—just to see the stars."

Libby's breath quickened, thinking of a night she, too, had stopped along that road and teetered on the brink.

His voice lowered. "Back then, I had lived in the city so long I'd forgotten what the Milky Way looked like. Out there, it was ink dark and the sky looked salted with stars. Like you could put your finger anyplace above you and touch a thousand. The ocean was a black hole, nothing but the sound of breakers rolling in a hundred feet below. It was like standing on the edge of the world."

Libby felt the pull of yawning space. He paused, and she thought the story was over, but he went on.

"Something magical happened that night. I looked down on the surf and saw this white ribbon of sea foam—phosphorescent in the dark, like those creatures that live miles deep. I couldn't believe what I was seeing. The only living thing in the black abyss. Wave after wave cast these lacy, glowing strands onto the shore, and each one broke up in a million sparkles and then dissolved back into the sea."

Libby's breath came through open lips. She wanted to tell him she understood the tragedy of a thing of beauty breaking apart, but she had no words. A chill ran up her arms and she hugged them to her.

He shifted his weight on the big cycle; its springs squeaked. Half his face was hidden in shadows. "You want to go riding tonight?"

Yes, she thought, god, yes. I want to feel the wind on my face and pretend I'm still young. I want to be someone else, just for a while, and remember nothing, especially my past.

When she didn't answer, he said, "I guess you can't leave Kiwi here asleep, though, can you. Want to wake her up? She's small enough we could put her in the middle." White teeth flashed in the dark.

Libby hesitated. "She has school tomorrow. Better let her sleep. But she'd be all right for a few minutes. Just a short ride."

"You sure?"

She nodded. He pointed to the step where she could swing herself onto the seat behind him. She climbed up and put her arms around his stomach. "Need a jacket?" he asked.

"No." The heat of his body was quite enough. The cycle's engine ripped the night. Kiwi had slept through that noise every night since they'd moved in, and Libby prayed she would again.

They didn't go far. A few miles down the interstate, he crossed over and started back. But the ride was everything she wanted—the wind, the moonlight, the deep-throated rumble of the cycle. She was breathing hard when he pulled into the Sleepy Iguana parking lot and killed the engine. The night went unnaturally still.

Shaun dismounted to help her off. "Careful of that muffler. It'll burn your leg."

His hands were strong but not rough. Something inside her began to slide away, a piece of herself she couldn't afford to lose. Too much of her was gone already. With both feet on the ground, she caught her balance. "Thanks for the ride. It was fun." But her voice didn't sound like fun; even she could hear the loneliness in it.

The street light glittered in his eyes. "Libby Seager. Why are you always sad?" His lips brushed her mouth so gently that later she would wonder if she had imagined it. Then he mounted the cycle and thundered away. She stood in the empty parking lot and watched him go, the streetlight elongating her shadow.

She didn't know anything about Shaun Balogun. Not where he lived or how he had ended up here or whom he had loved. Let alone how he had made and lost a lot of money. It was better that way. If she didn't ask about his past, maybe he wouldn't ask about hers.

Chapter 12

Kiwi's Journal

27 January 2009

LAST NIGHT I HAD THE DREAM about Mom moving away without me. I know why: Mom has latched onto another loser. I recognize the symptoms. This morning she forgot to send my lunch money, and on the way to school, she drove past the turn and we ended up at Myra's. She says she's just tired because she's been getting up to drive me to school. But she's always tired, and she only forgets things when she's thinking about some guy. It's Shaun the Bartender. Through my peephole, I can see and hear them on nights when there aren't many customers, and my mom's voice is starting to sound different. I only met Shaun once, and we didn't say much to each other. But he's Mom's boss—he has the power. He also has the ponytail, the tattoos, and a big honking motorcycle. I better stop before Mrs. Gomez catches me not paying attention. She's showing a film about agriculture in Mexico. I have no idea why. My stomach hurts; I'm gonna ask to stay in at recess.

Love,
Kiwi

28 January

I'm in social studies again, and I can barely stay awake. I've already read the assignment everybody else is reading, so it's okay to hide behind the kid in front of me and write in my journal. This class is boring, but that's not the only reason I'm sleepy.

Last night, after Mom came over from work and checked that I was in bed, I got back up as usual. Most nights I crash before midnight, but I wasn't sleepy, so I watched TV with the sound turned down low. Then I stood on the chair and looked through the spy hole.

About midnight I heard Denise go home. She's the other waitress. I ran to the upstairs window and watched her drive away. The parking lot was empty except for our truck and Shaun's black Harley-Davidson. No customers. Mom was alone over there with Shaun. I ran back down and looked through the hole.

I heard their low voices for a long time. Finally the light through the hole went out and I heard a door bang shut. I ran back upstairs and looked out the window. Being a spy demands a lot of exercise.

Mom came around from the front of the building, and Shaun was with her. They stopped by his cycle like they were talking, but I couldn't hear what they said. Under the light of the parking lot, the Harley looked like a space monster that could fly to the moon or slice your head off and wouldn't care either way. But Shaun patted the handlebars like it was man's best friend. He threw his leg over the seat and the bike rocked, ready to go.

But he didn't leave, and neither did Mom. She stood with her back to me—her hair looking like faded gold. Shaun started up the Harley and the window glass vibrated. He walked it backward, *thrum thrum thrum thrum*, and turned it toward the street. Just when I thought he would roar away, Mom climbed on behind him. My stomach started rolling downhill. She put her arms around him and her forehead against his shoulder. I couldn't see her face. He headed toward the interstate, with Mom's hair flying out behind her. She didn't even have a helmet.

The pink light of the Sleepy Iguana sign jittered on my face like it was laughing at me. I felt like the last kid on earth, watching her ride away. It's not the first time I thought I'd never see my mom again, but each time is worse than the last. I almost wished for her not to come back, just so we could get it over with.

Later—

It's recess, but I didn't feel like going outside, so Mrs. Gomez let me stay in again. I'm by myself in our homeroom.

After Mom left with Shaun last night, I stayed by the window until I fell asleep on the stairs. And guess what? She came home. She put me to bed, but I don't think she ever came to bed herself because at seven this morning she called up the stairs to wake me up for breakfast.

We sat at the table with our cereal bowls and orange juice, but she wouldn't look at me. She asked about my homework but kept watching her cereal like she'd never seen Honey Bunches of Oats before. Obviously she wasn't going to tell me about Shaun the Bartender. And I knew she'd get mad if I asked her about him. My stomach felt too shaky for a fight. I didn't want to start to yell or throw up.

I sneaked some coffee to help me stay awake in school today, but it made me feel worse. I wonder if kids can get ulcers. I hope it feels better this afternoon because Mr. Mathis wants to talk to me and weird Tran about the science fair. Tran's not too weird, I guess, just too smart to carry on a normal conversation.

Right now I need to put my head down for a while.

XXOOXO,

Kiwi

Thursday, 5 February

As soon as Mom left for work this evening, I came upstairs and started to pack. I was cramming underwear into my backpack when all of a sudden, Bones showed up. It was the first I'd seen of him since we moved. "It took you long enough to find me," I said.

"You've been busy." He looked at my backpack. "What are you packing for?"

"I'm going to the district science fair tomorrow. Tran and I have to be there early to demonstrate our projects. His mom is taking us, and Mr. Mathis is bringing the whole class later in the day. Kids from other schools will come, too, and the judges will award ribbons."

"Cool," he said. "Are you nervous?"

"Kind of, yeah."

"Why do you need your toothbrush on a field trip?"

"Because I'm not coming back."

"Uh-oh." Bones frowned. "Is that because your mom is dating the guy who owns the bar?"

"That's part of it," I said.

Bones sat down as if he was ready to listen. How many adults do you know who'll do that? Not many, that's for sure.

I told him there was a terrible repeating pattern with my mother. Sooner or later, she always disappeared with some perv. It was only a matter of time before she left me again. So this time, I was leaving first.

"Why would she leave you?" he said. "All moms love their kids."

I told him he was naïve for his age. (*Naïve* was my new word this week.)

"Mom used to love me," I explained, "even when I was mouthy or didn't clean up my room. But that all changed in San Jose. It's not her fault. I did something so awful even God won't forgive me."

Bones sat next to me on the bed and patted my hair the way Daddy used to do when I was little. That made my nose run, and we didn't have any tissues.

"How do you know God won't forgive you?" Bones said. "Did you ask him?"

"I can't. If I told you what I did, you'd understand why."

He looked even more worried. "That sounds scary."

"It is. You're the only one I can tell. I keep holding it inside like too much water in a big balloon. I feel like I'm going to rip open."

"We don't want that." He stretched out beside me. "Tell me."

So I did.

❧

The Spiderling

The move was the fourth one since third grade. Somebody we used to know in the Army lived there—a lady who was married to one of Dad's buddies. She helped Mom get a job in a department store. I liked the school, but we had this crappy apartment with a toilet that didn't work right and a shower with a bottom so black that you couldn't get it white no matter how much bleach you used.

Mom said her job was boring but better than waiting tables. On weekends she needed some fun, and so she started going out with people she worked with. That was okay until she met Rocket.

Rocket probably wasn't his real name, but I never asked him. He had black hair and thick arms with tattoos from the wrist all the way up his neck. His eyes were dark and mean. The first time I looked in them, I knew he was bad news. Mom couldn't see it, though, or she didn't care. Maybe she liked that he seemed dangerous. She started acting different, not responsibly. A couple of times, she didn't come home until morning, and I would stay awake all night too scared to go to sleep. I was only ten and not as independent as I am now that I'm eleven.

Before long, Rocket said he had an apartment he didn't use much where we could stay. I didn't like the idea but Mom was disgusted with the place we had, so we moved. His place was better. It had two bedrooms and the toilet worked. And lots of nights he didn't even visit.

But sometimes he did. And when Rocket and Mom got together, they drank too much and laughed too loud. He got her to smoke pot and gave her pills that he said would help her sleep. When I complained, she told me to mind my own business. Pretty soon she was taking pills morning and night. She started losing weight, and I swear her skin was turning yellow, but she wouldn't believe me.

I couldn't stand the way she sucked up to Rocket when he did visit. She waited on him like a slave and he treated her like one. It made me want to hurl. Rocket knew it too. He'd give me this snotty little smile when he sent her out to get him a beer or a sandwich or to the store for cigarettes. If I glared back, he gave me the finger. He'd sit in the apartment with his feet on the furniture. It was crappy furniture, but still.

One time he told me to go get him something and I didn't get up fast enough. He slapped the back of my head so hard I fell on the floor.

When I got up, he knocked my feet out from under me, and then he laughed. The fall chipped my tooth. Another time he tried to get me to take one of his pills. He said I'd see wild colors and feel great. When I told him where he could stick his pills, he pinched my boob till my eyes watered and then gave me a wedgie. He said I had a smart mouth, and muttered that one of these days he'd teach me a lesson. His eyes were dark when he said that and it scared me. He loved to make me cry, so I tried hard not to.

After the fall, I made a point not to be alone with him. I tried to tell Mom, but he never did bad stuff to me when she was there. He'd smile and call me Kiddo, but when her back was turned, he'd make threats with his eyes or a motion like he was slitting my throat. Mom thought I was lying about him to get attention because I'd done that once or twice before with other guys. I was like the kid who cried wolf when there wasn't one and then got eaten.

But as scared as I was for me, I was more scared about what was happening to Mom. We started fighting all the time, mostly about Rocket. The more we argued, the more she stayed away. One night when I was home alone, I woke to loud noises and screams. Sirens wailed outside and I heard feet running in the hall. I locked the doors and windows, turned off the lights, and hid under my blanket. I was shaking and hyperventilating. But after the police went away and it was quiet again, I got mad. I started to cry. The more I cried, the madder I got.

When Mom finally came home, I threw a megatantrum. I cussed Rocket and called her a bad name, and said awful stuff about Dad being ashamed of her. I threw every shoe I could find, and I yelled that if she didn't leave Rocket, I was going to do something terrible. My idea of something terrible was to run away or throw her makeup in the dumpster. I had no idea what a bad person I really was.

When I ran out of shoes to throw, Mom slapped me hard. Then she burst into tears; we both spent the rest of the night crying but in separate rooms. That was a horrible night and it didn't change anything. She was addicted to Rocket and his pills. I could see I was going to lose her and be an orphan. I fell asleep on the couch, dreaming I had come home from school and found my mom dead from an overdose.

The Spiderling

.Mom was still asleep the next morning when I got up, so I dressed and went to school and got in trouble for being late again. Because of detention, I came home later than usual. Rocket was asleep on the couch. Mom was always at work when I got home after school, but I had no idea why Rocket was there. He didn't seem to have a regular job.

I looked at him with his inked-up arm thrown behind his head and his mouth half open, and I got madder and madder. His booze breath polluted the whole apartment. I thought about my dream, about finding my mom dead, and I hated Rocket for what he'd done to her. Our fighting was his fault, and so were the nights I stayed by myself scared to death. He was an Olympic-class creep, and I hated him so much, I felt sweaty. But I was afraid of him too.

I didn't want to be there alone with Rocket. So I decided to sneak out before he woke up and stay gone until I was sure Mom was home. His jacket was thrown over a chair. I went through his pockets hoping to find money for a snack at the Quick Stop or at least some gum. Very quietly, I slipped my hand into a jacket pocket. It was empty. I tried the other pocket, and my hand touched something cold and heavy.

When I pulled it out, I was holding a gun.

I couldn't believe it. I held the gun flat on my palms. I'd seen a real gun before, but it was a rifle the Army issued to my dad. This one was short, like a policeman's.

What did Rocket do with that gun? Hold up stores? Did my mom know he had it? What if he got mad and shot her? Or maybe he meant to use that gun on me.

I aimed it with both hands like the police do on TV. Rocket snorted in his sleep and I jumped like a rabbit. That pissed me off, so I pointed the gun at him.

"Rocket," I said, but I whispered the name so he wouldn't wake up. "You are a waste of food and oxygen, and I wish you'd disappear."

It was another version of the Traffic Game. I didn't think about what would happen when I pulled the trigger. I just pulled it.

The explosion knocked me down. My ears rang so loud I couldn't hear. I thought I'd shot myself, and I sat there a minute to see if I would die. I felt like I was screaming, but I couldn't make any noise at all.

When I realized I wasn't shot, I got up and looked at Rocket. He had a hole in his neck, right below his jaw. It was bleeding but not too much, and his eyes were still shut. Like an idiot, I thought he couldn't be hurt too badly if it didn't even wake him up. Then I saw blood leaking from the back of his head and across the cushion and dripping on the floor. I started to gag. My head got dizzy. I didn't want to look at him, but I couldn't move. I couldn't even close my eyes.

I begged him, *Don't be dead, please don't be dead.*

Get up, I muttered. *Get up and take the gun away from me, you worthless bag of crap.*

The worst part, and the reason God's not going to forgive me, was that even while I prayed that he wasn't dead, part of me hoped he was. He was an evil, scary man, and the only way Mom would ever get away from him was if he was dead.

When I realized he was, I started to shake. I don't know how long I stood there like that, but I still hadn't moved when Mom got home.

She didn't scream. I remember the first thing she did was lock the door. She had to pry the gun out of my hands. I couldn't talk. She led me to the bedroom and wrapped me in a blanket on the bed. She had tears on her face. She leaned over me and said to be quiet, she would take care of everything.

She went back out to where Rocket was, and when she came back in the bedroom, she told me to get up and help her pack. We filled one suitcase, and she led me past Rocket and out of the apartment. I didn't look at him. I was wrapped up in the blanket like a mummy. Mom had to hold onto me and drag our suitcase down the stairs.

Outside, it was dark. We didn't have a car, so we took Rocket's. The last thing I remember about that night was curling into a tight ball on the seat and looking up through the windshield at the stars.

When my story was finished, Bones didn't say anything for a long time. Finally he said, "It sounds like your mom was trying to protect you as best she could."

"She was," I told him. "But how can she love a murderer? I broke her heart, and it was already broken because of my dad. She's better off without me."

"Where will you go?" Bones asked.

"I don't know." The seat-belt feeling was tightening my chest again.

Bones said, "No matter what happens, I'll always love you, Kiwi."

When I could stop crying long enough, I worked up my courage to ask Bones something that had been bubbling in my mind for weeks. I had to whisper it because it was too important to say out loud.

"Bones, are you my dad, come back to watch over me?"

He fell silent for a long time. "I might have been, in another life," he said. "But I'm not now."

"Why not? Why can't you be my dad now?"

He shook his head. "It doesn't work that way. If you run away from home, I can't go with you. But you're a smart girl. You'll figure out what you need to do."

I hoped he was right. My chest loosened up enough that I could take a deep breath. But it looked like once I slipped away from the science fair tomorrow, I'd be on my own.

So long,

Kiwi the Runaway

Chapter 13

Missing in Action

O N A FRIDAY AFTERNOON, the alarm on Libby's cell phone chimed. Time to pick up Kiwi from school. She slipped into jeans and a light sweater and pulled her hair back in a quick ponytail. Twisting the elastic band around and around, she remembered this was the day of Kiwi's field trip and wondered how the science demonstration had gone. Kiwi had seemed nervous that morning when Libby dropped her off at school, almost as if she might cry.

Near the school she parked at their usual meeting spot and shut off the engine. Children scattered from the building, boarding buses, heading for the line of cars parked along the street. Some trickled out into the neighborhood on foot. Libby turned on the radio and waited.

Kids wearing backpacks and carrying wrinkled papers disappeared into the waiting cars. Vehicles pulled away, then one of the buses. Libby thought, What's keeping you, Squirt?

In ten more minutes, the schoolyard was nearly vacant. She was irritated as she got out of the pickup and walked toward the entrance. Inside, the building was quiet except for a distant echo of voices. Libby turned down the hallway where she'd met Kiwi's science teacher. If Kiwi was hanging around anywhere, she thought, that's where she would be. Through an open doorway, she saw Mr. Mathis sitting at his desk, shuffling paperwork. Kiwi wasn't there.

He glanced up. "May I help you?"

"I'm looking for Kiwi," she said.

"Oh! Mrs. Seager." He stood up, but his smile quickly changed to a frown. "Tran's mom was going to drop her off at your house. She should have been there by now."

Libby pictured Tran's mom dropping Kiwi at the Sleepy Iguana and her face flushed. Kiwi hadn't told her she was riding home with someone else. "Maybe I just missed her."

"Let me check," he said and picked up a cell phone. He pushed a button, then said, "Mrs. Phenn? It's Mr. Mathis. Have you dropped Kiwi off at home yet?" He waited, his forehead creasing. "No, she told me you were taking her home. No, no, it's not your fault. Mrs. Seager is here now. We'll check with the director at the exhibit building."

By the time he hung up, a dark mass was rising in Libby's chest. "Where is she?"

The teacher met her eyes. "She told Mrs. Phenn she was coming home with the rest of us on the bus. She told me she was riding home with Tran. She had a note from you saying it was okay."

Libby shook her head. "Not from me. I signed her permission slip for the trip; she was supposed to ride with Tran's mom this morning. I thought she was coming back on the bus."

His jaw tightened as they both realized at the same time that Kiwi had planned this. "This is not like Kiwi." He looked betrayed. "Does she know anybody in Creosote City?"

Again Libby shook her head. In her ears a buzzing started like the sound inside a beehive. She thought of Kiwi fidgeting at the breakfast table, unable to finish her cereal. She wasn't nervous about the science fair; she was planning to run away. Suddenly her legs wouldn't hold her up. She sank into a student desk.

Mr. Mathis was punching more numbers into his cell phone. "I need to speak with the director, please. It's urgent." In seconds, he spoke again. "One of our students didn't get home from the science fair today.

I need you to search the building as fast as possible. Her name is Kiwi Seager, and she's eleven." He reeled off the digits of his cell number and closed the phone, then looked at Libby. "Let's go."

Creosote City was an hour northwest on the interstate. She followed him in her own vehicle in case she needed to stay. The teacher drove fast; this stretch of highway was notoriously ignored by law enforcement. After twenty minutes on the road, her cell phone rang. She grabbed it, hoping nonsensically to hear Kiwi's voice.

"She's not in the building," Mr. Mathis said. "They searched the restrooms, the storage rooms, everything. I told him to have the police meet us at the coliseum."

"Police?" The truck veered onto the cobbled warning strip of the shoulder; Libby steered it back. "Is that necessary?"

"Yes, it is," he said evenly. "In fact, they've already started looking for her."

"My gas gauge says empty. I may have to stop."

"I don't think there's a station between here and there," he said. "Call me if you run out and I'll circle back to get you."

She hung up and laid a curse on the truck: Don't you dare stop running. And it didn't, despite the warning light and the needle edging toward E.

When she reached the exhibit hall, two squad cars were parked in the breezeway. Libby felt sick. If Kiwi's name went out across the state as missing, would the San Jose police recognize it?

Only two other cars were in the lot. She and Mr. Mathis trotted toward the entrance. Inside, a uniformed policeman was talking to a balding man with a worried expression on his face.

"I'm Kiwi's mother," she said to the policeman.

His eyes softened. He introduced himself and the other man, the director of the coliseum, but the name didn't register. The director apologized as if Kiwi's absence was somehow his fault.

"We have units out looking all over town," Officer Davies told her. "We haven't seen her yet, but we did talk to a parent who thinks she saw your daughter leaving the grounds by herself this afternoon."

"Which way?"

"Toward the McDonald's," he said. "We've asked everyone there, but nobody remembers her. What was she wearing?"

Libby's mind went blank. "Jeans and sneakers," she began. "A pink-and-brown backpack."

When she faltered, Mr. Mathis spoke up. "A red knit shirt," he said. "She has long dark hair in a ponytail, backpack charms attached to her belt loops. And military dog tags around her neck."

Libby balked—Mr. Mathis had paid more attention to Kiwi than her own mother. She looked at him, her mouth open.

"I visited her exhibit and watched her demonstration this morning," he said as if to explain.

I should have been there, too, Libby thought.

"Dog tags?" Officer Davies said, pausing in his note-taking.

"Her father was killed in Iraq," Mr. Mathis told him. "He was a war hero."

Libby flinched, but she saw the officer's posture straighten and his mouth set in a tight line. Mr. Mathis had added that detail to ensure that Kiwi got their full attention.

Officer Davies addressed both of them. "Was Kiwi upset about anything recently? Is there any chance she has run away?"

Libby and the teacher exchanged a glance. "Yes," Libby said. She told him about Kiwi's deception. She was afraid he would ask what would prompt her to run away, but the officer only nodded.

"Do you have a photo of her?"

"Not with me," she said, but she didn't have a recent one at home, either. Kiwi had missed her school pictures last year.

"Will you issue an Amber alert?" Mr. Mathis asked.

The officer shook his head. "Not on a runaway. That's only if we suspect foul play. But we'll add her description to the police bulletin and send out a photo when we get one. We'll find her—the town's not that big." He hesitated. "Unless . . ."

Libby's heart flipped. "Unless what?"

"Unless somebody picked her up and got on the interstate."

Libby thought she might throw up. The officer told her to stay at the exhibit hall in case Kiwi found her way back. He was operating on the premise that she went AWOL on a lark and got lost. Libby hoped he was right. He took her cell number and promised to call if there was any news. Mr. Mathis offered to stand vigil in the building lobby with the director.

As for Libby, she needed to be alone. She wandered through the exhibit hall, down rows of tables strewn with leftovers from projects their creators had taken home after the fair. Only one table was not vacant.

Libby's breath jerked as she reached the table where Kiwi's project sat, still neatly intact. On a small easel, a certificate declared her project to be the first-place winner in the sixth-grade division. There was a little drawing of a blue ribbon, but the ribbon itself was gone.

Chapter 14

Kiwi's Journal

TO WHOEVER FINDS THIS JOURNAL:
Please tell my mother, Libby Louise Seager, that I love her, and I'm sorry I caused her so much trouble. But don't let her read my journal. It might make her sad.

Please tell Mr. Ian Mathis at Sand Flats Elementary School that I apologize for lying to him. He's one of the best teachers I ever had.

So that somebody will know, this is what happened the day I left home. . . .

Friday, 6 February 2009

Tran and his mom and I got to the district science fair about 8:30 this morning. A lady gave us name tags and took us into a huge exhibit hall. Rows and rows of tables were set up with tall screens behind them. The lady helped us find our tables, and we went to work setting up for our demonstrations. Tran's table was three tables down and across the aisle from mine. Mrs. Phenn's English is hard to understand, but she's really nice. I told her I was supposed to ride home on the bus with our class later on, and she said okay.

We practiced our demonstrations, and then it was time for the judges to come through. Some kids followed them around and watched the other demonstrations, but Tran and I stood behind our tables and waited. Tran's face looked shriveled. He's a nervous person even on regular days.

After each demonstration, the judges and their groupies clapped politely. The judges made notes and congratulated each kid for his project and then moved on to the next table. They came to Tran, but I couldn't see his demonstration for the groupies. His project was about detecting certain compounds using a sensor and a computer program that strobes different colors. Everybody clapped, so I guess it worked.

My project was about using solar energy to purify water without a bunch of chemicals. I'd been thinking about it ever since I read an article about prescription drugs in the water supply. When the judges came to my table, I tried to smile like Mr. Mathis had told me. I started the purification process (using a heat lamp for the sun). While they watched that, I explained how the process could be adapted on a lot bigger scale to handle a whole town's water supply, without using hardly any electricity. My project didn't explode or flash pretty colors, but Mr. Mathis had said it was good science. He said it might not work in a rainy climate, but it would darn sure work in the desert.

At the end, I poured some of the purified water into tiny plastic cups and gave everybody a taste. I drank some, too, because by then, my mouth was awful dry. Some of the kids were afraid to try it until they saw the judges drink. Then they said, *Wow!* and *Could I have another sample*? It was like they'd never tasted pure water before.

When the judges were gone, I slumped on my chair and looked down the row at Tran. He smiled and gave me a thumbs-up.

They had lunch for all the kids, and that's when they awarded the ribbons. I got a blue ribbon for first place in my division! I felt a little bad, though, because Tran had worked even harder on his than I did on mine. But he got a red ribbon, so our school looked good.

After lunch we went back to our tables. Buses started to arrive, and kids trooped through to see the exhibits. My blue ribbon and first-place certificate were on a little stand beside my table. My class went through, and I did the whole demonstration for them, even though they'd already seen it at our school. Then Mr. Mathis herded them outdoors to a courtyard where the sponsors of the fair had put out snacks and drinks.

When my class went back to their bus, I picked up my backpack and stuck the blue ribbon inside. I waved at Tran and left my table. But instead of going outside, I went into the restroom and waited until I was sure the bus would be gone. Then I just walked away.

I remembered seeing a McDonald's down the street that morning. I wanted some chicken nuggets and fries because the lunch they'd served us was pretty lame, and I was too nervous to eat anyway. I had $41.75 I'd saved from my paper route, but I figured I'd better ration it. So I just got a Coke and kept walking.

At first, I felt cool being on my own. Independent. I told myself that nobody in the world knew where I was that minute. But then I got a hollow feeling in my stomach like when I get to school without my homework or say something stupid that hurts somebody's feelings.

I spent the afternoon in the Creosote City Walmart. It's a good place to keep a low profile because nobody pays any attention to you there. All kinds of people were pushing carts up and down the aisles, so I didn't feel lost. No matter what else changes, Walmart is always the same.

I wondered if my class was back at school yet and how long it would be until someone noticed I was missing. Probably not until Mom showed up at school to get me, if she didn't forget. I tried to be mad at her again for hooking up with Shaun the Bartender, but I couldn't. I was already lonesome. I wondered if she'd be mad or sad or just relieved that I was gone. Maybe she wouldn't report that I was missing so she could go on with her life. That's what I wanted. Sort of. But I also hoped she'd miss me like crazy. I sat on my backpack in the pet aisle and watched the goldfish swimming circles in their blue tanks, waiting for someone to give them a home. The goldfish had no options, but I'm not a fish. I've got skills. It was time to step up and make a plan.

One option was to play the Traffic Game on the interstate and let some big honking truck take me out. I pictured my body flying through the air and landing in a heap in the ditch. I wonder if you'd feel the pain when every bone in your body snapped or if the impact would knock you instantly unconscious. But the truth is I'm scared to die. As Bones pointed out, if I'm going to hell for the rest of eternity, why be in a hurry to get there?

So I was going to stay alive. With that decided, did I want to spend the rest of my days as a homeless person in Creosote City, California? If not, I needed to catch a ride somewhere. I didn't know if the city had a bus or train station or if I had enough money for a ticket or where I wanted to go. But where I went didn't matter much. If Mom did report me missing, people would be searching here. I needed to get out of town.

From the Walmart, I could see a big truck stop close to the highway. My grandfather in Alabama was a truck driver before he retired and died. He said drivers are the salt of the earth. I knew what he meant: What would the earth be without salt? There would be no point to potato chips, no fun in French fries. I felt the same way about ketchup. I wished Grandpa was still alive and I could catch a ride in his big rig.

When I got to the truck stop, I was thirsty again, so I bought an orange slushy and some chips. I sat on a bench in front of the building and watched the big trucks roll up to the diesel pumps. I didn't realize how big and loud and smelly those trucks were until I saw them up close. The ones that didn't need gas parked in a slanted row away from the building. A Transformer could have pushed one over, and they'd all have fallen like dominoes.

In one truck cab, a big dog hung its floppy face out the window and smiled at me. Maybe I could find a stray dog someplace, and we could be homeless together. My one requirement was to be homeless near a school. School was something I could depend on.

Cars were stopping for gas, too, so I watched for a family I could catch a ride with. But people with children might be suspicious of a kid my age being alone. They'd probably ask questions. So I decided to target one of those alone women who want to help everybody or an old man who looked like a grandpa. I sat there a long time, working up my cover story, but nobody who came through looked suitable. My slushy was gone by then, and I was still thirsty. I was digging in my pocket for money by a pop machine outside the building when a big hand reached in front of me. The hand held out a bunch of quarters.

"Need these?" a voice said. "Go ahead, I've got lots of change."

I followed the arm up to a face that was shaved and smiling. He was younger than a grandpa but older than my dad or Bones.

"Thanks," I said and took the quarters. I fed change into the machine, and a bottle of water dropped out.

"Water?" he said. "Smart. Most people don't drink enough water."

"That's a fact. Especially purified water." I took a big drink and looked him over. He had blue eyes and short hair with a little too much gel. His clothes looked clean and neat, almost like he'd ironed them. The short sleeves of his T-shirt were rolled up on his biceps like old lady stockings.

"Are you a truck driver?" I said.

"Correct." He smiled again. "Name's Jack."

"How come you don't have tattoos?"

"Don't like 'em. Make your arms look dirty."

"Amen to that," I said.

"What's your name?"

The lie came out slick as cat snot. "Ruby," I said. "Thanks again for the quarters." I sat back down on the bench, but he didn't go away.

"You've been sitting here the whole time I was gassing up my rig. Are you waiting for somebody?"

"My dad," I said. "I guess he's still in the bathroom."

He frowned. "Do you want me to check on him?"

"Nah. He's probably got diarrhea again. Trust me, you don't wanna go in there."

Jack laughed. "Thanks for the tip. I'll be inside getting a burger. Let me know if you need some help."

He went inside and I sat there deliberating. Was Jack the salt of the earth?

The sun slipped down behind the building, and the shadows of the trucks got longer and longer. Maybe I should go back to Walmart and hide in the bathroom until they closed. I could spend the night in the bedding aisle. I once read a book about a lady who lived in a Walmart. It worked out okay until she had a baby in there. I don't know if it was a true story or not. After she had the baby, people found out and she had to leave. But I was never going to have a baby, so maybe nobody would notice me if I spent a few hours there.

That was the plan I'd decided on when Jack came back out. He was drinking a soda and holding a white sack that smelled like a hamburger. I was starving. He saw me looking at the sack. "Still here, huh?"

"Yup."

"Your dad's not with you, is he?" I didn't answer.

I could smell the warm beef patty, the mustard, and the dill pickle. I'm usually not a fan of hamburgers, but right now it smelled great. My mouth started to water and my eyes did too.

"Where you headed?" he asked.

"San Jose." The name just popped out.

His eyebrows hitched up. "Coincidence. That's where I'm headed too." He shrugged his shoulders and started to walk away. "This burger's for you if you want it."

I sat still for a few seconds and my eyes began to water even worse. *San Jose*. The name went click in my brain. I picked up my backpack and followed the smell of that hamburger like a rat behind the Pied Piper of Hamelin.

Jack's truck has a bunk up behind the seats in the cab. That's where I am now, writing this down. He said on long hauls, he can sleep there instead of getting a motel room. After I ate the hamburger, he suggested I crawl up in the bunk and get some sleep. It was dark by then, and I was exhausted. He said he'd be driving all night.

There's barely enough light from the dashboard to write. We're barreling down the highway at sixty-two miles an hour, despite the signs saying the speed limit for trucks is fifty-five. I hadn't seen any signs for San Jose yet. I guess it's still a long way away. I was almost asleep awhile ago when something seriously weird happened. Jack had been quiet for miles, and then I heard him say, more to himself than to me, "Tomorrow we'll find a place where you can take a bath."

My eyes slammed open. His voice sounded different from before, not like the same person. Scary.

I shivered. All of a sudden all I wanted was out of this truck! What was I thinking, getting in with some guy I didn't know?

I couldn't jump out at sixty-two miles an hour, so I pulled a blanket over me and turned my back so he would think I was asleep. Surely he would have to stop and pee sometime, and then I'd escape. I hoped.

Pray for me.

Kiwi

In the middle of the night, the truck finally stopped. Jack pushed on my shoulder and said, "Wake up, kiddo. Bathroom stop."

I lied and said I didn't need to go. I tried to sound sleepy, but I had yet to even close my eyes. He said, "Suit yourself," and got out and slammed the door. The locks clicked. He left the truck running, but it was dark inside the cab.

As soon as he walked away, I climbed down onto the passenger seat. We were parked beside some other trucks at a rest area. This was my chance. My heart was going *boom boom boom* in my ears.

I reached for the door handle and pulled, but the door wouldn't open. I yanked harder—nothing.

I crawled across to the other door and tried that one. It wouldn't open either! Why would you have childproof locks in a truck? I hunted on the armrest for the unlock button, but it was so dark I couldn't find anything. I was afraid to push stuff on the dashboard—an alarm might go off or the truck might start to roll. But I was going crazy, so finally, I pushed something anyway. A light came on by my feet. That's when I saw a magazine had slid out from under the driver's seat. There was a naked woman on the cover, and I can't write down what she was doing. I opened the magazine and saw sick pictures—some of them showed kids my age! I was in big trouble.

With no warning, my hamburger ejected. I hurled all over the magazine and the floor. When it stopped, I was shaking. If I didn't get out of this truck before Jack came back, going to hell would be the best thing that might happen to me.

I looked toward the building where Jack had disappeared, but I still couldn't see him. I yanked the door handle again and pounded on the window button. Everything was locked! Then I remembered a little sliding window up behind the bunk.

I scrambled up there and slid the window open. It was covered by a screen. Diesel fumes blew in and made my stomach hurt more. I tried to punch out the screen with my fist, but I couldn't. So I got on my back, doubled up my legs, and took a deep breath. Then I jammed both feet into the screen as hard as I could.

The whole screen popped off.

My backpack was too fat to fit through the window. Real fast, I threw out shoes and clothes. When it would fit, I stuffed it through the opening and heard it drop.

For once I was lucky to be small. I wiggled halfway through the window, but then my hips caught. I heard men's voices coming toward the building.

I grabbed hold of a bar on the trailer behind the cab. When I pulled myself through, my jacket tore and skin scraped off my side. I half fell and half climbed down between the cab and the trailer and landed on the pavement beside my pack. The blood on my shirt looked black in the parking lights. I ran on my toes so I wouldn't make noise, between the big trucks and away from the lighted building.

Behind the lot was open desert with nothing to hide in but creosote bush, which is only about knee-high. I ran until my side hurt so much I doubled over and fell. I rolled behind the biggest bush I could find and landed on my back, panting and looking up at a bazillion stars.

So here I am, writing by moonlight. If I stay real still, nobody looking out over the field should be able to see me in the dark. I hope. If Jack finds me . . . well, I can't even think about that. My side hurts so bad I have to cry, but not out loud. Thank goodness I still have my journal and Moxie in my backpack.

It's quiet and lonesome out here in the desert, and I'm scared. I can't believe how stupid I've been. I didn't plan where to go or how to get there. And I climbed in a truck with a stranger. If I don't do better, I'll be one of those anonymous skeletons they find out in the sand. I wish Bones would show up and keep me company. But I have a sad feeling he can't find me under this big endless sky.

Bones said I was a smart girl and would figure out what I needed to do. I didn't understand—but now I do. Or maybe I knew all along.

Jack may have lied when he said he was headed for San Jose, but I didn't. I have to go back and tell the truth about shooting Rocket. Then Mom won't have to stay on the run to protect me. And she won't have to live with a murderer. Telling the truth is what Dad would want me to do.

Now that I know where I'm going—if Jack doesn't find me—the next problem is that I have no idea where I am. And no clue how to get to San Jose.

Love,
Kiwi

Chapter 15

Sins of the Mothers

FOR THE NEXT THREE HOURS, Libby paced the terrazzo floor of the Creosote City coliseum. Fifteen minutes before she was due at the Sleepy Iguana, she phoned Shaun to tell him why she wouldn't be coming to work. The concern in his voice made her eyes tear.

"Take all the time you need," he said. "Anything I can do to help?"

"I don't think so. The police are all over it." She promised to keep in touch.

Standing behind glass walls, Libby stared past the empty parking lot toward the town beyond, where lights had begun to flicker on. She imagined Kiwi out there somewhere in the dark, walking the streets. Where would she go? How could a mother not have seen this coming? Kiwi had been quiet lately, but she'd had quiet spells off and on for the last three years. She didn't like Libby dating Shaun, if you could call it dating, but that was nothing new. Kiwi objected to anyone Libby dated.

Her fists clenched. In what way had she failed her daughter this time? Didn't Kiwi care that she was hurting her mother too? Or was that her intention? Libby checked the silent cell phone for the third time in five minutes. Surely Kiwi would get scared and call soon. But as night thickened outside the glass walls, so did her breath. She thought of Deacon, in the unknown place where souls might go. I'm so sorry, Deacon. I need your help. I don't know how to do this without you. The lights of Creosote City shimmered before her.

By midnight, there was still no trace of Kiwi. Officer Davies looked tired when he returned from the search and advised Libby to go home. He assured her they would keep looking overnight. A search crew was combing the town street by street, and a bulletin had gone out to state police. He promised to call if they found any clue, no matter the hour. He assured Libby that they had gone through every closet and cranny of the coliseum with a search dog, and now the manager needed to lock up the building for the night.

Libby had a choice: She could either sit at the police station the rest of the night or go home. She chose home.

Ian Mathis left ahead of her in his green Honda. She respected him for staying so long. Still, she couldn't deny a petty resentment for the intensity of his concern. He was not Kiwi's parent; it wasn't his fault she had lied to them both. He wasn't the one who had taken off on a motorcycle in the middle of the night. He hadn't neglected to give Kiwi the attention she needed or to praise her when she did well. Libby owned all that guilt herself, and the teacher's blamelessness made her feel even worse.

Within minutes on the highway, she lost sight of Mathis's car. There were no streetlights and the stars looked flat and hard. Libby's vehicle was the only moving thing in a vast desert landscape. She felt utterly lost, like the night she had run away from her own mother.

The darkness beyond her headlights sucked her back fifteen years, to the summer before her junior year in high school. The fight she and her mother had that night wasn't any worse than a thousand others before it, just the final scene in a decade of competitive bickering.

She had come home an hour past her curfew the night before. As if the curfew meant anything; often her mother wasn't even home. Dayleen had been fired twice for drinking on the job, both before and after her husband had left her. It was no big deal. Lots of parents drank. But Dayleen also slept around, and that did bother Libby. She suspected her mother was doing it for money. Their argument turned ugly, and she had called her mother a whore. Dayleen slapped her, a resounding blow that made her eyes water and her cheek go numb. She wanted to take the words back, to say "I'm sorry," but she was struck silent by the savage look on her mother's face.

She hates me, Libby thought. She wishes I had never been born.

Libby packed an old gym bag and left that night. Dayleen sat at the kitchen table with her bourbon and Coke and didn't try to stop her. Maybe she thought their anger would wear off and Libby would come back. Maybe she didn't care.

The only friend Libby could trust was spending that summer with her father in a different state, so Libby spent the night huddled inside a cluster of shrubs in the city park. Winos haunted the park, most of them harmless but some of them insane. She was more afraid of roaming gangs. A beat cop walked by and urinated into the bushes, barely missing her shoes. She was afraid of him too. She stayed awake all night in her prickly cave.

Libby's tires drummed on the warning strip at the road's edge. She corrected her steering and blinked her eyes hard. Kids didn't think about consequences. Was Kiwi trembling in the bushes this minute, hungry and scared? Where the hell did she think she would go? What if she'd been kidnapped by some deviant freak?

At that moment, the pickup's engine sputtered twice and died. After all was said and done, she had forgotten about the empty gas tank. Shit, she thought. *Shit shit shit!* Why couldn't she do anything right?

Libby swiped at her eyes and coasted to a stop on the shoulder. Dousing the lights, she sat in the dark and bounced her forehead against the steering wheel. She was about halfway between Creosote City and Sand Flats, with no container to carry gas even if she walked thirty miles to a station. What kind of inept human being ran out of gas on an isolated road in the middle of the night? Exhaustion rolled over her. This is why people drown themselves, she thought. They give in and sink. And finally take one long, last deep breath. Too tired to fight her way back up, she felt the heaviness of water in her lungs.

But she couldn't quit now, with Kiwi missing. She forced a deep breath, blew it out, and picked up her cell phone. Thankfully, the battery wasn't dead. A minor miracle.

By the third ring, Shaun hadn't picked up. It was 1:00 a.m. and he would still be at the bar. If he didn't answer, she'd have to phone Myra and wake her. She hadn't talked to Myra in weeks and hated to call in the middle of the night asking a huge favor. She dreaded the disapproval that she often imagined in Myra's tone, whether it was there or not.

On the fifth ring, Shaun answered.

She stopped tapping the wheel. "Beware of offering help to idiots," she said, her voice hoarse. "I've run out of gas on the highway."

"Is Kiwi with you?" She almost loved him for asking that question first.

"No. They're still looking. The police sent me home."

"Where are you?"

"About halfway between you and Creosote City." She switched on the headlights. "I can see mile marker 153, if that helps. There's no gas station on this whole godforsaken road."

"I can get there in less than an hour," he said. "Put on your trouble lights and lock your doors."

Her nose burned. "Thanks." Libby tossed the phone on the seat and put her head back, exhaling a shaky breath.

When she opened the door, a rectangle of light flashed on the road, extinguishing when she slammed the door again. Her shoes crunched gravel. She walked to the back of the truck and sat on the bumper. She would put the trouble lights on later so Shaun could find her.

Right now, all she wanted was fresh air, the stillness, and the dark. She propped her head back and stretched out her legs. In the cloudless sky was a constellation whose name she didn't know. It might have been a bear or three sisters, but Libby saw instead the shape of Kiwi's face. Her breath came sharp and hard while her daughter's life flashed before her eyes. She saw Kiwi as a baby, then as a toddler. Precocious, resisting sleep, a mystery from the day she was born. Libby felt the tiny hands grasping her hair, saw the utter love in those trusting eyes. With a cruel clarity, Libby knew that her sorrow over losing Deacon had become an excuse not to face the hard task of living without him. In her selfish grieving, she had abandoned Kiwi to cope on her own.

"My God," she told the stars. "I'm as bad a mother as Dayleen."

The realization floored her. When Kiwi was born, she had vowed that her daughter would always feel loved and protected. With Deacon's help, that had been an easy promise to keep. Alone, she had failed. Her body felt stripped, like a tree struck by lightning, but when she looked down, her skin was marble-white in the darkness. She remembered her mother's bony arms and freckled skin. These were not her mother's arms, and she was not Dayleen. Libby's mistakes were not because she didn't care.

She hugged herself, shivering. "Please stay safe until I find you, Kiwi. Give me another chance."

When the single headlight appeared on the long horizon, Libby was back in the truck with the trouble lights on. The light slowed as it grew closer, and she recognized the deep-throated rumble of Shaun's Harley. He did not own a four-wheeled vehicle. In the past week, she had learned that he'd once worked as a website and computer-game designer in Sacramento but had gone off the grid when he lost his young wife to cancer. Their similar loss became a kind of bond.

Shaun made a U-turn and pulled off the highway in front of her. She locked the truck, pocketed her cell phone and keys, and approached the bike.

"You okay?" he asked.

"I guess."

"We'll get your truck tomorrow."

He handed her a flannel shirt and a helmet. She put them on and straddled the seat behind him. The engine revved, and Shaun glanced over his shoulder at miles of empty highway before he pulled onto the road. In seconds, they were streaking through the chilly night. Libby locked her arms around Shaun's stomach and felt the bones of his spine against her chest. She closed her eyes.

Kiwi is wrong about him, she thought. He's a good guy. It's a wonder that I'm attracted to him at all.

Chapter 16

Kiwi's Journal

Saturday, I think.

THIS MORNING I WOKE UP curled in a ball on the ground with desert all around me. I was freezing cold and almost panicked until I remembered how I had gotten here. Then I freaked out! I'd gone and fallen asleep. Jack might have come looking for me and stumbled right over my body!

I stood halfway up and peered toward the truck stop in the distance. His rig was gone. And I was thirsty.

There wasn't much left in my water bottle, and I drank it all. I didn't feel safe, but nothing is quite as bad in daylight as it is in the dark. I stayed low and started to crawl away from the highway. My side hurt and I was hungry, but I couldn't fix that. So I just kept crawling, dragging my backpack behind me in the dirt.

I thought of a book I once read called *My Side of the Mountain* about a boy who went to live in the woods all by himself. He learned what plants to eat and how to catch little animals and cook them and all kinds of stuff about nature.

Maybe I could do the same thing in the desert. I was pretty sure I was hungry enough to eat a lizard but not without cooking it first.

I looked around, trying to get my bearings. The desert seemed to go on forever in every direction. Finally I saw an old building and headed for it. It looked to be an abandoned filling station. But you can never be too sure. A lot of junk was piled where the pumps used to be, and two dirt roads crossed beside it.

I crouched in the weeds, watching and waiting. Something smelled awful. A clattering on the other side of the building caught my attention. I crept closer and looked around the corner. A pair of big gray dumpsters sat beside the road, and the lid on the closest one was hanging open. I heard the noise again, thinking some animal was in there rooting around. Maybe a raccoon. They're curious and they'll eat anything.

I waited to see what would come out. But when a head popped up, it was no raccoon. It was an old lady with wild gray hair and filthy overalls over a ruffled pink shirt. She looked around a second, like a prairie dog popping up from its hole, then down she went again. A dumpster diver! She must be homeless, like me. But what an icky way to make a living.

Something came flying out of the dumpster and landed on the ground. It looked like a kid's stool that used to be painted red. Then out came some clothes and a pair of yellow flip-flops. I could see a strap was blown out on the flops, but I guess she hadn't noticed that.

After a while, her head popped up again, and she started to climb out. She had some trouble because she was carrying what looked like purple glass, and she was trying not to break it. She finally got her legs over the side as the dumpster started to teeter. I thought for sure it would tip over on her. But before it could, she dropped to the ground. Pretty limber for an old lady.

She picked up her treasures and carried them to an ancient car that I hadn't even noticed. The sedan was parked along the road past the dumpsters, so I sneaked out where I could watch her. The car was dusty brown and as long as a boat. She opened the trunk, and I could see it was already full of junk. She took stuff out and started to repack.

Right then my stomach sent me a message, and I ran behind the building for a few minutes.

When I emerged, I heard the dumpster lady say, "Well, hello there, Evangeline."

I looked all around to see who she was talking to, but nobody was there but me.

"Can't you talk, dearie?" the dumpster lady asked.

"I can talk," I said. "But my name's not Evangeline."

"I know that." She laughed as if it was all a huge joke, a big belly laugh, the kind babies do, the kind that when you hear it you have to laugh too.

"My name's not Birdie, either," she said, "but you can call me that anyway. Everybody does."

I wondered who "everybody" was.

"I was about to have some breakfast," she said. "Care to join me?"

I had already let my hungry stomach get me in trouble once, so I just stood there and listened to it growl.

Birdie opened a door to the back seat and brought out a flowered cloth and a small cooler I'm guessing she'd found in a dumpster. She spread the cloth on the ground behind the car, set the cooler on it, and pulled out two Dr Peppers and a pack of peanuts. Then she stood, unfastened two hooks on her overalls, and let them drop.

Thank goodness, she had on baggy gray pants underneath. They weren't nearly as dirty as the overalls. She stepped out of her dropped pants, rolled them up, and threw them in the back seat. Then she came out with a baby wipe packet and carefully washed her hands.

I walked down the dusty ditch toward her.

"Baby wipe?" she said, and tossed a packet at me.

I caught it and began to wash my hands too. Before I could finish, however, I heard a scream and looked up to see a hawk swooping out of the sky. Its wicked talons stretched down, down toward a baby bunny crouched beside a clump of weeds. Bunnies are born to be hawk food, but I didn't want to see it happen.

I let out a scream: "Noooooo!"

The bunny froze, but Birdie sprang into action. She grabbed up the tablecloth, upsetting her picnic into the dirt, and lunged toward the hawk. She waved the cloth in the sky and shouted, "Shoo! Git!"

The hawk wheeled away, screaming, but my heart was beating so loud in my ears, I could hardly hear its squawks.

The bunny was still too scared to run. Birdie approached slowly and scooped the rabbit up. She cupped the bunny gently, talking in a childish voice. I walked up to get a closer look at them both.

Close up, Birdie's eyes were an amazing bright blue that looked almost artificial. And sparkly. But something was missing in there. Birdie's face was wrinkled, but her eyes looked as innocent as a little kid's. Maybe they were too beautiful to see ugliness in the world.

I peeked between her rough fingers. The bunny hunched down as far as he could, and he was trembling. On his head, he had a tiny white diamond. Sunlight shone pink through his ears.

"He's so soft I can't even feel him," Birdie whispered.

I stuck my finger out and stroked his back. He was softer than spiderwebs.

"Maybe we can keep him for a pet," Birdie said. "Feed him milk with a spoon."

I doubted the chances of that plan. I had tried to save wild baby birds before. "I'll bet his mom is looking for him," I said, hoping that was true. "Maybe we should put him back where she can find him."

Birdie's frizzy hair bounced when she nodded. "Good idea. She'll protect him from the hawk."

Not for long, I thought. But I didn't think Birdie wanted to know that. She wanted to have saved him.

We walked into the field a short way and set the baby rabbit underneath a bush where he would be hidden from above. Then we dusted off Birdie's picnic and had peanuts and warm Dr Pepper for breakfast.

Bye for now,
Kiwi the Desert Rat

Another day in southern California

It turned out that Birdie's old car actually ran. After we ate breakfast, I helped her cram the new stuff she had found into the trunk. The red stool wouldn't fit, but she refused to give it up. She said it was perfect for climbing in and out of dumpsters. She wedged it into the back seat, which was packed to the ceiling, and cleared out a place for me to sit in front. By then, I had figured out Birdie was harmless, and if not, I was convinced I could outrun her.

We checked on the little rabbit one more time before we left. He was already gone.

Come to find out, Birdie wasn't homeless like I had thought. But her house looked like nobody lived there, except for the decorations in the front yard. Birdie took recycling to a whole new level.

The first thing I saw was a bunch of old cowboy boots stuck upside down onto the branches of a dead tree. She had two wooden wheels, an old toilet with a cactus growing out of it, and a metal sculpture of a roadrunner made from rusty spoons. Birdie said people threw away too much good stuff and that if we kept doing that, the world would run out of room. All the land would be covered by garbage dumps and cemeteries. She said she was going to have herself cremated to save space for the living. Not until she was dead, though.

The toilet planter and the spoon sculpture were interesting, but my favorite was the bottle tree. Birdie had collected hundreds of colored bottles—brown and blue and green and a few red ones—and had threaded them onto the branches of another dead tree. (There weren't any live trees in Birdie's yard.) When we drove up, the morning sun shone through the bottles and sent watery, colorful reflections dancing over the front of the house. It was beautiful.

Birdie parked right by the front door. She opened the trunk and added the purple glass vase she had found that morning to the bottle tree. We stood there for a minute admiring what Birdie called the generosity of colors. Her eyes were as bright as those sunlit bottles.

Her front yard was full of desert plants. To me, they looked just like the weeds in Myra's backyard. Weed. Plant. I guess it's just a matter of your point of view. The stucco was crumbling off the house, and the front door had once been painted blue. It wasn't locked. When she pushed it open, the air smelled like dirty feet. I took a deep breath of outdoor air before I went in.

It was cool inside. Birdie's house had a living room, one bedroom, a tiny kitchen, and bathroom—all of them stacked as high as she could reach with junk. I followed her down a narrow trail through the living room. If there was a sofa in there, I couldn't see it. What I did see was boxes and boxes of empty fruit jars, old coat hangers tied together with string, a kid's potty chair, and a bunch of old lamps, some with shades and some without. There were stacks of clothes and books and old throw pillows. I picked up one of the books and sneezed three times. Somewhere ahead of me in the maze, Birdie sang out "ge-sund-heit!"

The best thing I saw was in a tall cabinet with glass doors that was crammed full of salt and pepper shakers. Blue chickens and red fish and oil wells and skunks, all in pairs with little holes in their heads. There was a set that looked like real china, painted with tiny flowers and a gold rim. And a set shaped like a woman's boobs with red-painted nipples. I wanted to look at them all up close, but Birdie had disappeared and I was afraid of losing her. I followed the trail to the kitchen. Her stove was stacked with pans and dishes she'd collected. So was the kitchen table and the chairs and the walls. I guess she stood up to eat. Or else she ate out—meaning outdoors—like we did this morning.

The light switches didn't work, but the refrigerator did. She got out a cold Dr Pepper for me. I'd already had one for breakfast and would have preferred water, but I said thanks and popped the top. Birdie got herself one and said, "Let's sit outside in the ramada."

That was a new word for me, and not the last one of the day. The ramada turned out to be a little patio with a wooden roof over it. Or what was left of a roof. We sat in the shade behind the house and drank our Dr Peppers and looked out over a dry ditch. The ground was scattered with grayish brown bushes and yucca plants. Birdie said the farmers around here irrigate their crops and that once you add water to the soil, it will grow lots of things.

Talking to her was funny. She would say something very intelligent, like explaining about the farming, and the next minute she'd say something that made no sense at all. Once she said, "Oink around the clock."

"What?" I asked, thinking I hadn't heard her right. But she just looked out over the miles like she didn't hear me either.

The next minute she was back to normal. She told me she once had a husband and a little boy, and they were both killed in a car crash when the boy was younger than me. She had lived out here by herself ever since. I wondered if that was what happened to Birdie's mind. The sadness or the lonesomeness—either one might have done it. Or she might have had that disease I can't spell that makes you forget things.

We watched a cactus wren looking for bugs in a mesquite bush.

"Do you live in town?" she asked me.

I didn't know which town she meant, but I didn't live anywhere now, so I said, "No, I'm just traveling."

She nodded like that made perfect sense. "You meet very interesting people when you travel," she said.

Truer words were never spoken.

"Where are you headed next?" she asked.

I took a swallow of Dr Pepper, wondering how to answer. Birdie had shared everything she had with me, even the story about her family. I decided to tell her as much of the truth as I could.

"San Jose," I said. "I used to live there."

She turned her wild blue eyes on me. "Me, too!"

What a coincidence! She smiled real big, and I noticed one of her front teeth was chipped. "I'll drive you there!" she said.

I told her that would be great.

Birdie jumped up. "Wait here. I'll get my things."

She was gone only a minute. When she came out of the house, she was carrying an old purse that looked like flowered curtains. She hadn't changed clothes, but then, I wasn't so clean myself.

"I'm ready," she said. "Better use the ladies' room before we go. It's a long drive."

The bathroom wasn't as gross as I expected, and the toilet actually flushed. The bathtub was stacked full of random stuff, but the sink was usable. I washed the dust off my arms and face and brushed my teeth. I hadn't thought to put a hairbrush in my backpack. Mom would have a fit if she saw knots in my hair.

I followed Birdie around the house to her car and asked her if we should unload it before our trip. But she said there might be something in there we would need. After that, we climbed into Big Brown and headed down the road.

Birdie drove poky slow on the road—and forty miles an hour around the corners! I hung on while the tires skidded sideways on the gravel. It was like riding a Tilt-A-Whirl at the county fair. We followed the dirt road to a paved one and then the paved one to a highway that was divided down the middle. It didn't look like the same highway Jack had taken, and I was glad of that.

We rode with the front windows partly down and junk blowing around in the back seat. A big bus zoomed past at one point, leaving us in a blast of stinky fumes.

After a while I looked over at the gauges on the dashboard.

"Birdie?" I said. "I think you're about out of gas."

"Nah," she said. "That gauge hasn't worked for years. I got gas a week or two ago."

We went about ten miles more before the car started to choke and lose speed.

"Dadgum," Birdie said. "Somebody must be stealing my gasoline at night."

She guided Big Brown down the next exit ramp toward a service station. The car died as we turned in, but we coasted right up to the pumps.

"I've always been lucky," Birdie said and gave one of her belly laughs.

"I should buy the gas, since you're driving me," I said. "I have some money."

"No worries," she said. "I have a gas card. You pump and I'll pay."

She reached into the big flowered purse and pulled out a credit card. I wondered if she had found the card in a dumpster. She squinted at the directions on the credit-card reader, leaning up close and then far back. That worried me a little about her driving. I reached for the card, and pushed it in and out of the slot for her, expecting bells and alarms to go off. But nothing happened except a message: *Remove nozzle from pump.* I'd never pumped gas before, but I'd seen Mom do it a hundred times.

I filled up the tank, and then the machine flashed *Thank you* and asked if we wanted a receipt.

Not only do you meet interesting people when you travel, you learn new skills and see interesting contraptions. I went inside to buy some snacks for lunch, and then we hit the road again.

There wasn't much to look at. The land was flat, with hazy mountains zigzagging along the horizon. Big Brown shivered if we hit fifty miles an hour, so Birdie kept it about forty. Every car and truck on the road passed us, and a few of them blasted their horns, to boot. Birdie just smiled and waved.

We ate in the car, not worrying about the crumbs. Birdie sang funny songs. She'd sing a verse once and then repeat it so I could join in. We sang *Do you know the way to San Jose* over and over. Birdie's voice strained on the high notes, but I could tell she used to be a good singer. I wondered what she was like before her family died.

When the sun went down, Birdie said we had to stop. She didn't see well enough to drive at night. We parked in a rest area, and Birdie dug around in the back seat and found us each a blanket. Mine smelled like old spaghetti. I shook it out good, and when no more bugs fell out, we got back in and locked the car doors. Birdie let her seat down, stretched out her legs, and began to snore. My seat wouldn't lean back, so sleep was slow coming.

That's where we are now. It's not quite dark and Birdie is snoring, so I decided to write in my journal. Once in a while, another car pulls into the rest stop, and people get out and look at me funny. I smile and wave, like Birdie did on the highway. It's interesting: If you want people to ignore you, just act *really* friendly.

It's cozy in here, with the doors locked and the sky streaked in gold and pink where the sun went down. What are the odds of crawling out of a creosote bush field and finding someone as cool as Birdie and catching a ride to San Jose? Maybe Birdie's good luck is rubbing off on me.

When it got too quiet, however, I started to think about Mom and what I would have to do when I reached San Jose to make things right. That made my stomach hurt. So I tried to keep my mind busy with something else. I found a map of California in the side pocket of Birdie's car and spread it out on the dashboard. An outdoor light blinked on beside the bathrooms, but it's still bright as day in here.

I found San Jose on the map, but I couldn't tell how far away it was because I don't know where we are. Guess I'll have to take it one mile at a time.

Tomorrow: Further Adventures with Birdie and Big Brown.

Love and good night,

Kiwi

On the way to San Jose

I knew something was wrong as soon as we woke up this morning. I said "Morning, Birdie," and she looked at me as if I was from another planet. Her eyes were an empty blue sky. She didn't say anything for a long time, content to watch the trucks zooming past. I didn't rush her.

Finally she whispered, "Where are we?" like it might be a secret.

"We're on the way to San Jose—remember?"

"Why?"

I decided to change the subject. "How about a Dr Pepper?" Maybe when she was more awake, her mind would come back from wherever it had gone.

She nodded. "Yes. I'm thirsty."

"Let's wash up first."

I led Birdie to the ladies' room at the rest area. I splashed cold water on my face and hoped Birdie would try it too and wake up. But she just washed her hands. We came back to the car, and I got our Dr Peppers and the bag of peanuts I'd bought yesterday, Birdie's favorite breakfast. We didn't have ice in the cooler, so the pop was lukewarm. The familiar taste seemed to brighten her up. We sat on the curb and watched the traffic go by.

Finally she said, "Who are you?" Not like she was afraid, but like she needed reminding.

I considered my answer. "Evangeline," I said.

"Oh, yeah." She nodded. "Well, you'll have to drive. I'm not myself today."

Holey cheese! Another day, another new skill. I folded up both our blankets and stacked them in the driver's seat so I could see over the steering wheel. Birdie showed me how to push the seat up closer. I knew about the gas and the brake. Driving isn't rocket science. But I'd never actually steered a car down the road before.

I turned the key twice before I got Big Brown started. The second time, I twisted the key too long and the car made an awful sound, like a shovel dragging across concrete. Birdie helped me adjust the mirrors and showed me how to put the gearshift in reverse. We were the only car at the rest stop this early, a lucky thing.

I backed out of our parking place very carefully, stopped with a jerk, and slid the little needle to the letter D. When I pushed on the gas gently, nothing happened. So I pushed a little harder, and we shot forward! I stomped the brake.

"Easy does it," Birdie said. Then she put her head back on the seat and closed her eyes. I didn't know if she was still tired or couldn't watch.

Driving wasn't as easy as it looked. I took a deep breath. If we were going anywhere today, it was up to me. So I pushed the gas again, slow and careful, and turned the wheel toward the entrance ramp to the highway. Too much. We headed toward the ditch, but I steered back and lurched toward the other ditch. Big Brown's steering wheel turned about three inches before anything happened. I didn't think that was normal.

Out on the highway, cars and trucks streaked by, going about a hundred miles an hour. My breakfast threatened to come up.

"Birdie?" I said. "I've never driven before. I probably shouldn't be doing this."

No answer.

Birdie had gone to sleep.

I turned off the motor and we sat there on the ramp. And sat there. Wind rocked the car, especially when one of those big trucks went by. The sun got higher and the car got hotter. I tried to work up my courage to start the car again and drive out onto the highway. But I had the feeling that if I did that, I would smash Birdie's car or we'd be killed or both. My eyes got runny. How was I going to get to San Jose?

I said Birdie's name a few more times, then pushed her arm a little bit. Then a little more. Finally I yelled, "Birdie!"

Her beautiful blues snapped open. "Good morning," she said. She looked around like it was a new world. Finally she realized I was sitting on the stack of blankets and holding onto the steering wheel. "Scoot over and let me drive," she said.

I hopped out and ran around to the passenger side while Birdie scooted across the seat. She stuffed the blankets in the back, and off we went. She stayed awake after that. We toddled along at forty miles an hour for a long while. Finally I saw a sign that said Bakersfield, five miles. My heart sank. I remembered seeing Bakersfield on the map last night, and it was at least six inches from San Jose.

I pointed at the sign. "Let's stop at Bakersfield and take a break."

It was a long five miles. Birdie got off the highway and drove to a fast-food place and parked the car. People looked at us when we went inside, but Birdie walked up and ordered grilled cheese sandwiches like she didn't notice. I asked for a salad instead of fries. I was actually getting sick of junk food. Who knew that could happen?

Birdie paid with a crumpled bill she pulled out of her baggy purse, and we sat in an empty corner of the store to eat. Half way through her sandwich, Birdie announced, "I have to go home today."

Grilled cheese stuck in my throat. "This isn't San Jose yet. The sign said Bakersfield."

"I don't know how to get to San Jose."

"You used to live there, remember?"

"No. I used to live in San Miguel."

Uh-oh. I blinked real hard. "Birdie, you've been very nice to me. Thank you for all your trouble. But if you go home, how will I get to San Jose?"

A little of the blue spark came back into her eyes. "When I was a little girl, my mother and I rode the bus all the way to Los Angeles."

"Do you know where a bus station is?"

"No idea," she said.

"I'm not sure I have enough money left for a bus ticket," I said.

"Don't worry. I have plenty." She plopped her flowered purse open on top of the table. "See?"

Money spilled out. Her purse was packed full of crumpled wads of bills—most of them were ones, but some were fives and tens. A woman three tables down stared at us.

I snapped Birdie's purse shut. "Don't show everybody your money," I whispered. "Somebody might decide to rob you."

Birdie just laughed. "Nobody robs me. They know who I am."

Oh, my—poor Birdie.

While she finished her sandwich, I dumped my trash in a bin and went to the counter. The girl taking orders looked like she should have been at school. But then, so should I.

I said, "Could I please speak to the manager?"

"Was something wrong with your food?" she asked.

"No, it was fine. I just have a question for him."

She gave me a suspicious look, then turned around and yelled, "Hey, Ben. Somebody wants to talk to you."

Ben looked a whole two years older than the gum-chewing girl. But he smiled and asked how he could help me.

"I need to find the bus station. Could you give me directions?"

He looked blank for a second, then he turned around and shouted, "Hey, Juan! Do we have a bus station in town?"

A big dark-skinned man looked up from where he was grilling burgers. "Eighteenth at G Street," he said. "Off Truxtun."

"Thanks," I said. "How do we get to Eighteenth and G Street?"

Ben looked blank again, so Juan wiped his hands off on his apron and came up to the counter. He pointed his big brown arm toward the window. "Turn right on this street here, and keep going a couple miles until you see an exit for Chester. Go right on Chester a mile or so, and then left on Truxtun. By then, you'll see signs that point to the bus station."

I borrowed a napkin and wrote it down. "Thank you, sir," I said. "You've been very helpful."

Juan kind of smiled. "You and your grandma be careful now."

I went back and sat down. Birdie had finished her sandwich.

"I got directions to the bus station," I told her. "The cook thinks you're my grandmother."

Birdie smiled. "Okay."

We used the restroom and refilled her Dr Pepper for the road. There wasn't much traffic, and in a few blocks I figured out why. It was Sunday.

The bells in a stone church were ringing when we went past, and people in nice clothes were going inside. I found myself wishing that I could go in with them. I would have welcomed the safe feeling that has always washed over me when sitting in a pew in church against a background of organ music and a pastor's soothing voice. A few prayers wouldn't have hurt either.

I watched for our exit to Chester and told Birdie where to turn. When we got to Truxtun, it was divided into two one-way streets, and we went down the wrong side. But the streets were empty, and when we got turned around, there was G Street and the bus station. Birdie parked and we went inside.

The station was much cleaner than I expected. Rows of metal chairs faced a wall of glass doors along the back, with a number over each one. But I didn't see any buses. Four little Hispanic kids were playing tag around a woman on a gray bench. She looked exhausted from ignoring them. Other than that, Birdie and I were the only ones there.

We went up to the ticket counter, which was as high as my chin. The lady behind it looked like a white raisin.

"Is there a bus that goes to San Jose?" I asked.

"Two o'clock. Schedule's up there on the wall." Her eyes were big behind her glasses, and she didn't smile.

"How much is a ticket on that one?"

"Round trip?"

"No, one way."

"Two of you?"

"No, just me."

Her eyes flashed up to Birdie, and she looked like she disapproved.

Someone else came in and got in line behind us. I caught a glimpse of a battle dress uniform and boots. An Army guy. That gave me an idea.

"Is there a military discount?" I asked the ticket lady. "I have an ID card."

"How old are you?" she said.

Uh-oh. It was a trick question, and I didn't know the trick. Was there an age limit for traveling by yourself?

I looked her right in the eye and said, "Twelve." I'm too small to get by with fudging very much, and twelve's the adult age for movies.

"There are rules for a child traveling alone," the raisin lady said, and she pushed a paper across the counter. "Read that, and if you meet all the requirements, come back and I'll sell you a ticket. It's forty-five dollars, plus a five-dollar fee for an unaccompanied child."

I looked at the paper and saw a list of eight rules, plus some other instructions in small print. The ticket lady glanced over my head at the customer behind us. "Next!"

"Just a darned minute," Birdie said, stepping closer to the counter. "My granddaughter needs to get home, and I have money." She opened her flowered purse and held it up so the ticket lady could see. Two wadded-up dollar bills fell out on the floor.

"Step out of line, please," Raisin Lady said.

"Come on, Birdie," I said. "We'll have to sit down and read this paper."

The soldier behind us picked up the dollar bills and handed them back to Birdie.

"Thanks," I said, and he smiled. I liked his high-and-tight haircut and desert camo uniform. He looked a little like Bones, except bigger.

"You're a military kid, huh?" he said.

"I was. Before my dad got killed."

His eyes were a deep green. "In the line of duty?" he said.

"Yes, sir. Iraq."

His mouth shut in a tight line. He gave me a little nod and looked up at the ticket lady.

"She isn't traveling alone," he said. "I'm her chaperone."

The raisin lady puckered her mouth. "Whatever you say, soldier. You paying too?"

"No, I am," I said quickly.

I pulled three ten-dollar bills out of my pocket, which was all I had left, and snagged a ten and five out of Birdie's still-open purse. I counted out forty-five dollars on the ticket ledge.

Raisin Lady pushed one of the tens back to me. "Thirty-five with the military discount." She gave me the ticket.

"Thanks a lot," I said to the tall soldier.

"No problem," he said. "We'll sit together on the bus."

Birdie and I moved away from the ticket window. I handed Birdie the ten, but she said I should keep it because I might need something to eat. Birdie forgot a lot of things, but she always remembered food.

The schedule on the wall showed six hours and five minutes to get to San Jose. From the snack shop in the station, I bought a sandwich in a cellophane package and a bottle of water. I zipped them into my backpack. It was already one o'clock.

I asked Birdie if she could find her way home, and she said, "Sure. I'll just go back the way we came." I worried about that, but her eyes were bright again, and all I could do was hope for the best.

"I wish you were going with me," I told her.

She smiled and touched my hair. "You'll be fine with your new friend. Tell Elgin hello when you get to San Miguel."

Oh, my. "I sure will," I said.

She turned around like she'd heard someone call her name, and then walked out of the bus station without even saying good-bye. I was pretty sure I'd never see her again, and that was sad because I liked Birdie.

I'm sitting on a bench in the station writing all that happened today in my journal. A bus just pulled up outside; I can smell the diesel exhaust. It must be ours because the soldier is motioning to me.

Guess I'm really on my way to San Jose.

Love,
Kiwi

Chapter 17

Second Revelations

AT 5:20 A.M., THE CELL PHONE by the sofa rang. Libby had been asleep barely two hours but came instantly awake. The caller was Officer Davies with the Creosote City police.

"We've heard from a Walmart employee who thinks she saw a girl matching Kiwi's description in the store yesterday," he said. "The girl was in the pet aisle, looking at the fish. Later the employee found something the girl might have dropped. If it's your daughter's, we'll have a starting point to trace her."

"What is it she found?"

"The lady says it's a charm like kids put on their backpacks. She put it in the store's lost and found. I'm meeting her at Walmart at 8:00 a.m."

"I'll be there," Libby said and hung up.

She raked her fingers through her tangled hair. In the silent apartment, Kiwi's absence felt tangible. What if the charm was Kiwi's? Could she have left it as a clue? Would Libby even recognize it?

She phoned Shaun without thinking of the hour. His cell rolled immediately to voice mail. "I need to be in Creosote City by eight," she said. "They might have found something."

If he didn't phone back in twenty minutes, she would call Myra. It was Saturday; at least Myra wouldn't be at work.

Libby took a quick shower and toweled her hair but didn't bother with the blow dryer. She put on a clean shirt and jeans. In ten minutes she was walking to the gas station a block from the Sleepy Iguana. She bought a gas can, filled it up, and was screwing on the cap when her phone vibrated. Shaun. She told him what the policeman had said; he promised to pick her up in fifteen minutes.

She was waiting in front of the bar when he rolled to a stop. He took a small blanket from the saddlebag. "Hold the can between us and keep it covered, in case it's illegal to carry gasoline on a bike," he said. "I've never done it." The sun was not quite up as they pulled away from the bar and headed for the highway.

They found her truck sitting on the shoulder of the road as she'd left it, not even a sticker from the state police on its window. Shaun poured the gasoline into the tank and put the can in the truck bed.

"I'll follow you," he said.

"Thanks for your help. You don't have to go with me."

"I know." He mounted the bike and waited for her to pull out and turn around.

Libby had been to the Creosote City Walmart several times before. A dozen vehicles sat in the parking lot, one of them a police car. The sun was a fierce yellow star above the horizon as she and Shaun approached the building. Officer Davies stood near the customer service desk with a middle-aged woman in a flowered shirt. Libby watched him look Shaun over, registering the ponytail and motorcycle boots. The tail of Shaun's iguana tattoo curved out beneath his sleeve. She read the cop's eyes: possible suspect.

He introduced himself. "I'm Officer Davies."

Shaun shook the man's hand, his forearm flexing. "Shaun Balogun. I'm Ms. Seager's employer."

The officer nodded and turned to Libby. He extended his other hand, and in his palm lay a plastic figurine attached to a short chain and clasp, like a key chain. The figure was painted with camouflage clothes, an olive green helmet and black boots. An Army man.

Her voice cracked. "It's Kiwi's. She's had that charm since we lived in Fort Lewis, years ago."

The officer nodded and put the charm in his pocket.

"So Kiwi was here yesterday," Shaun said, looking at the woman Officer Davies hadn't bothered to introduce.

"Apparently so," the woman said. "Do you have a picture?"

Damn. In the few hours Libby had been home, she had forgotten to look for one. Instead, she described Kiwi to the woman.

"Yes, that sounds right. She was by herself," the woman said, "but that's not unusual here, so I didn't think anything about it."

"What time did you see her?" the officer asked.

"Close to three o'clock, right before my break."

"And how long after that did you find the charm?"

"Maybe an hour. No longer."

"You've been a big help. I'd like to talk with all the cashiers who were working yesterday between three and four o'clock. Can you arrange that?"

"I'll tell my manager." To Libby, she said, "I sure hope you find her soon." She gave Libby a consoling look before walking away.

"This could take all morning," the officer said. "You might as well get some breakfast."

Libby started to object, but Shaun touched her elbow. "Good idea. We'll check back in a couple of hours." He led her from the store. "Let's fill up your truck with gas. Two gallons won't last long."

They drove to a truck stop nearby, and Shaun went inside to buy coffee.

Libby was running out of cash. She hadn't used her credit card since she'd left San Jose because it was traceable. She'd have to use it now to fill up the truck. It didn't matter; with Kiwi's name in the news, their secret would soon unravel. Libby shoved the nozzle into the gas tank and watched the numbers on the pump tick past like something inevitable unwinding. She was certain to be arrested soon, maybe Kiwi, too. God, please let me find Kiwi first.

A familiar green Honda pulled into the truck stop and parked away from the pumps. Ian Mathis got out and trotted toward her. The teacher was holding a colored envelope in his hand. Still twenty feet away, he was already talking. "I saw your truck! I went by your apartment, but you weren't there. Thought you might have need of these." He stopped beside her, breathless. "They're Kiwi's school pictures. They came yesterday, but Kiwi wasn't there to get hers."

He handed her the envelope. In a cellophane window, Kiwi's face was framed by a blue background, her corkscrew ponytail trailing over one shoulder, a sprinkling of freckles across her cheeks. Her mouth was smiling politely, on command. But Kiwi's expression shamed Libby where she stood. The camera had captured the haunted look in Kiwi's eyes.

When Ian Mathis saw her reaction, his voice softened. "I'm sorry," he said. "But the police wanted a current photo."

Libby nodded without looking at him. "Yes, thank you." Her voice was choked. "I'll take one to Officer Davies immediately."

He hesitated. "Is there any news?"

She explained about the backpack charm. Shaun came out of the store carrying two large coffees with lids. Each man looked surprised to see the other. Ian introduced himself and Shaun said something, but Libby wasn't listening to them. She couldn't take her eyes from Kiwi's photo.

"If there's anything I can do, please call," Mathis said as he said good-bye.

When he had gone, Shaun nodded toward the pictures in Libby's hand. "May I see them?" He studied Kiwi's face. "Let's take these inside. I talked to a cashier in there who saw a girl with a backpack here yesterday."

Libby's head snapped up. She left the pickup parked at the pump and followed Shaun into the store.

The woman's name was June. She was thin, with a cigarette voice and the leathery face of a desert dweller. She looked at Kiwi's picture and nodded. "Sure could be her. The girl bought a drink and chips and sat outside on the bench like she was waiting for somebody. After while she was gone, but I didn't see her leave."

"Did you see anyone with her?" Shaun asked.

The woman shrugged. "No. But there could have been. I just don't know."

Officer Davies arrived within two minutes of Libby's phone call. He talked to the clerk and phoned his captain. Another officer arrived and began to canvass everyone who worked at the store as well as the customers coming and going. He was showing Kiwi's photo to them all. Officer Davies took another photo to be sent out to state police.

"Do you think she'd accept a ride from a stranger?" he asked Libby.

"After yesterday, I don't know what she might do." Then something occurred to her. "Her grandpa was a truck driver."

Davies nodded, his eyes narrowing. "We've got a computer guy at the station. We'll trace the truck routes that passed through Creosote City yesterday and get names of the drivers."

To Libby it seemed an impossible task. Several highways converged here and the truck stop served them all.

"There's a room at the department where you can wait if you like," Officer Davies said.

Creosote City police headquarters was on Main Street, a squat building with a flat roof. A civilian receptionist led Libby to a small room where a vinyl sofa and one rolling chair faced off with a soda machine. When the door closed, Libby caught a reflection in the glass and for an instant didn't recognize herself. Her hair had dried wild on the motorcycle ride; she looked like an old rock star, thin and sallow-faced.

Shaun arrived a few minutes later with breakfast from a fast-food place. Libby didn't think she could eat until she smelled the bacon. She gave him a grateful smile. She appreciated Shaun's company, sort of, but part of her wished he'd go home so she could be alone. At least he wasn't a talker.

Shaun settled in the rolling desk chair and ate his breakfast. Above the door, a round clock ticked off the seconds. It was half past ten. Kiwi had been missing less than twenty-four hours, but it felt like days. And how long have I been missing? Libby thought. Three years?

Again she had the feeling that inevitable events were in motion. That she would never have the chance to be a better mom. She remembered the long cut on Kiwi's arm, and her breath shook.

The hours passed with no news. They took turns pacing the narrow path between the sofa and the pop machine. Shaun took her outdoors for a walk, but she was afraid to stay gone long.

Before his shift ended, Officer Davies came into the room. "We've got the list of truck drivers, and we're tracking them down. It's against the law to take a rider, let alone a child, so if one of them picked her up, he wouldn't admit it. But one driver might have seen her with another one. State police units have been notified to check trucks on all the highways that pass through here."

The hopelessness of finding one little girl in such a vast area settled like a boulder in Libby's chest.

"You should go home and try to rest," the officer said.

"Can I stay here?"

"If that's what you want." He glanced at Shaun, who gave him nothing. "I'll see you tomorrow, then."

Libby resumed her pacing. If Kiwi was still okay, where would she try to go? What was she thinking? Finally Libby sank onto the plastic sofa and laid back her head.

In her dream, Deacon was pushing Kiwi in a swing at a park Libby didn't recognize. Green trees filled the background; a merry-go-round spun off to one side. Kiwi was younger, happy, asking to go higher and higher. Deacon was newly back from Officer Candidate School, a freshly minted second lieutenant. He was wearing the single gold bar on his BDU. Libby was not in the dream.

Kiwi asked him what he had learned at his school, the same thing he asked her every day.

Deacon didn't tell her about the endless drills, the obstacle courses, or the rigorous efforts of the instructors to break the soldier recruits, to wash them out. Those were the things he had told Libby. To Kiwi, he said, "OCS was the hardest thing I've ever done. But I learned something important there."

"What was that?" Kiwi asked.

"OCS taught me why it's worth it to do the right thing, even when no one is watching."

Libby jerked awake on the sofa in the police station, the dream still alive in her head. She didn't remember lying down, but her shoes were off, and there was a pillow under her head. Shaun still sat in the chair by the desk, reading a newspaper and drinking coffee. It was six o'clock, a Sunday morning.

"Have you been up all night?" she said.

He shrugged. "I dozed awhile."

"Nothing new, I guess?"

"No. I would have roused you."

Libby sat up. "Where'd you get the coffee?"

"I'll bring you some. Black?"

"Please."

While he was gone, she tried to extract something shimmering just below conscious level. Something from the dream.

The clock ticked. Her heart thudded in her ears.

By the time Shawn came back with her cup of coffee, she had the answer. "I think I know what she's doing," she told him. "She's trying to get to San Jose."

Chapter 18

The Road Back

ABOUT MIDMORNING, OFFICER Davies checked in with Libby, but he had nothing to report. Once again, he suggested that Libby go home and get some rest. "I can't keep waiting, doing nothing," she said. "I think Kiwi might be trying to get to San Jose, where we used to live. I'm going to go look for her."

The officer pressed his lips together. "Do what you gotta do. But stay in touch."

Libby promised, and Officer Davies left the room. When he had gone, Shaun met her eyes for a long moment. She waited for him to say she was crazy, that going to San Jose on a hunch made no sense.

Instead, he said, "I'll go with you." His eyes were calm, despite being on his fifth coffee of the day.

She thought about driving those long miles through the desert alone and how much better it would feel to have him with her. She was getting too attached, too indebted. That couldn't be good.

"What about the bar?" she said.

He shrugged. "Denise and her husband can run it for a few days. They've done it before. Otherwise, it'll just be locked up for a while."

"I don't want to waste two hours driving back to Sand Flats to pack a suitcase," she said. "I'm going to leave from here."

"Then I'd better find someplace to park the Harley."

She listened while Shaun phoned a biker friend and arranged to leave the motorcycle at his shop. Then he phoned Denise and woke her up. She had to consult with her husband about running the bar. "Whatever," Shaun said. "You know where the key is."

Libby frowned at this, but the bar was not her problem.

At the biker shop across town, Shaun rode into an open garage door and disappeared into the shadows. When he came out a few minutes later, he was carrying a California map. He climbed into the cab beside her, and Libby pointed the truck toward the highway. No change of clothes, not even a toothbrush, and Libby's mouth already tasted like bad salmon.

Beneath the slanted February sun, the desert spread out flat as a runway, except for the dried gray skeletons of creosote bushes. Not a tree anywhere, but always the brown mountains on the horizon. How can people live here, Libby thought, and then remembered that's exactly what she'd been doing for five months.

Half an hour later, a few stunted Joshua trees dotted the landscape. Shaun said they weren't trees at all, only an improbable species of yucca. They passed Edwards Air Force Base and a forest of wind turbines that climbed the mountains behind the town of Mojave. Libby wondered if she was getting closer to Kiwi or farther away. What if she had guessed wrong?

On the other side of a winding mountain pass, the land began to change to orchards and occasional row crops. They stopped at the edge of Bakersfield for lunch. The sun was bright and warm, the shadows cool. Shaun bought a twelve-pack of bottled water.

"Always good to have water in the desert. Want me to drive?" he asked.

She shook her head. Her back ached, but she needed the small measure of control that came from being at the wheel. With Shaun navigating, they drove northward toward Interstate 5. He slumped on the seat and propped one knee against the dashboard, watching miles slide past through hooded eyes. "So," he said. "Kiwi doesn't want you involved with me. Is that why she took off?"

Libby glanced at him. "We aren't involved."

"We could be. Kiwi doesn't trust me?"

"She doesn't trust anybody." It was a flippant answer. "No. That's not right. She trusts most people too much. But she doesn't like me dating or the men I've dated. She doesn't want anyone trying to replace her dad." Libby checked the rearview mirror and realized she was looking for cops, a habit since San Jose. "To be fair, I've hooked up with some real losers."

Half a mile went by. "Maybe you don't want anyone to replace her dad, either," Shaun said.

Libby had no answer for that.

"For the record," he said, "you don't have to tell me one damned thing unless you want to. But if you do, I'll listen."

An odor like scorched ammonia sifted through the cab. Shaun sat up fast and leaned over to peer at the temperature gauge.

"Pull over!"

The needle pointed to *hot*. Libby hadn't even noticed. She pulled the truck onto the shoulder and stopped. Semis whooshed by, rocking the vehicle as they both climbed out on the passenger side.

"Stand back." Shaun protected his hand with the tail of his shirt as he carefully unlatched the hood. Steam rolled out in a smelly cloud. "Busted radiator hose." They watched until the steam subsided, then he propped the hood open and leaned over the engine to confirm his guess.

"What now?" she said.

"When it cools off, I'll pour our bottled water in the radiator. But we'll have to get the hose fixed or we'll burn up the engine." He squinted down the highway, first east, then west. There were no towns in sight, no service stations. Not even a road sign. "Let's take a look at the map."

He traced their route with his finger. "No towns for fifty miles ahead. We'll have to ease back to Kettleman City." He folded the map and stuck it over the visor.

"I don't want to go backward!" Libby said.

"Sorry. There's no alternative."

When Shaun judged the radiator cool enough, he added the water. "Let me drive," he said.

Libby relinquished the wheel. Shaun negotiated a U-turn across the grass median and merged into the right lane with the emergency lights blinking. Libby sat cross-legged beside him, despising the truck.

She should have dumped the damned thing months ago for a car with good gas mileage. While she was stuck with truck repairs, Kiwi was out there only god knows where fending for herself. Stay safe, be smart, Libby thought, sending a message into the universe. I'm coming. She repeated the mantra over and over in her head.

Back in Kettleman City, which was actually a very small town, Libby waited in the cab while Shaun went inside a quick-stop to inquire about where to get the radiator fixed. She checked her cell—no messages, and the battery was getting low. She'd brought a charger, but not the kind that worked in the truck.

Shaun came back looking discouraged. "Afraid nothing's open. It's Sunday."

"There's no Walmart?"

"Nope. There's one auto-parts store that opens at eight tomorrow morning. We're stuck for the night."

She banged the heel of her hand on the dashboard. "Dammit!"

Shaun added more water to the radiator and without further discussion headed for two motels that sat along the highway. He stopped at the one that looked less expensive, and she handed him her credit card. They could save money by sharing a room, but she didn't want to suggest it. She sat in the truck sulking while he went into the motel office. He came back with one key and didn't say a word.

The room had two double beds and smelled like bleach, which was probably a good thing. Shaun took first turn in the shower. When it was Libby's turn, she washed her underwear with a bar of soap and then hung her bra and panties on the towel rod. She put her shirt and jeans back on. It was barely dusk, but she felt whipped and ready for sleep.

She came out of the bathroom to find no Shaun and a note on the bed. For a heart-stopping moment she thought, he's taken my truck and left me here. But the note said he'd gone out to find food.

The Spiderling

Libby plugged her cell phone into the charger, digging behind the headboard for the outlet that motels always tried to hide. Leaving the room dark, she crawled into bed and flicked through channels on television, hunting for a local news feed to see if they said anything about a missing girl. She found only sitcoms and cable news.

Shaun returned with pizza and beer. He had also bought two bottles of water, toothbrushes, and an extra-large T-shirt that said Pismo Beach. He tossed the shirt to her. "I thought you might want that to sleep in."

She held up the shirt, staring at multicolored kites that floated across its back. She wanted to say that she appreciated his thoughtfulness and his company, but she knew that her voice would break. She stared at those bright little kites, speechless.

The bluish light from the TV illuminated his smile. "What? You got something against Pismo Beach? It's not like they had a lot of choices." His eyes were dilated in the dim room. It was a dangerous moment for Libby. But then he said "Let's eat" and set the pizza box on the foot of her bed.

They polished off a pepperoni-with-extra-cheese and the six-pack. Shaun crammed the cartons into a trash can, unwrapped one of the toothbrushes, and went into the bathroom. After her turn to brush, she found him sprawled facedown on the other bed, both pillows pushed aside, eyes closed. His back was smooth and brown above the sheet, his jeans and T-shirt draped over a chair. She stood still, wearing the Pismo Beach shirt, but for only a moment. Then she crawled into the other bed.

The beer had relaxed her and the sheets were cool. She clicked off the TV and glanced over at Shaun once more. Hearing his regular breathing, she turned away from him to face the wall. And thought of Kiwi.

The day she'd brought her new baby home from the hospital, Kiwi was so small and fragile Libby was afraid she'd break. How did her baby get to be so tough? But Libby knew that answer. Kiwi had endured a lot of heartache in her eleven years. Some of it was Libby's fault, some of it just shitty luck.

She wondered what Kiwi would do if she somehow managed to get to San Jose. Would she visit her old school, her old friends? Or did she have something more important to do—like going to the police?

How would Libby protect her then?

In the sharp otherness of the motel room, Libby came to a decision. If she could find Kiwi safe again, she would do the right thing for her daughter, what she should have done before. Deacon's mother, Justine, knew how to love a child; she had raised a loving and responsible son. Kiwi would be safe with her grandmother while Libby served time in prison for killing Rocket.

Chapter 19

Kiwi's Journal: On the Greyhound

THE BUS IS AWESOME. The seats sit up high, and the windows are so big I can see for miles. The powder-sugar-topped chocolate mountains outside my window are far away. Closer up, however, are orchards with the trees lined up like soldiers in perfect rows. Stanton says we're riding through the southern end of the San Joaquin Valley, food basket of the nation.

Stanton is the soldier who saved my bacon back at the bus station. We talked nonstop for the first hour on the bus. I always talk a lot when I'm nervous, and boy, had I been nervous climbing onto this bus. I had to ask Stanton how to spell *Joaquin*. He said it rhymes with *Wa-keen*. Stanton named a bunch of things they grow in the valley: grapes for raisins, almonds, pistachios, oranges, grapefruit, carrots.

But wherever people don't water the fields, it's still a desert.

Some people love the desert, and I think Stanton's one of them. To me, the desert is like those bronze statues of some ancient guy you'll never know, all the same color with a hard face and hollowed-out eyes.

We've been riding two hours and twenty-two minutes, according to Stanton's Swatch. He's on his way to visit his sister's family in San Jose.

He likes the bus, too, because he flew thirteen hours getting home from Afghanistan, and he's sick of airplanes. He's on leave for one more week, then he has to go back. Makes me scared to think about it, so I won't.

I've been trying to remember the words to that poem about the wisdom to accept the things you can't change. I've decided that's my new philosophy of life. If you can't change something, don't think about it.

New subject: the Army.

Army people take care of each other. It's like the world's biggest family—where the people might be different but they're also the same. It isn't just the dad or the mom who's Army. The whole family belongs, kids and all. You move someplace and meet new people, and then you have to leave them behind and move someplace else. That's the hard part, but everybody you know is doing the same thing. And after a while, you know people all over the country. My dad had friends in Washington, D.C. and Kansas and Louisiana that he used to email—guys he was in basic training with or officer school. Even kids can have friends all over the place, if they're old enough to have a computer and email. I got mustered out too young for that. Back then I just complained about changing schools and being temporary. I wasn't old enough to appreciate being part of that big family. Now I miss it.

Stanton is a perfect example of what I mean about the Army. He asked me what unit my dad served with in Iraq. I told him Fifth Stryker Brigade, Second Infantry Division out of Fort Lewis, and we started to compare dates and places. Sure enough, Stanton has a buddy from San Jose who was in that same unit. His buddy's not in the military anymore, but he served in Iraq about the same time as my dad. And if he went over with the same unit, there's a good chance his buddy actually knew my dad!

I asked for his friend's name so I could write it down, and he said, "Sergeant Jeremiah Redbone Summernigh." Here's the spooky part: I'm dead certain *I have heard that name before*. How could anybody forget it? It has a rhythm like a rap song. I'll bet anything Dad knew Sergeant Summernigh when we were living in that duplex on Fort Lewis before he went to Iraq. He might have come to our house, even. So I asked Stanton what Sergeant Jeremiah Redbone Summernigh looked like.

"Like he could save your soul or break you in half," he said, but he laughed when he said it.

I asked him to be more specific.

"He's part black, part white, and part Chickasaw Indian," Stanton said. "Not too tall and square as a brick. His voice is quiet and he laughs like a little kid. I haven't seen Jeremiah for a long time, but I know he served as a medic in Iraq."

I got the same tingly feeling I got when Bones showed up in my room the first time. Meeting Stanton and both of us being connected to somebody who probably knew my dad—that was a sign. I knew now I was on the right road: I'm supposed to go back to San Jose and admit what I did.

It's dark now, and the driver had turned off the lights inside the bus. Except for Stanton and me, everybody else was asleep. I offered to split my sandwich with him, but he said no thanks. Good decision. I couldn't eat it, either.

While I've been writing, Stanton has been looking out the window, watching the dark. Maybe he's thinking about his buddies back in Afghanistan. I've been thinking too. About the interesting people you meet when you travel and how you learn something from each one.

I've learned a bunch from Stanton, but I learned from Birdie, too, like that junk has value and that being alone too much isn't good for your mind. And I kinda learned how to drive! I even learned something from Jack: A guy who is clean-cut and doesn't have tattoos can still be a sleazeball. Which also probably means that not all guys with long hair and tats are necessarily creeps. Stanton has a couple tats, and he's definitely a good person. I don't think you can tell much about people from looking only at their outsides.

I'm trying to stay awake, but my eyes keep falling shut. If I go to sleep, the next thing I know we'll be there, and it's showtime. I wish I knew what will happen to me after I tell the police I'm a murderer. It's the right thing to do, but when I think about it, my throat closes up so I can barely breathe. Doing the right thing is wicked scary.

I miss my mom. I hope she's okay and not too worried about me.

Love,

Kiwi

Sunday night, San Jose PD

Well, I did it. I turned myself in. I'm in a tiny room all by myself in the San Jose police station. I'm so tired, but I want to write everything down while I still can.

When the bus arrived in San Jose, Stanton collected his Army duffel from the driver, and I followed him into the bus station. The clock in the station said 8:32, but it felt like midnight. Stanton's sister was waiting for him. I watched them hug and laugh, and she was crying. I was glad for Stanton. It would feel great to have someone that happy to see you. I didn't want to interrupt them to say good-bye, so I kept walking. But I didn't get far before he called after me.

"Kiwi! Who's supposed to meet you?" he said.

I could see he felt responsible for me and that he wouldn't be able to go home with his sister if he thought I was alone. So I told him I was supposed to catch a cab.

He frowned. "Do you have enough money?"

Actually, I had no idea. I didn't know what cabs cost. I only thought of it because I saw some outside when the bus drove in.

He told his sister he'd be right back. Stanton walked outside with me, and we found a couple of cabs sitting by the curb. "I need a ride," I said to one of the drivers.

"Where to, young lady?"

I couldn't let Stanton know I was going to the police. Thinking fast, I gave the cab driver the street address where our old apartment was when we lived here. Stanton asked the driver how much, and he said, "Thirty ought to get it."

Yikes! I had no idea cabs were so expensive.

Stanton got thirty-five dollars out of his billfold and gave it to me. "You sure you'll be okay? Will someone be home when you get there?"

"Sure," I said.

How did I get so good at lying? It's lucky my nose isn't made of wood. But there's a difference between lying to protect someone else and lying for a selfish reason. I'm an expert—I've done both. Unfortunately, I've learned lying feels lousy either way.

I thanked Stanton for everything and smiled when I told him I'd be fine. Then I hugged him around the middle and got into the cab real quick so he couldn't see my face. The driver shut the door. Stanton waved and turned back toward his sister.

When the driver got in, I told him never mind the address I gave him, to please take me to the police station.

He looked over his shoulder at me. "The police?"

"Yes, sir. I have some business to take care of there."

"Whatever you say." He swung the car out into traffic, pitching me sideways on the seat.

I'd ridden in a cab before, so I knew they smelled bad. This guy had used way too much lemon air freshener. I asked if he could please open a window. He did what I asked, but he didn't say anything. Obviously, he wasn't going to be one of the interesting people I met on my travels.

I watched the headlights flash past on the street. By now I was having a lot of trouble breathing. I considered jerking the door open and jumping out on the street. But I'd promised Bones I'd try to stop hurting myself. I didn't want to add promise breaker to my list of sins. Hell's supposed to be for eternity, but if God decided you'd served enough time there, I'm sure He has the power to send you somewhere else. I bet you aren't allowed into heaven, though.

The cab pulled up to a building and stopped.

"San Jose Police Department," the driver said.

Holey cheese. That was way too fast!

I looked out the window on the street side. There was a black iron fence right next to us. "Which building is it?" I asked.

The driver pointed to a big gray one behind the fence. Finally I saw a gate and a wall with Police Administration Building written on it. The driver asked for twenty dollars, which seemed like a lot for such a short ride. I climbed out and he drove away.

I stood on the sidewalk looking through the bars of a fence with little spears along the top. The airport must have been close because a jet flew over so low the air shook. I wished the plane would fall out of the sky right on top of me. I tried to take a deep breath, but my chest had that seat-belt feeling again. I inhaled just enough air to remember the smell of San Jose. I used to like this place once upon a time. But that was Before Rocket.

I slung my pack on my back and forced my legs to climb the thirteen steps up to the building. I opened a glass door and went in. The place was vacant, only a bunch of empty seats and some ticket windows like at a movie theater. Behind one of the windows sat a mostly bald officer with tiny glasses. A sign said *Start Here*.

So I did. The officer looked at me over his glasses when I got to his window. On TV, the detectives are always the ones in charge, so I said, "I need to speak to a detective, please."

"Our detectives are pretty busy," he said. "What's this about?"

I had practiced this on the bus. "I have information about a murder."

His eyebrows went up. "A murder?" the officer said.

"Yes—about a man who was shot a few months ago."

He frowned. "You here by yourself?"

"Yes, sir."

"Okay. Wait by that door and someone will come get you."

And then he picked up a phone and made a call.

About a minute later, I heard a lock click and the door opened. A different officer said, "Come with me," and I followed him through a maze of hallways and down some stairs. The whole place was quiet, library quiet. Finally we got to a tiny room with a mirrored window, a small table, and two chairs. The walls were bare; the room, empty.

"Detective Delgado will be with you in a minute," the officer said, and he left me.

I was having difficulty breathing in the cold little room with the door shut. My head felt swimmy too. I tried counting my breaths and rehearsing how I was going to tell the detective about Rocket. About what I had done. I decided on the direct approach, with no excuses. The Army way.

Finally, the door opened, and a tall man with dark eyes and a zipper haircut came in. He was wearing slacks, a striped shirt with a tie, and a gun on his belt. The sight of that gun made my chest tighten.

He said, "Hi. My name's Nick. Who are you?" He had a soda straw in his hand but no cup.

"I'm Kiwi," I said. "Are you a detective?"

"Yup. Detective Nicolas Delgado. Call me Nick. Nick's a lot easier." He smiled. "Kiwi who?"

"Kiwi Seager."

He sat down and crossed his legs. He had on sneakers with no socks and, for some reason, that made me feel a little better.

"Okay, Kiwi," he said. "What was it you wanted to talk to me about?"

I took a big breath and looked him in the eye. "Back in September, a man was shot in an apartment on Cortez Street. His name was Rocket."

Detective Nick fiddled with his straw, winding it through his fingers. "I remember that," he said. "Rocket had a long history in the drug business, if I recall."

I nodded. "That sounds about right. Anyway—I'm the one who shot him."

"You shot him?"

I could see he had doubts. "I didn't intend to kill him," I said. "I didn't think the gun would really go off."

Dang, I had sworn no excuses. I tried to do better. "I did hate him, and I pulled the trigger, so I guess I murdered him."

"Wow," he said. "That's heavy."

"It sure is." But I felt lighter now that I'd admitted it. In fact, I felt like a helium balloon. I grabbed the sides of the chair so I wouldn't float off. "Murdering someone changes everything," I said. "Have you ever shot anybody? For your job, I mean?"

Detective Nick frowned. He looked down at his hands turning the straw end for end on the table. "Yeah, I did once. I was pretty messed up about it afterwards."

"Me, too," I said. My nose started to twitch; I had to fight not to cry.

"This is serious stuff, Kiwi. We need your mom or dad here. Where are they?"

Uh-oh, I thought, but I said, "I'm not sure. Mom might be out looking for me or she might still be in Sand Flats. She's been trying to protect me ever since it happened, but it's messing us both up. So I came here to do the right thing."

"To do the right thing?" he said.

"My dad was a soldier, and he said it's important to do the right thing, even when nobody else knows."

"Wow. Your dad sounds like quite a guy."

"He was."

"Was? He's not around anymore?"

I shook my head. I didn't think I could tell him about Dad right then. It would sound like another excuse, and I'd start to cry for sure.

"So you ran away from home to do the right thing," he said, and I nodded. "How did you get here?"

I told him about leaving the science fair and meeting Jack and Birdie and Stanton, the short version. He listened carefully and asked several questions about Jack and made some notes. When I was finished I thought he'd ask more about the shooting, but instead he sat there tapping his straw like he was thinking. I watched him a minute. "Are you trying to quit smoking?" I said.

He looked up. "How the heck did you know that?"

"My dad carried around a pencil when he quit. He said it gave him something to do with his hands."

He smiled and stuck the straw behind his ear. "You have some blood there on your jacket. What happened?"

I lifted up my torn pocket and showed him my side. "I scraped it getting out of Jack's truck."

"What's that on your arm?"

My jacket sleeves are too short, and he could see part of my scar. I showed him that too. "I fell out of a tree," I said. "It's nearly healed, though."

"Looks like you had stitches."

"Yeah, thirteen of them." I pulled down my sleeve.

"Kiwi, before we talk about this guy Rocket, I have to explain your rights now. And first I need to be sure you can understand them. Okay?"

He asked some dumb questions then, like, "If you make an A on your homework, is that good or bad?" And "Do you know what stealing is? Is that right or wrong?" And then, "If you shoot someone, is that good or bad?"

I got all the questions right. He said I didn't have to say anything, and I could have an attorney if I wanted one. I didn't. I felt like I could trust Nick, and I wanted to tell him what happened.

He took my picture and looked through my backpack and asked some more questions. He wrote the answers down on a worksheet and then finally got back to Rocket.

I told him the whole story about the shooting and how Mom and I ran away into the desert. I asked if he was going to take me to prison.

"Well, it isn't prison. You'll go to juvenile hall tonight."

"Kids' jail?"

"Sort of. It's next door to this building." He didn't seem in a hurry to send me there, though. "I need to check some things first. Are you hungry? The detectives usually send out for burgers about this time. You want one?"

Now that I'd unloaded my secret, I was hungry as a caterpillar. "Do you think I could I get a grilled cheese instead?" I said.

"Sure. What to drink?"

"Water, please."

"Okay. I'll be back in a few minutes. You okay? Are you cold?"

I guess I was shivering. I thought about sitting in here by myself with the door closed. "Do you have anything I could read? Any kind of book or a newspaper?"

"You're a reader, huh?"

"You know what Groucho Marx said," I told him.

"No. What did he say?"

"Outside of a dog, a book is man's best friend. Inside a dog, it's too dark to read."

He laughed. "You're a little young to know who Groucho Marx is."

"I don't know him," I said. "I just like that joke."

"I'll find you something to read," he said. At the door, he turned around. "Kiwi, I'll notify your mom. But do you have any family here in San Jose I could get hold of for you? Anybody you'd like to call?"

I thought a minute and opened up my journal.

"Sergeant Jeremiah Redbone Summernigh," I said. "But I don't know his telephone number."

Nick reached out and sort of tousled my hair. Nobody had done that to me since I was a little kid. I used to hate it, but this time, I didn't mind. I had finished my first ever conversation with a police detective, and I thought it had gone pretty well, considering how scared I was.

In a little while, a lady officer came in and gave me the a copy of the *San Jose Mercury News*. I said thanks and she left. I would read the newspaper later, if I could stay awake, but first I wanted to write all this down in my journal.

Truth be told, I can't believe I'm here. I feel like I'm in a movie or a dream. This room is spooky quiet. I still don't know the rules of this place. I hope they don't take my journal away from me at the juvenile jail. It's my last friend.

Love,
Kiwi the Inmate-to-be

Chapter 20

Your Truth or Mine

IN THE DARKENED MOTEL ROOM, the trill of Libby's cell phone jarred her awake. She grabbed the phone from the nightstand, yanking the plug from the charger. It was 11:53 p.m. "Yes?"

"Libby Seager?"

"Yes. Who is this?"

"Detective Nick Delgado at the San Jose Police Department. I saw the missing persons report on your daughter and talked with Officer Davies in Creosote City. Kiwi is here in San Jose with me."

Libby's wail woke Shaun. He sat up on the edge of his bed facing her, rubbing the sleep out of his eyes.

"Is she okay?" Libby said. "Can I talk to her?"

"Physically, she's fine. But we have another issue. How soon can you get here?"

San Jose was two hours away. When the auto-parts store opened at eight, Shaun bought a radiator hose and a pair of pliers. In twenty minutes, he had the truck repaired and they were on their way. They arrived at the police department before noon. Libby paced the reception area, a stark and busy place with rows of metal seating, until Detective

Delgado came out. He was tall, dark-haired, and wearing sneakers. As with Officer Davies before him, Delgado gave Shaun the once-over. Ingrained cop behavior, Libby guessed. The detective had said to call him Nick. His eyes were penetrating but not unkind.

"Mrs. Seager, I need to speak to you privately about your daughter."

Shaun offered to wait in the reception area. Delgado led her down coffee-scented hallways into the belly of the station. Libby flashed back to her days as a troubled teenager and felt the sensation of entering a maze where there was no way out.

Finally, the detective stopped at a door marked "Witness/Victim Waiting Room." I'm not either one, Libby thought. I'm the perp.

Inside, a television played with the sound off, and a toy box stood in one corner. The detective pointed her to a sofa.

"Kiwi came here last night on her own," he said. "She's been processed into the juvenile center and spent the night there."

Libby's fears were coming true one by one. She pictured Kiwi in some kind of cell, and her stomach started a fistlike clamping.

The detective met her eyes. "What do you know about the death of a man known as Rocket five months ago?"

Her shoulders fell. Kiwi had told him. Libby looked down at her hands. Her cuticles were bleeding. "I was living with Rocket." Never had she had felt more worthless than she did at that moment.

"Kiwi says she shot him," the detective said.

She took a deep breath and met his eyes. "I was afraid she might. It isn't true."

"That thought occurred to me," the detective said. His tone was matter-of-fact, no surprise or judgment in his eyes. "If you have exculpatory information, we need to get your statement right away."

"What's *exculpatory*?"

"Evidence that she didn't shoot this guy."

Libby nodded and felt herself swaying like a boat on the ocean.

"I'll tell you everything I know," she said. "But first I want to see my daughter. And I want a lawyer."

Chapter 21

Kiwi's Journal

Monday—I think

I SPENT LAST NIGHT IN kid jail. That definitely makes the list of Top Ten Worst Nights of My Life. But it doesn't matter anymore because this morning I met Sergeant Jeremiah Redbone Summernigh. I know he's the reason I was supposed to come back to San Jose.

Kid jail isn't like I imagined. There aren't any bars. It's a tiny room with only a bed and a toilet and a locked door with a little window in it. The toilet is stainless steel and there's no seat. You have to sit on the cold edge of the thing. So gross!

They took my clothes and gave me a white bunny suit. It's like a one-piece pajamas with a zipper up the front. They wouldn't let me keep my journal even though I begged them. (Jeremiah got it back for me this morning.) They took away everything that was mine: Moxie, my dog tags, my dignity.

I told the big police lady that those tags were the only thing I had left of my father, and if they lost them, I would sue the police department and the President and her in particular. She just rolled her eyes.

So I asked if she enjoyed humiliating children. "Some of them I do," she said and gave me a mean look.

It was already night, so as soon as I got in my room, they turned off the lights. If it wasn't for a night-light that stayed on, I'd have gone ballistic. I wrapped up in the stinky blanket and tried to make myself small. The air vent made a ticking sound all night like the whole place was set to blow up. I wished it would.

I didn't know if I would be there forever or if they'd take me to see a judge or if I'd ever see Mom again. Except for Detective Nick, nobody told me anything. What if they left me in that nasty little room and never came back? I cried myself to sleep.

This morning, the mean lady herded all the kids into a cafeteria for breakfast, which I couldn't eat. Nobody talked to me. Afterward one of the guards came and said, "You have a visitor. Come with me."

I was so happy about not having to go back to my cell that I didn't even ask who it was. The guard led me to a visiting room. Detective Nick and another man were there.

"Morning, Kiwi," Detective Nick said. "This is Mr. Summernigh."

Holey cheese! I couldn't believe they had actually found him.

Sergeant Jeremiah Redbone Summernigh looked Army tough even in jeans and a loose shirt. He also seemed kinda familiar, in the way that Army guys sort of look alike. He commented on how grown up I looked, and his high-pitched voice was a shock because it didn't fit his body. I knew right away I'd heard that voice before.

"Hello, Sergeant Summernigh," I said.

"You were a little thing the last time I saw you," he said. "You probably don't remember me."

A memory blinked on in my head. "You played reveille through your nose," I said.

His laugh was a whoop. "My one claim to fame!"

Detective Nick smiled at me. "I'll leave you alone a few minutes if you're okay with that, Kiwi."

I nodded. He went out, but I could still see him through a pair of big windows, and he could see me. There was a policeman out there too. The sergeant and I sat down at a table.

Sergeant Summernigh's eyes are the color of Starbucks coffee, straight up. "You knew my dad," I said to him.

He reached over and put his thick fingers on my hand, very gently. "Kiwi, I admired your father as much as any man I've ever known. We were in Iraq together."

"I want to know everything," I said. "Mom couldn't talk about it. But I have to know."

His Adam's apple scooted up his throat like a cat under a blanket. "I was a medic, and I was with him when he died," he said. "Ask me anything you want."

And so I did.

First I asked him how it happened, what it was like when the bomb went off, and why the bomb was there. He talked to me like a grown-up, in Army language.

He told me about the IEDs—improvised explosive devices—that were planted along the roadsides. Sometimes the Al-Qaeda did it or sometimes local militias or war lords. War was confusing, he said, and you couldn't always tell who was the enemy and who wasn't. They never learned who set the bomb that took my dad.

My dad's Jeep was blown up and then it burned. Jeremiah got there right afterward, but it was already too late for Dad. He was unconscious and died quickly, which Jeremiah said was better than dying slowly if you were too messed up to get well. Two other men died too. Another one lost his leg.

He told me how they took care of the bodies and about the special ceremony they have for fallen soldiers, with their rifles standing up between their empty boots. They hang the soldier's helmet on top of his rifle, and behind it are crossed flags. Jeremiah said that ceremony was one of the hardest days in his life. Then he talked about what a good man my dad was.

I wiped my face on my bunny suit and kept asking questions. After we got past the hardest stuff, Jeremiah told me about the unbearable heat and the sandstorms and how there was less violence in the winter, and how everybody looked forward to that. Then he told about the time my dad put a rubber scorpion in the bunk of one of his buddies, who found it in the dark and woke up the whole platoon, yelling and cussing. When he told that, I could hear my dad's laugh.

Jeremiah said Dad used to keep a picture of Mom and me in the top of his helmet. Sometimes he and Dad would pray together because Jeremiah was kind of a chaplain too.

While he was talking, my dad's face gradually came back to me. I had almost lost my memory of how he looked, but now I can summon his face up at will. I see the dark stubble of his beard and the brown mole up high on his left cheek. I remember his voice and the way he smelled and the soft curly hair on his arms.

I began to understand something important too: This conversation was the real reason I had come to San Jose. The rest of it, about Rocket and going to prison, didn't matter. I was meant to come here and meet Jeremiah and find my father again.

By the time Detective Nick came back in, I had composed my face and Jeremiah had me laughing. He said he would help me and Mom any way he could. I asked him to look out for Mom when I went to prison.

Jeremiah asked to talk to Detective Nick outside for a minute, but before he left, he told me one more story about Dad.

He said my dad loved fried chicken more than anything except his family and his country. When they served fried chicken in the mess hall, there was never anything left on Dad's plate but a pile of bones picked clean. His buddies nicknamed him Bones.

So there you have it. I thought I'd lost him, but Dad has been with me all along.

Love,

Kiwi

Chapter 22

A Reunion of Strangers

THE VISITING ROOM—with its generic sofa and chairs, a round table, curtains on the windows—looked more like a hospital than a detention facility. The first face Libby saw was not her daughter's. It was that of a square-built dark man, his haircut cropped close, something Asian about his eyes.

"Hello, Libby," he said.

"Jeremiah?" She had met him back at Fort Lewis and then again on the day of Deacon's funeral. There was no forgetting that burnished face or the triple name attached to it. "What—? Why are you here?"

"Kiwi asked to see me," he said.

He stepped aside and she saw Kiwi then.

Her daughter was sitting in a straight-backed chair at the table and writing in her lavender notebook. She was wearing a white institutional jumpsuit, a mass of tangled hair falling into her eyes. Her expression sent goosebumps up Libby's arms. Kiwi looked tired but peaceful, as if her skin were giving off a soft light.

Libby couldn't draw breath.

The room dissolved around her.

Libby dropped to her knees and gave a little cry of relief. Her baby girl was okay.

Kiwi looked up, saw her mom, put down her journal, and rose slowly from her chair. Without a word, she came and gave Libby a hug.

"Oh, Kiwi." Libby's voice broke.

It was the first hug they had shared since San Jose, maybe even longer. Kneeling, Libby was shorter than her daughter. She pressed her face into Kiwi's chest. The dog tags were gone, and Libby imagined the fight that loss must have caused.

Kiwi was the first to let go. She extracted herself from Libby's arms and returned to her chair while Libby hunted for a tissue in her pockets. Jeremiah Summernigh handed Libby a paper napkin from the table.

"How did you get in?" Libby asked him. "The lawyer had trouble getting permission for me to see my own daughter."

"I managed to persuade the deputy chief that Kiwi should be allowed a visitor," he said with a slight smile. "He's an old Special Forces guy."

A sharp knock interrupted their brief exchange. A woman rushed in, running late. The room suddenly felt crowded. "I'm Sarah Longstaff with the public defender's office," the woman said with a nod to the detective. "Detective Delgado."

"Sarah," he said.

She put her briefcase down and took a seat. "Hi, Kiwi. I'm Sarah."

Sarah Longstaff looked forty-five and fierce, the kind of woman who had chosen public defense as a career, not as a stepping-stone to something more lucrative. That's good, Libby thought. Fierce is good.

"My client would like to see her daughter alone," she announced.

Libby could tell the detective didn't like it, but there was nothing he could do. Kiwi was a minor. Jeremiah moved toward the door.

Kiwi glanced up at him quickly. "Do you have to leave?"

"Yes. But I'll be back later," Jeremiah said. He handed Libby a card with his phone numbers.

Libby thanked him, still baffled by his presence. When the men left, she addressed the attorney. "Can they hear what we say in this room?"

"No. Anything we talk about here is absolutely private."

"Good—I would like to talk to Kiwi alone."

The lawyer hesitated.

"Please," Libby said. "Just step out for a few minutes."

Ms. Longstaff scowled, but she picked up her briefcase and headed for the door. When the door closed behind her, Libby took the chair across from Kiwi, who was sitting quietly with her hands folded. Libby put her hands on the table too.

"You've been chewing your nails again," Kiwi said.

Libby curled her fingers under. Kiwi didn't meet her eyes. "Why did you leave me?" Libby asked.

Kiwi shook her head.

"What did you tell the detective?"

"I told him I killed Rocket."

Libby's hands curled into fists and she closed her eyes. She felt too tired to breathe, and too sad. No matter what happened now, she had lost the battle. She and Kiwi would be separated for a very long time. The best she could do was try to keep Kiwi out of state custody.

"You didn't kill Rocket, Kiwi. I did."

Kiwi frowned. "Don't do that, Mom."

Libby leaned in as close to Kiwi as she could. She lowered her voice. "Listen to me. When I came in that day and found you, I took the gun out of your hands and led you to the bedroom. Remember? I wrapped you in a blanket because you were shaking, and I left you on the bed while I went back to the living room."

She waited, and finally Kiwi nodded. "He was still alive, Kiwi."

"No, he wasn't."

"He opened his eyes and looked at me. He couldn't talk and he was bleeding, but he was still alive. I could have called 9-1-1 and tried to save him. But I looked at his eyes, and they were threatening me even with a bullet hole in his neck." Her voice turned cold. "I picked up a pillow from the sofa and held it over his face."

Kiwi twisted her face. "Mom! Stop it! That's not true."

"I pushed down with both hands and my knee." Libby pictured it, could almost feel it. "It was my chance to be free of him."

"You're lying."

"You didn't kill him. He was still alive."

"No he wasn't! I'd been staring at him forever when you got home." She was angry. "He was dead as a mackerel. Roadkill! Toast!"

"I finished him. He might have lived otherwise."

"I told Detective Nick the truth." There were tears in her eyes. "You can go on with your life now, and I don't care what they do with me. I took responsibility for my actions, like Dad always said."

"But you didn't kill him, Kiwi. I will tell the detective that. You can't take responsibility for something you didn't do."

Libby reached for Kiwi's hands, but she pulled away. She sprang to her feet and pressed her back against the wall.

"I wish you hadn't come here," Kiwi said.

Libby hugged herself, shivering, wishing she could hug Kiwi instead. "Kiwi. Sweetheart. Let me do this one thing right. Please. Let me do one responsible thing for my daughter."

In the moment before Sarah Longstaff tapped on the door and re-entered the room, Kiwi's tears spilled over.

"Sorry, Mom," Kiwi said. "I can't."

Detective Delgado took Libby to an interrogation room with one-way glass and a video camera in the corner. The room was tan and claustrophobic. "You don't have to be here," she told the attorney.

"Of course I do," Ms. Longstaff said. "Don't be stupid."

Delgado filled out a form with personal information, then sat back in his chair. "Tell me about the shooting. Where did this happen?"

Libby named the street but couldn't remember the house number. She described the living room where Rocket died, told about the pills he supplied her, her fear of violence if she didn't do what he wanted. "I was afraid of him. I never meant for Kiwi to be alone with him." All of this was true.

Delgado listened without interrupting. His eyes were as benign as a wall—another cop thing. She had dealt with street cops before but not detectives. He seemed less cocky, more professional.

"Why would Kiwi tell me she shot him?" he asked.

"To protect me. She's already lost her dad, and she's afraid of losing me too. Kiwi didn't shoot Rocket," she said. "I did."

He glanced at the attorney, who was scowling. "Stop now," she said.

"No. I need to do this," Libby said.

Delgado quoted her Miranda rights. She had transformed from a witness to a suspect. He photographed her, took her cell phone, then asked more questions.

"Tell me exactly how it happened, every detail you can remember," he said, and she knew the video camera was rolling.

"I came home from work one afternoon and found Rocket on the sofa, drunk and furious, but very much alive. Kiwi was aiming his own gun at him. He was swearing, threatening, but he was afraid to move." She swallowed, working to keep her voice level. "I took the gun away from Kiwi and sent her to the bedroom. As soon as she closed the door, Rocket said, 'I ought to kill you both.' He lunged at me and I pulled the trigger."

"Were those his exact words? I ought to kill you both?"

"Yes. And I believed he would."

"That's self-defense, pure and simple," Ms. Longstaff said. The detective ignored her.

"But he was unarmed?"

Libby shrugged. "As far as I know. He was big, though, over six feet."

"Had you ever shot a handgun before?" he asked.

"No. I've shot rifles. But he was so close, it would have been hard to miss."

The detective watched her as she talked. She couldn't tell if he was convinced. She might have to repeat the story several times. Her voice was calm, but she was starting to shake. "Can I have a blanket or something? It's freezing in here."

He ignored this too. "What happened after you shot him?"

"He fell back on the sofa. I wasn't sure where he'd been hit. I held the gun and waited to see if he got up. When I thought he'd stopped breathing, I went to check on Kiwi."

"Where was she then?"

"Still in the bedroom with the door shut. She was wrapped up in a blanket, even her head. She couldn't talk and her eyes looked wrong. Glassy, like she didn't know where she was." Her voice choked when she told this part; she could still see the way Kiwi had looked that day, like she'd gone blind. "I made her get up and we packed a suitcase. I found Rocket's car keys and led Kiwi out of the apartment. She was still wrapped in the blanket. I covered her face so she couldn't see Rocket when we left."

"What happened to the gun?"

"I took it with us," Libby said. "In the middle of the night, I threw it into the ocean somewhere along Highway 1."

"Did Kiwi see you do that?"

"No. She was asleep in the car."

He nodded. "Why was Kiwi pointing the gun at him?"

"I never asked her."

"You never asked?"

She slid her icy hands beneath her thighs on the chair. "She hated him because she thought he was hurting me. And . . . she said he'd been mean to her. I thought she was exaggerating so I'd leave him." She stopped, forced a deep breath. "I know I shouldn't have run, but I was too scared to think. I just wanted to get Kiwi away from there."

His gaze rested on a corner of the ceiling for a long minute. Libby wondered if someone was watching behind the mirrored window and whether the detective had a wife and kids at home or was married to his job. Stubble shadowed his angular chin. She wondered if Kiwi thought Nick Delgado was a good man.

Ms. Longstaff watched him too. "So are you going to file charges or not?"

"We'll review the crime report. See whose story matches evidence from the scene. There wasn't much."

"Are you going to talk to Kiwi again?" Ms. Longstaff asked.

"Yup."

"I want to hear it."

He shrugged. "You can watch from the observation window."

He laid a legal pad and pen on the table in front of Libby. "Write down your account of everything that happened, every detail you can remember."

"Why?" the lawyer said. "You've got it on tape."

He just looked at her.

"It's okay," Libby said.

When they'd gone, she reprised her story on paper, trying to remember the questions Delgado asked and answer them exactly the same. Then she sat at the table, clicking the tip of the ballpoint pen in and out. In and out. And suddenly she remembered Shaun.

In the alter-world of the police station, she'd totally forgotten about him. He had been waiting for hours, probably expecting her to appear any minute with her runaway daughter in tow. She had told him nothing about Rocket or the shooting.

She wondered if he was still there and what would happen if she walked out of the room to find him. But she didn't move.

Forty-two minutes later, the attorney came back. It was late afternoon and Libby hadn't eaten all day. Her head ached. If she laid her face on the table, she could have slept sitting up.

Sarah Longstaff picked up the tablet containing Libby's confession. "Let's hold onto this for a while." She stuck the legal pad in her briefcase. "Mr. Summernigh has made arrangements to take Kiwi home with him for the night, with your permission. Apparently he has some pull with the deputy chief. He lives here in San Jose with his wife and two kids, and he'll be responsible for bringing her back tomorrow. Is that okay with you?"

"Does Kiwi want to go with him?" Libby asked.

"Yes, she does. She appears to have taken to him. The other choice is the cell in juvenile hall."

"Jeremiah was a friend of my husband's. It'll be okay. Better than jail, for sure."

"I'll tell the detective. Meanwhile, you'll be stuck in a holding cell overnight."

"I need to talk to my friend who came with me. Shaun's been waiting in the reception area all this time. He'll be worried."

The lawyer asked for Shaun's last name. "I'll try to get permission for him to come in a few minutes." She tapped her pen against the briefcase. "Nick wants to have Kiwi talk with a psychologist. Without you or me present."

Libby came to attention. "Why?"

Sarah frowned like that was a stupid question. "She's either killed a man or lied to protect a mother who killed a man. Either way, that's messed up. Not to mention her encounter with a probable pedophile."

"What? What pedophile?"

"The truck driver she hitched a ride with had child pornography in his truck. Apparently he didn't intend to let Kiwi go. She escaped on her own."

"On her own?" A dark edge crept into Libby's vision. "How did she escape? Did they catch him?"

"I don't have all the details, but she promised Nick that the man didn't touch her. She gave them a good description, and they're looking for him. But unless he already has a record, all they can do is get him fired for taking a rider. Even if they find him, they have no proof he's committed a crime. Yet."

Libby's head filled with horrific thoughts. She squeezed her eyes shut in an effort to keep the thoughts at bay.

The lawyer took a breath and exhaled slowly. "The chief wants a psychologist's opinion on Kiwi's state of mind. Probably to get an idea of how truthful she's capable of being."

Libby thought of several possible results from such an interview, none of them good. Her breath shortened.

"I don't want that," she said. "Kiwi's been through enough. Can I deny permission?"

"You can. But they might get a judge to overrule you."

"I told them what happened. Why can't they leave her alone?"

"Let's see. Because maybe you're protecting Kiwi like you say Kiwi's trying to protect you?"

"He should take my word for it. I'm the adult."

"Are you?" Sarah Longstaff said, rising to leave again. "After listening to Kiwi, I have to say I'm not so sure."

A few minutes later, Shaun entered the room. Libby was ashamed of how glad she was to see him. She wanted to run into his arms and have him hold her until this nightmare with Kiwi was over, but this was neither the time nor the place. She stayed in her chair.

"I'm so sorry," she began, but he silenced her with a finger to his lips. His face showed no annoyance about having waited all afternoon in a police station. Libby would never understand Shaun Balogun.

"Tell me what's going on," he said. "Is Kiwi all right?"

"She seems to be. But she . . ." Libby faltered over the words. How do you tell someone your grade-schooler has confessed to murder? She would have to start at the beginning to make him understand, and where did it begin? With Rocket or somewhere before that? When Deacon was killed? When Libby became a mother, unequipped?

"Kiwi and I are in trouble."

"I gathered that," he said mildly.

"It looks like I'll be here overnight." An understatement. "If you want to go home, I understand."

"I'm in no hurry," he said. "But the cop in reception is starting to look at me funny. I could drive back and bring you and Kiwi some stuff from home, if you want. Clothes, pajamas, whatever."

Libby dropped her head onto the table. "You've got to stop being good to me," she said. "I don't know what to do with that."

Shaun came behind her chair and kneaded the muscles in her neck and shoulders. The pressure was gentle, but she was so tense that at first, it hurt. Her breath shuddered.

"Relax," he said, "relax." And when she finally did, the pain dissolved into the warmth of his hands.

His voice as he continued was low. "The first night you walked into the bar, I thought, there's a woman who's been to hell and back. And she's not all the way back yet." He rested his hands on her shoulders. "Not everyone in the world has bad intentions, Libby. Some people can actually be trusted. You'd just as well start with me because I'm the only one here."

⁂

After Shaun left, Sarah Longstaff came back to the cubicle, which Libby had already begun to think of as her cell. Funny how adaptable humans are. She had already memorized a faint brown stain that looked like a small crab in one corner of the ceiling and felt the slow progress of sundown in her bones although the room had no window. On the tabletop, someone had carved:

Sal was here,
I am innocent,
Cops suck.

It read like a little poem.

The attorney dropped a sack on the table.

"I brought you a sandwich," Longstaff said.

"Thanks," said Libby. She was so empty her hands shook when she picked up the sandwich. Turkey and bacon with Swiss cheese. She bit into it like a wolf and carefully observed the lawyer while she chewed. The collar of Longstaff's pink blouse looked wilted, her suit not as crisp as this morning. Libby read the woman's stylish watch; it was after seven.

"You work long hours," Libby said.

The lawyer's smile twisted. "What can I say? Working for folks who can't afford my services is my life."

"And nobody appreciates you," said Libby with a deadpan face.

"Exactly." The lawyer laughed, the first sign of humanity Libby had seen from her.

Longstaff shifted a hip on the chair and leaned back. "Detective Delgado wants to interview you again. He'll be here in a few minutes. They're going to sweat you, see if your story changes. By tomorrow afternoon, they'll have to file charges or kick you loose, unless you love this place and choose to stay on your own."

Libby nodded. "Kiwi has a grandmother in Alabama. When they arrest me, I want Kiwi to go live with her. I'll give you her name and phone number."

The lawyer looked at Libby, openly assessing her, and Libby imagined seeing herself through Sarah Longstaff's eyes. Lousy mother. Lousy provider.

No wonder the woman disliked her.

But the attorney's tone was respectful when she spoke again.

"You're actually prepared to go to prison, aren't you?" Longstaff said, and her face said that was a surprise.

Libby chewed, swallowed. "Can anybody prepare for that?"

· "Not unless you've been there before. And you haven't. I checked."

Libby shrugged. "I've been through worse."

Sarah Longstaff met her eyes as if to argue, but changed her mind.

"I'll tell Nick we're ready," she said.

Detective Delgado sat down at the table, crossed his legs, and looked at Libby. "Okay, tell me from the beginning how this shooting happened."

"You don't have to say anything, Libby," Longstaff said. "If they had any evidence, they'd have issued a warrant months ago." Her lawyerly advice sounded like a recording.

"It's okay," Libby said. She repeated the story she had told him before, keeping every detail exactly the same.

"Had he ever threatened you before that?"

"Yes. And Kiwi said he threatened her. I didn't believe her."

"What kind of gun was it?"

"I don't know, but I can describe it," she said, and did so.

"Where is it now?" he said.

"Still in the ocean where I threw it, I guess, like I told you before."

The detective was drawing spirals like a tornado on a notepad. "Are you willing to take a lie detector test?"

"You don't have to," her lawyer said quickly.

Libby thought a moment.

"I don't trust those things," she said. "I'm too nervous."

Longstaff nodded her approval.

＊

When both the detective and the lawyer had left for the night, a cop came in and Libby was searched again and installed in a stark holding cell. At least they let her keep her own clothes. Alone with the tepid fluorescent lighting and the drone of used air, she lay back on the bunk and hoped Kiwi was okay at Jeremiah's house. She wondered whether they would see each other tomorrow. Kiwi had escaped from a pedophile! My God, was there anything the child couldn't do? Her eyes filled, and she smiled. Kiwi was her hero.

Then she thought about Shaun, driving eight hours back to Sand Flats. He would need to sleep, gather the list of items she'd given him from her apartment, and drive eight hours back. If he came back.

Somehow, against all odds and prior experience, she believed he would. It was unaccountable, this new optimism building slowly from within, warm as a sunrise. Libby was facing a prison term, yet she felt stronger than she had since Deacon's death.

For once, maybe for the first time, she was doing what was best for Kiwi.

She stretched her legs and prepared to pass the night, not expecting sleep. She recalled the night her mother had locked her in a closet so she wouldn't sneak out with her friends. Libby had been thirteen at the time, just two years older than Kiwi was now. In the claustrophobic dark of that closet, Libby had pulled out chunks of her hair.

This holding cell was larger than a closet, and the light stayed on.

She could do this. Piece of cake.

Chapter 23

Kiwi's Journal

A day in February—no idea which one.

TONIGHT I AM SLEEPING over at Jeremiah's house. I'm glad to be here, but the truth is, I'd have gone anywhere to get out of Juvie Jail. I feel sick when I imagine spending years and years in there. I wonder if those years might count against my time in hell. If I'm a jailbird long enough, would God judge that I had atoned for my sins and maybe cancel the order to send me to hell? That's the only possible bright side I can think of about being locked up in that bare little room with the repulsive toilet.

It's also something I can't change, so like Scarlett O'Hara in *Gone with the Wind*, I'll worry about that tomorrow.

I know I'm lucky that I got to come home with Jeremiah. His wife is named Anita and they have two kids. Perry is ten, and Wendell is a teenager. Perry let me have his bedroom, and he's sleeping in Wendell's room. They didn't even seem mad about it. My friend Karen back in Sand Flats had a teenage sister, and if you put them in the same bedroom, they'd fight like wildcats. But Wendell is quite a bit older than

Perry and seems laid back. I'm on the top bunk in Perry's room right now, writing all this in my journal. Jeremiah got Moxie and my dog tags back for me too. Jeremiah is magic.

This morning, he was still with me in the visiting room when, with no warning, Mom walked in! I didn't even know Detective Nick had found her or whether she would come if he did. She looked skinny and tired. Her face was paper white. Seeing her was such a shock, I couldn't move. I wasn't sure she'd want a hug, but I gave her one anyway. But I didn't want to break out blubbering in front of Jeremiah and Detective Nick, so I got away as fast as I could and went back to my chair. I was sure happy, though, that she'd come to see me before I went to prison. I'm going to miss her a lot.

After that things got crazy. Some lady came in and said she was my lawyer. I guess Mom hired her. Then Mom made everybody leave, and she tried to tell me she's the one who killed Rocket! She said she smothered him with a pillow. I don't believe her, but I can't get that horrible picture out of my head.

Adults make everything so complicated. I came here on a simple mission, but all these people got involved and now it's out of control. I can't let Mom go to prison. If I'm in jail, I'll probably end up being one of the tough kids everybody's afraid of, but I'll stay alive. I don't think Mom could do that. I think she'd die in there, and it would be my fault.

Jeremiah says that when he has troubles, he tries to do what's right and then relax and put everything in God's hands. That sounds easy, but it isn't. God and I are not all that tight. If he's so good and wise, how could he let my dad get killed in Iraq? What good could possibly come from it? Even Jeremiah didn't have an answer for that.

Before I left the police station, I had to go over the whole story about Rocket with Detective Nick again. I think he helped Jeremiah fix it so I could stay at his house tonight. But Mom wasn't allowed to leave yet, so I don't know where she's staying. Shaun the Bartender came to San Jose with her, she said, but I never saw him.

The Summernighs have a nice house, but thankfully, it's not fancy. I wouldn't feel comfortable in somebody's fancy house. They have a dog named Toastmaster who is a total sweetheart. He's part beagle and part wiener dog, with short legs and a long tail. I was hoping Toastmaster would sleep in my room, but Perry says he always sleeps with their mom. Their mom, by the way, is a terrific cook. We had chicken and rice for dinner and about three kinds of vegetables. I ate like a pig.

The first thing I did when I got here was take a hot shower and wash my hair. I felt so much better with clean hair. And I like this bunk bed. The sheets are blue with yellow stars and moons. I guess Perry likes astronomy because he has the solar system pasted all over the ceiling of his room. He said when I turn out the lights I'll see the Milky Way, and the stars and planets will glow in the dark. He also left me a night-light in case I need it. I like Perry. If we went to the same school, I bet we could be friends.

The whole Summernigh family has been so nice. But every few minutes, I think about Juvie Jail and my arms start to shake, like when you're so cold you can't stop shivering. When this happened at dinner, Miss Anita put her arm around me and held me close until it stopped. Then we went back to eating like nothing had happened. I wish my manners were that good.

I think I'll turn out the light now and look at Perry's stars. Jeremiah suggested I try to talk to God when I'm scared or lonesome. Considering what I've done and what God lets happen in this world, that doesn't seem a conversation worth having to me. Maybe I'll try talking to Bones instead.

Love,
Kiwi

Shrinky-Dink Day

When I woke up this morning, I smelled bacon. I love bacon, especially when it's crisp and not floppy. I smelled something else good, too, which turned out to be blueberry waffles. Yum! If I lived here, I'd be as fat as Patrick Star on *SpongeBob*.

Jeremiah was sitting at the table drinking coffee and reading his newspaper. I sat at the table with him while Miss Anita made me a hot waffle. She asked me if I slept well. I must have because it was already eight o'clock, and Perry and Wendell had left for school.

Jeremiah said we were supposed to go back to the police station at two o'clock. My lawyer would meet us there. Then he folded up his newspaper and laid his brown arms on the table. "But before that," he said, "I'm supposed to take you to see a psychologist at 10:30 a.m. A lady named Dr. Marks."

"Oh, man!" I said. "Will I have to go through the whole story again?"

"Yes, you probably will. Just tell the truth. That's always the best approach."

I wasn't so sure about that, but I nodded. What if I tripped up and said something I shouldn't? How would I even know?

"So you know what a psychologist is?" he said.

"A head doctor. Can't they give me a lie-detector test instead?"

"I don't think they use those on kids," he said. "The doctor will talk with you, probably about an hour. Detective Nick says she's a nice lady."

Dr. Marks had reddish hair, and she was small and slim. She smiled like she wanted me to like her, but we weren't going to be together long enough for that. I can't remember all the questions she asked. But she started with Mom and Dad and school, and then she asked about Jack. I thought I was going to get a pass on Rocket, but she finally got around to him. She wanted to know how I felt about him and whether he'd ever "touched me where he shouldn't." Good grief—why don't people just go ahead and say *molested* or *raped*?

"Not like you mean," I said. "But he hit me a couple of times, and he could threaten you with a look. I stayed away from him as much as I could."

I thought about the time he'd pinched my boob, but I didn't really have boobs at the time, and I didn't want to explain about that. I hated thinking about Rocket, let alone talking about him. Dr. Marks was a stranger. It was none of her business how Rocket used to shove me around or make me stay in my room so he could slap Mom around. The way I saw it, Dr. Marks was one of those too nice people who are easily rattled. People like that irritate me. I bet nothing bad had ever happened to her. I felt like shocking her, so I gave her some attitude and talked tougher than I usually would. But I didn't tell her much.

Jeremiah was in the waiting room reading his newspaper when I came out. I was tired, though all I'd done was sit in a chair. He took me to a pizza parlor for lunch, then we killed time at a park feeding the pigeons. I watched some kids on a school playground close to the park and wondered if I'd ever get to go to school again.

When we arrived at the police station, Detective Nick had been called out on a case, but Sarah the Lawyer was in the house. I asked to see Mom, but she said it wasn't possible at the moment.

"Why not?" I said. "Is she okay?"

"Which one of those do you want me to answer?" she said, and then she didn't answer either one. Jeremiah interrupted and asked if he could take me back home.

"She's in your custody," she said, "until Nick and the D.A. make up their minds about filing charges. I'll call you."

So we went back to Jeremiah's house. I watched *SpongeBob* while Jeremiah made some phone calls about his work. Perry and Wendell were in sports after school, so they weren't home yet, and neither was Miss Anita.

Jeremiah was still on the phone when the doorbell rang. So I said, "You want me to get that?" and he said please.

I opened the door and there, of all people, stood Shaun the Bartender.

"Hi, Kiwi," he said. He was taller than I remembered.

"How the heck did you find me here?" I said. "And why?"

It sounded rude, but he smiled. "Your mom asked me to bring you some stuff from home." He held up a brown paper sack.

Jeremiah came to the door and Shaun introduced himself. "I'd like to talk with Kiwi a few minutes, if that's okay," Shaun said.

"That's up to Kiwi," Jeremiah said.

I thought Shaun might have a message from Mom or knew where she was staying. So I said okay, and Jeremiah invited Shaun to come in.

Jeremiah led us out to the patio. It was a nice day so it was on the sunny side and warm out there.

"If you need me, Kiwi, just give a yell," he said. He went back inside, but I noticed that he left the door open.

Shaun and I each claimed a patio chair in the sunshine. He set the brown sack by my feet. "Some clean clothes and stuff," he said. Score one for the bartender.

"Thanks," I said. "Did you see Mom today?"

"Not yet, but I saw her yesterday afternoon. She asked me to check on you and let her know how you're doing."

"I'm fine," I said. "Jeremiah's family is nice."

"That's good. I'll tell her that."

Shaun and I had probably never said more than a dozen words to each other before. He had strange eyes, but I have to admit they were interesting. They were dark blue, like the deep ocean. With his long hair, he looked kind of like Jesus with tats. I could see how Mom got fooled into liking him.

"So what did you want to talk to me about?" I said. "Is Mom still trying to take the blame for Rocket?"

He shrugged. "I don't know who Rocket is or why she's there."

"Really?" I snorted. "No wonder you're still hanging around. You don't know what we've done."

"Don't need to know," he said. "Libby will tell me when she's ready. Or not."

I gave him a look, but his face was open, like he meant it.

"She did tell me she'd had some bad experiences with men," he said. "So I understand why you don't want me around. I want you to know that I won't do anything to hurt her. You might not believe me, but I care about your mom."

Something mean rose up inside me. I didn't trust what he was saying, and I figured I knew how to drive him away.

"Really? Then maybe you should know what happened with Rocket," I said. "He gave my mom drugs and treated her like crap, and she still wouldn't leave him, so I shot the bastard. Now she's trying to tell the police that she did it. She wants to save me, but it's too late. I can deal with prison or hell or whatever else they throw at me. But Mom can't. She's not that strong. Otherwise she wouldn't keep hooking up with guys like Rocket."

My voice was getting loud, so I stopped. With the door open, Jeremiah couldn't have missed hearing me, but he didn't come out. I'd already told him the whole ugly story about Rocket, and he was my friend anyway. I was betting Shaun wouldn't be that kind of friend to Mom.

Shaun's voice got real quiet.

"She must really love you," he said.

"What? How did you get that out of all the stuff I just told you?"

He looked straight at me and his eyes got ten miles deep. "My wife died of cancer when she was younger than your mom," he said. "I lost everything else, too, because I didn't care anymore. I finally landed in Sand Flats, hiding from the world, trying to get my head right. See, I have some idea of what you and Libby went through when you lost your dad."

I squirmed in my patio chair. This was the last thing I wanted to hear. "No, you don't," I said, as mean as I could. "You have no idea." Tears started dripping off my chin. "But I'm sorry about your wife."

"I'm sorry about your dad," he said.

He swallowed a couple of times. I thought he was going to say something more, but instead, he seemed focused on a white jet trail in the sky. That was fine with me, but then he shifted his attention back to me.

"Kiwi, I'll make you a deal," he said. "I'm going to stick by your mom until this thing with the police shakes out. She needs somebody to be there. But afterward, no matter how it ends, if you still think I'm bad for her and want me to leave, I'll walk away."

"Liar," I said.

"No. I'll never be a hero like your dad, but I do keep my word."

He left then, and I came straight to Perry's room to write all this down. Sometimes this journal is the only way I can deal with the stuff I don't understand. And while I wouldn't want anyone to know it, most days it seems like the longer I live, the less I know about anything.

Love,
Kiwi the Confused

Second night at the Summernighs

After dinner, I came back to my borrowed bedroom and emptied the sack Shaun the Bartender had brought from home, well, what used to be my home. I was glad for the clean clothes and pajamas and underwear. It was weird to imagine Shaun going to our apartment and finding my clothes like he was a member of the family. But compared to the crazy stuff that had happened lately, Shaun was last on the list. What I found in the bottom of the sack was way weirder.

Underneath the clothes, there was something heavy. I dug down to it and found Mom's Royal Gorge box. The one she told me was full of memories. Why would he bring me this? Then I found an envelope with my name on it. Inside was Mom's charm bracelet with the key to the box, and a note in her handwriting:

> Kiwi—
> I don't know when I'll see you again, so I asked Shaun to bring you this box. There are some letters in it that I should have given you a long time ago. I'm sorry I've been such a lousy mother.
> Love, Mom

Did she mean that?

My shaky hands had a hard time fitting the tiny gold key into the lock. I carefully opened the lid. Right on top, like they were the last things Mom put in, were two letters. I thought they would be from Dad when he was overseas. But they weren't from Dad—they were from Grandma Seager.

I admit I was disappointed. Why in the world would Mom hide letters from Grandma? I'd read dozens of her letters. Lots of times, I wrote her back. But now that I thought of it, I hadn't seen a letter from her for a long time.

I held the envelopes side by side. These two hadn't come with the checks because they had their own postmarks. And they were addressed to me, not to Mom, nor to Mom and me both. Mom had opened my mail and then hid it from me. Why? I read the letters over and over. Grandma had sent the first one right after we got to Sand Flats. Here's what it said:

> Dear Kiwi,
>
> I didn't get a school picture from you last year, and I hope you'll send one soon. I keep asking your mom to bring you for a visit. Maybe at Thanksgiving? Surely at Christmas? I could send money for gas or airplane tickets. I'm hoping you can convince her to come this year. But if you can't, maybe you could come by yourself.
>
> I hear all the time about children who fly alone, and the flight attendants take good care of them. Libby could put you on a direct flight, and I'd be here to meet you. I know you're fearless like your dad, not a Nervous Nellie like your grandma. (I've only flown once in my life, and I was so scared it was embarrassing.) But you're brave and independent—I know you could do it. You'd probably think it was fun!
>
> If you can convince your mom, I'll send the airplane ticket.
>
> Love, Grandma

That one made me smile. If I'd read it before, I would have bugged Mom to let me go. I guess she didn't want to hear it, so she just hid the letter. But it wasn't right to hide somebody's letters from her own grandma. Grandma Seager must have waited and waited for me to answer, and when I never did, she'd have thought I didn't want to come.

The second letter was dated a couple months later.

> Dear Kiwi,
>
> I haven't heard from you in a long time, and I'm worried. I tried to phone, but Libby never called back. Are you okay?
>
> I've been thinking that perhaps you should come

live with me for a while, until your mom can work out her grief and settle down somewhere. Do you remember this big old house and how you used to play on the stairs? And the veranda where we watched the fireflies come out in the evening? We could have fun together, like we did when Grandpa was alive. We have excellent schools in our town too.

There's plenty of room for you and Libby both, and I've talked to her about this. But she won't come. Maybe this house has so much of Deacon in it that it makes her sad. I'm worried about her, but I'm even more worried about you.

Please write soon, or phone me and charge the call to my number. Here it is: (205) 555-1313.

I love you,
Grandma

The more I thought about it, the madder I got that Mom never showed me these letters. It wasn't the first time she'd betrayed me, either. Didn't she choose Rocket instead of me? Why wouldn't she be happy for me to go live with Grandma?

I looked through the other things in the Royal Gorge box. A baby picture of me, a pressed flower that was crumbling apart, and a newspaper clipping about someone who had died in a car crash. I think it was my mom's mom.

In the bottom of the box was a photo of Mom and Dad and me at some Army ceremony when I was one or two years old. Dad had on his uniform and goofy Army hat and was holding me in one arm. I had on a frilly pink dress and white patent shoes and doggy ears. Dad was smiling, I was pulling out one of my hair ribbons, and Mom looked stressed out. Pretty much the history of our family.

Love,
Kiwi

Chapter 24

Libby and the Lawyer

LIBBY SPENT THE NIGHT dozing off and on in the holding cell. Early the next morning, a policeman led her to the conference room to meet with her attorney. Her mouth tasted like cardboard, and her neck ached. She hoped the police didn't intend to question her again. She was way too groggy to keep her facts straight.

Sarah Longstaff brought a cardboard tray with two coffees and a paper bag balanced on top. She placed a coffee in front of Libby and ripped open the side of the bag to reveal a croissant and a creamed-cheese Danish. She motioned for Libby to choose. Libby picked the croissant.

"Long night?" Longstaff said, sitting down.

Libby looked at her with bleary eyes. "I appreciate the coffee."

The attorney's hair was tumbled and damp, and Libby caught the fresh scent of shampoo. Her own hair felt ropy, her armpits sticky despite the chill of the room. This was her third day in the same clothes. No wonder people always looked guilty in their mug shots.

Longstaff slapped a file folder onto the table. "I've been doing some reading," she said and took a heroic bite of Danish.

Libby looked at the folder. "About what?"

The lawyer chewed twice and swallowed. "About Roger Kitridge Hogan. Alias Rocket."

At the unexpected mention of his name, all blood and rational thought drained from Libby's brain. Rocket. She saw him as she had for the last time, the handsome face slack and ashen, his power gone. From the distance of time, she marveled at the colossal stupidity of getting involved with him.

"He had a long rap sheet," the lawyer said, "and nobody around here mourned his passing. The police suspected one of his associates of turning on him. His death was written off months ago as a drug deal gone wrong."

Libby frowned, trying to sift out the lawyer's point. "They weren't looking for Kiwi and me?"

"Nope. You girls waltzed in here and stirred up a dead case."

Longstaff blew across the surface of her coffee and took a loud sip, eyeing Libby above the cup's rim.

Libby said nothing, caught by the irony. She had been hiding from an enemy who didn't exist.

"If your story is true," the attorney said, "it's self-defense, and there's no witness to dispute it. But if Kiwi's story is true and they charge her, that's problematical. She would go into the juvenile justice system and be there a long time. I have never seen a kid come out of that experience better off than when she went in."

"Kiwi's trying to protect me," Libby said, but Longstaff continued as if she hadn't spoken.

"Nick is putting Kiwi with a psychologist today, but neither of us believes Kiwi is a danger, let alone a sociopath. He wants to hear what the shrink has to say, but with no more evidence than they have now, the D.A. might decline to prosecute. I've had a persuasive discussion with her about it."

Libby sat forward in her chair. "What? What does that mean? Are you saying they might let us both go?"

Longstaff shrugged. "It's possible. For one thing, I think Nick talked to Kiwi too long that first night without the consent of her parent. Her lawyer could argue that anything she told him then would be inadmissible. If they charge you, we can plead self-defense. You're guilty of fleeing the scene of a crime, but you aren't likely to get jail time for that."

Libby was not accustomed to the breaks falling her way. She stared at the lawyer, stunned. Had the optimism she was feeling yesterday somehow created its own luck?

"The facts are too sketchy to prove anything," Longstaff continued. "And the department can save the taxpayers a lot of money by leaving Rocket's case alone." She crammed the last bite of Danish into her mouth and rolled up the sack. "Besides, Nick has a couple kids of his own and a huge respect for the military. I don't think he sees any advantage in charging either one of you. Of course, his boss and the D.A. have the last word, so don't start counting your chickens."

Never had Libby imagined the possibility of such an outcome. She was reconciled with doing time in prison and sending Kiwi to her grandmother. What if she and Kiwi got a second chance to stay together? Could Libby break the pattern of bad parenting that ran in her family like a genetic defect?

It seemed too much to hope for, but Libby hoped anyway.

Chapter 25

Kiwi's Journal

Last day with the Summernighs

AFTER I READ Grandma Seager's letters last night, I stayed awake most of the night, thinking about her big house with the creaky floors. I remember an upstairs bedroom where the wind through the windows smelled like flowers. Dad and Grandpa would sit on the porch after dark and talk about Army stuff. I could tell by his voice that Grandpa was proud of his son. Even Mom seemed to relax in their house, maybe because there were four adults to help her look after me.

The last time we were there was for Dad's funeral. My memory of that visit has fuzzy edges, but I remember two things: Jeremiah down on one knee presenting Mom the folded flag, and the sad sound of taps from a single bugle.

Finally I put Grandma's letters away and crawled down from Perry's bunk bed. I peeked out into the hallway and saw a light on somewhere in the house. I found Jeremiah in the den, working at his computer. He works for a construction company that has projects in other countries, where the time zone is like eight hours later. So if he emails them at night, it's already morning there.

I told him about the letters and asked him if I could phone my grandma.

"Sure you can," he said. His face was dark and shiny in the lamp light, and it made me homesick for someplace I'd never been. I wondered if Perry and Wendell knew how lucky they were to have such a father. "It's after midnight in Alabama. You don't want to wake her up tonight, do you?"

I was too lonesome to be considerate of Grandma's sleep. "You know what?" I said. "I'll bet she won't care. She's a grandma."

Jeremiah smiled. "You're probably right. My granny wouldn't have cared, either." He handed me his cell. The phone rang a bunch of times before a definitely sleepy voice answered.

"Hi, Grandma Seager? It's Kiwi."

She woke up fast. "My stars, I can't believe it," she said. "It's so good to hear your voice!"

I'd forgotten about Grandma's southern accent. She sounded like banana cream pie tastes. "I'm sorry to call so late," I said, "but I only just now found the letters you wrote me a long time ago. I'm sorry I never answered."

"It's okay, honey," she said. "How are you? Is everything okay there?"

That was a hard question. "Not exactly. Mom and I are back in San Jose. I'm kind of in trouble with the police."

"The police! Did you do something wrong? You can tell me, honey. I'll love you no matter what."

That made my nose run. Jeremiah reached out and patted my shoulder. But I could not tell my grandmother I'd shot a man. I wasn't going to lie, either. "I did something awful," I said. "I'll probably be in jail for a long time."

Jail sounds like where you go for spray-painting a wall or shoplifting, not as bad as prison. But my news was still a shock to Grandma.

"Oh, Kiwi! Surely they won't put you in jail!"

"I think they have to," I said. "I hope you'll write letters to me while I'm there. I promise I'll write back, if they let me."

The line went quiet for a few seconds. Her banana-pudding voice wasn't so soft when she said, "I want to talk to your mother."

"She's not here right now."

"Where is she?"

"At the police station, I think."

"You think." Another pause. "Where are you, exactly?"

"I'm at a friend's house. Do you remember a Sergeant Jeremiah Redbone Summernigh? He came to Dad's funeral."

"I do. He was very kind."

"I'm on his phone, so I better not talk too long. But I wanted to tell you that I remember your house, and Grandpa, and the fireflies."

"I'm very glad you called, Kiwi. Before you go, could I please have a phone number for Mr. Summernigh?"

I repeated the number Jeremiah told me.

"Please tell him I'd like to call him tomorrow—when it's daylight," Grandma said. "I love you, sweetheart."

I said I loved her, too. But the truth is, I don't really know her. What I love are my memories of her and Grandpa.

11 February 2009

There's a calendar in Perry's room, and I finally figured out what day it is—February 11. Three days before Valentine's. Back when I was young, we used to spend a whole afternoon at school making construction-paper cards for our parents and friends. I wonder what my class at Sand Flats Elementary is doing for the holiday. It feels like years since I was there, but according to my math, it's been only five days.

This morning I straightened up Perry's room and left him a thank-you note on the bottom bunk. I put on the clean clothes Shaun had brought me. The shirt doesn't go with these jeans, but that's the least of my problems.

I packed the Royal Gorge box and Grandma's letters in my backpack, and then Jeremiah and I drove downtown to the San Jose Police Department.

In the lobby, Jeremiah handed me off to my lady lawyer. I was hoping he could stay, but he'd already missed two days of work and said he would have to see me later.

Ms. Longstaff always looks like she ate pickles for breakfast. I asked her where Mom was. She said, "Don't worry, you'll see her this morning," in a voice that sounded like be careful what you ask for.

I was glad and not glad about seeing Mom. I was mad at her for hiding Grandma's letters, but I was also worried about her. She probably felt like that about me, too. Maybe we'd both be better off when we were separated. I was beginning to get used to that idea.

Ms. Longstaff and I went inside and found Detective Nick. He sent us to a room I hadn't been in before, with a nicer table and chairs and drapes on the windows. It looked like a room where Big Decisions were made. That must be why Ms. Longstaff was so snippy. Could they hold a trial in here? Maybe a judge would sweep in wearing his big choir robe and sentence me straight to hell, skip the prison part.

I was ready to get it over with. Ever since Jeremiah gave me back my dad, I haven't been as scared as before. I know Dad's with me, no matter what happens.

Ms. Longstaff and I sat down at the table. A minute later, Detective Nick came in. Right behind him was Mom, and then came Dr. Marks, the psychologist. Then a man I'd never seen before, but he was wearing a suit instead of a robe.

Yikes. It looked like a drug intervention on reality TV, but without the drugs. My heart started jumping like popcorn.

"I need to pee," I said.

Ms. Longstaff gave me a mean look. "Can you wait?"

"I don't think so," I said. "Don't get up, though. I know where the bathroom is."

"Right." She sighed and shoved her chair back.

I probably wouldn't have gone AWOL anyway, but there was no chance with her trailing behind me. I soaped my hands twice while she stood there with her arms crossed, but pretty soon there was nothing to do but go back to the meeting room. As soon as we sat down, the man in the suit introduced himself and took over. I assumed he was Nick's boss because he used complicated language like he was somebody extra important. But thanks to my good vocabulary, I understood all the words. Here's what he said, as accurately as I can remember:

"Detective Delgado and I have consulted with the district attorney's office about the new information concerning the murder of Roger Kitridge Hogan."

For a second, I didn't know who the heck he was talking about. I'd never heard Rocket's full name before. Then he said: "The accounts from Mrs. Seager and her daughter are conflicting, and there's no proof as to which story, if either one, contains the actual facts. Therefore the district attorney has declined to prosecute. And because of the special circumstances, the D.A. agreed not to file child-neglect charges under certain conditions. If Mrs. Seager agrees to abide by the conditions, she and her daughter will be free to go."

Free to go?

Was he kidding? How can you confess to murder and be free to go?

I looked at Mom, but she was staring at Suit Man. She looked like a baby bird. Detective Nick picked up the lecture. "Dr. Marks and I agree that both Kiwi and Mrs. Seager are in need of psychological counseling. Dr. Marks recommends parenting classes for Mrs. Seager. These services should be available to military families at little or no expense. We're going to ask Ms. Longstaff, as their legal representative, to see that this happens."

"Hold it," Longstaff said. "I'm a public defender, not a babysitter. I can't be responsible for what my clients do with the rest of their lives. These conditions of yours have no legal weight."

They ignored her. "If they don't get the counseling," the Suit Man said, "the D.A. can change her mind about bringing charges. If not for murder, at least for child neglect."

Ms. Longstaff was seriously ticked off. "You're blackmailing my client. And me, too!"

"Sarah," Nick said. He waited until Ms. Longtaff calmed down and looked at him. His voice was quiet but sharp. "Keep your eye on the ball here. Think of it like a plea agreement. We're trying to do what's best for Kiwi, give her a chance at a decent life."

Ms. Longstaff didn't have an answer for that.

I thought about telling her that compared to prison, talking to a counselor didn't sound that bad. Dr. Marks had been pretty nice, even though I wasn't nice to her. But I was also willing to bet Mom would never go to a shrink. An Army doctor tried to get her to do that after Dad was killed, but she never would.

Then—to prove that I don't know anything—my mom spoke up and said, "I accept the conditions."

My mouth fell open. Ms. Longstaff tossed her ballpoint pen onto the table.

"But I need to keep my job in Sand Flats," Mom said. "It's within driving distance of Edwards Air Force Base or Twentynine Palms. Maybe they have counseling services there."

Dr. Marks spoke up. "I can help set that up. And I'm willing to keep track of Libby and Kiwi's progress and report back to the department. It might be easier for me to do that than for Ms. Longstaff." She sounded pleasant and reasonable, like a schoolteacher, which made Ms. Longstaff sound like a jerk, and she looked even madder.

"Thank you, Doctor," Suit Man said.

Dr. Marks turned her blue eyes at me. "How about you, Kiwi? Do you accept these conditions?"

Everybody got quiet and looked at me.

My voice sounded wobbly. "Instead of going to prison?" I said. "Who wouldn't?"

But I was thinking: Is counseling a suitable punishment for somebody who's committed murder?

Suit Man stood up like everything was settled. "If Dr. Marks will make the arrangements with Mrs. Seager and Detective Delgado," he said, "please excuse me. I'm late for another meeting." He hurried out the door.

Sarah Longstaff got up and left too.

The rest of us sat around the table like the wreckage after a storm. Except for Dr. Marks, who looked perfectly calm.

Detective Nick let out his breath in a long hiss. "Kiwi," he said, "I don't think they need us. How about a soda pop and a doughnut?"

I wasn't sure I could stand. But I never turn down a doughnut. We left Mom and the shrink to work things out.

⁂

I sat at Nick's desk the rest of the morning and wrote everything that had happened up to that point in my journal. It was afternoon before Mom came and said we could go home. She looked a lot better than she had this morning. She tried to smile but was careful not to give me a hug. That was okay. I didn't want to hug her, either.

We walked out of the police station together. It felt odd to be alone with Mom again. I was wondering what it would be like when we got back to Sand Flats and tried to act normal. Then I looked up, and there was the answer to my question.

Shaun the Bartender was leaning against Mom's truck.

I stopped where I was. He saw us and stood up, and the way he and Mom looked at each other made my stomach drop. She hugged him, and they circled up, holding hands and talking.

Hi-ho the derry-o, the Cheese Stands Alone.

Home again, home again, jiggety jig.

On the drive back to Sand Flats, Mom and I had to squeeze together in the shotgun seat, and Shaun drove. Nobody talked. To fill up the silence, Shaun tuned the radio to a country music station that was total vulture vomit. I sat next to the door and stared out the window.

Before we got too far, I asked to use Mom's phone so I could call Jeremiah. After all he had done for me, it wasn't right to disappear without a word. But Jeremiah didn't answer and the phone battery was low, so all I could do was leave a quick message. I should have left a thank-you note for him and Miss Anita like I had for Perry. I'd probably never see any of them again.

We had to stop in Creosote City so Shaun could get his Harley. Mom and I drove the rest of the way after that by ourselves. She kept watching for Shaun in the rearview mirror, which made it pretty easy to avoid a conversation. I owed Shaun one for that.

The sun had long since set when we arrived home. Shaun went on to his house, thank goodness. I heated up some canned potato soup for Mom and me. She ate a little but said she was exhausted and we should go to bed early, so we did.

We lay there in the dark, thinking our own thoughts. After a while Mom said, "Do you want to go to school tomorrow?"

Wow. I'd totally forgotten about school.

"What day is this?" I asked.

"Thursday, I think."

"I better go," I said. "I'll have a lot of homework to catch up on."

I wondered if Mrs. Gomez and Mr. Mathis knew where I'd been and why. And if the other kids would look at me funny.

When I knew Mom was asleep, I got up quietly and came downstairs to write in my journal. It was almost full.

That's where I am now, downstairs by myself. The apartment was closed up while we were gone, and it smells like dirt. I opened the back windows to let in some fresh air. From here I can see the empty land behind the building. The desert is always the same after dark—dry and still, like nothing lives there. The tired old moon is fading away at one edge.

So I guess this is how it's going to be with Mom and me. We don't have to hide from the police anymore, but we still don't feel like mother and daughter. I doubt that will ever change. We're like two separate moons: We travel through the same space and time, but we never share the light we hold inside.

Night,

Kiwi

Chapter 26

Second Chances

O N AN APRIL AFTERNOON two months after the episode in San Jose, Libby drove toward her second appointment with Dr. Kelvin, the psychologist approved by her military insurance. His office was in Creosote City, which was closer than any military base but still an hour's drive each way. Kiwi rode silently beside her, reading a book. Libby envied her ability to read in a moving car.

They had back-to-back appointments with the doctor every Friday after school. Libby didn't like seeing the same psychologist as her daughter; it made her feel exposed. But the arrangement was convenient, and perhaps the doctor could get better insight if he saw things from both of their perspectives. He was supposed to be an expert in family counseling. Libby thought of the sessions as penance. She had given up feeling guilty about Rocket, and she hoped the doctor could help Kiwi get to that place.

In preparation for the weekly drives, Libby had sold the gas-hog. Shaun helped her locate a man who was willing to buy the truck even though the title wasn't officially signed over to her. With the money, she had bought a used Honda that got twenty-eight miles to the gallon and could fit into any parking space. Kiwi hated the car, of course. Because it was brown. She objected to nearly everything Libby did these days, a possible omen of the teenage years to come. Kiwi would be twelve next month.

A warm desert wind flooded the interior of the Honda. Libby thought of the cruel summer ahead, when her skin would feel reptilian no matter how much body lotion she slathered on. She daydreamed of the ocean, of fertile turquoise waters pounding black rocks along the Central Coast. If she left Sand Flats, would Shaun go with her? She had no clue whether Kiwi would be happy about moving or would sink into sullen rebellion.

Kiwi was undergoing a growth spurt, although her body hadn't yet begun to develop a female shape. As she drove, Libby considered a surprise party for her daughter's birthday but quickly discarded the notion. It would probably go better if Kiwi was in on the planning. Maybe she would like to invite a friend or two from school—if she had friends. She never talked about school these days. When Libby questioned her, Kiwi shrugged or gave one-word answers. Libby didn't know how to reach her. She was afraid if they couldn't form a good relationship soon, it would be too late. But she had no sense of what a normal mother-daughter bond felt like. Was it always part adversary, part friend? This was something she should discuss with Dr. Kelvin.

She took a deep breath and glanced over at her daughter. "What would you like to do for your birthday?"

Kiwi kept reading. "Nothing—maybe get a tasteful tattoo."

Libby snorted. "Yeah, right."

Kiwi hated tattoos; this much Libby knew. "You could have a friend over for a slumber party," she said. No reaction. "Or we could just invite Shaun and Myra for cake and ice cream."

Kiwi rolled her eyes.

"Too lame?"

"I'll be twelve, not six," Kiwi pointed out. Then she looked up from her book, as if she was considering. "Let me think about it."

"Okay. Just keep in mind our financial limitations."

"I always do," Kiwi said, with the preteen sarcasm that Libby was learning to detest. She was not fond of the change in Kiwi's wardrobe, either: nothing but knee-split jeans and black stretchy tops painted with skulls and acid-rock hallucinations. Never mind that Libby had dressed much the same as a teenager. She wanted something better for Kiwi.

Libby gave up on both conversation and fresh air. She rolled up the windows and pushed the A/C button. The cool air felt like a reprieve. She turned on the radio. Kiwi closed her book and gazed out the window, tapping her thumbs. She's tense about seeing the psychologist, same as me, Libby thought, wishing she knew what they talked about. Kiwi's immortal soul? Libby's crappy parenting?

Libby would have preferred a woman psychologist, but Dr. Kelvin was an okay guy. Kiwi seemed to like him. How would Libby know if he was helping her daughter? This attitude of Kiwi's had started the week they returned from San Jose, before she was seeing the counselor, so Libby couldn't blame it on him. But it wasn't getting any better.

They were only three minutes late arriving. Dr. Kelvin's waiting room was decorated in old-fashioned shades of blue and beige that were probably meant to be soothing. Maybe he had a wife who chose the colors. He got to poke around in her psyche with no restrictions, but she knew nothing about him beyond his appearance and soft, nasal voice. He had dark, curly hair worn slightly long and black-rimmed glasses. Probably in his forties.

Kiwi ignored the low table covered with building blocks and coloring books in the waiting room. Instead, she slipped into a chair in the corner and returned to reading her fantasy novel about wizards and muggles. Libby was first up.

An inside door opened, and Dr. Kelvin leaned out. He waved to Kiwi. "Come in, Libby. Hot today, isn't it? Would you like something to drink?"

Libby accepted a soda and plopped down in an overstuffed chair. The walls of the room were a neutral cream, the carpet flattened by the weight of dysfunctional lives.

"How are you feeling this week?" he asked. Libby had noticed that he liked to start with something innocent and work up to the painful stuff. On her last visit, she had wanted to talk about how to handle the continental drift between her and Kiwi, but he kept probing the subject of Deacon's death. Finally she had snapped at him. "Has somebody you loved ever been violently killed?" she said. "You don't move on. That would be a betrayal."

Dr. Kelvin had tented his fingers below his chin and looked at her, letting her hear the echo of her words in the quiet room.

"You feel that to stop mourning for Deacon would be less than he deserved," he said. "A betrayal."

She nodded. Her ribs felt broken.

"If Deacon were here right now," Dr. Kelvin said, "what would he say in response to that?"

"I don't know."

"I'll bet you do know." He waited again.

Libby sighed. She could almost hear the words in Deacon's voice. "Deacon would say that what happened to us sucked, but it is what it is. He would want me to make the best life I can for myself and Kiwi. He'd expect me to do that."

"And have you done it?"

"No."

"Do you want to?"

"For a long time, I didn't. I felt like it wasn't fair for me to be okay after what happened to him."

"What do you think now?"

She gave him the answer he expected. "I think it's time. Past time. For Kiwi's sake."

The doctor nodded. "Okay. But what about for Libby's sake?"

She shrugged.

"You didn't cause your husband's death, Libby. And you couldn't prevent it. There's absolutely no reason you should feel guilty for being alive. I think he'd be the first to tell you that. He was a soldier, a very good one from what I understand, and he accepted the risks that came with the job."

That day, Libby had left his office feeling like a filleted fish.

But today, Dr. Kelvin hadn't brought up Deacon. Instead, he said he wanted to talk about her sorry-ass parents. They spent most of the hour discussing why Libby had left home at sixteen and never returned. Finally, exhausted by the trip down memory lane, she said, "Can we talk about Kiwi?"

"Sure," he said. "We just can't talk about Kiwi's sessions with me."

"I understand that. But how's she doing? She's been sort of, I don't know, sarcastic and critical these days. She wasn't that way before she ran away. It's hard to have a normal conversation with her."

Dr. Kelvin reminded her that Kiwi would be a teenager before long and that a certain belligerence came with the territory. He asked if she'd like him to talk with Kiwi and discuss possible causes for her attitude.

"Please do," Libby said. She left the session feeling less battered than the week before, but then they had yet to discuss the elephant in the room—the death of Rocket, aka Roger Kitridge Hogan. Apparently psychocounseling was a slow, tedious process.

"Your turn," Libby said to Kiwi when she came out.

Kiwi scanned Libby's face and seemed okay with what she saw. She hopped up from the chair and disappeared into the inner sanctum. No one else was in the waiting room. Libby slouched on the sofa and closed her eyes. Her body felt like lead.

It seemed like only minutes later when Libby awakened and Kiwi had returned. She was escorted by Dr. Kelvin, both of them smiling.

"See you next week," he said.

"Awesome, possum," Kiwi responded and headed out the door.

On the ride home, Kiwi was chipper and talkative. Libby wanted to ask what they talked about in session, but that was off-limits. So she tried an oblique approach. "It's good to see you happy," she said.

"Dr. K and I talked about the science fair," Kiwi said. "He actually saw my project on purifying the water supply. He said it was cool."

Libby blinked. "Dr. Kelvin went to the district science fair?"

"Sure. His son had a project there too."

"He has a son?"

Kiwi gave her the Look. "Yes, Jeremy. He's in sixth grade. And a daughter named Amanda who's in first."

So that was what they talked about? The sixth-grade science fair and the doctor's family?

Libby was miffed, but before she could think of a proper response, Kiwi said, "I've decided what I'd like to do for my birthday."

She sighed, shifting gears. "Okay. What?"

"I want to have nachos and Cokes over at the Sleepy Iguana. There's nobody from school I want to invite, but we could invite Myra, like you said. And Shaun, since it's his bar."

"I don't know about having a birthday party for a twelve-year-old at a bar. . . ."

"Why not? Our apartment is too small." She wrinkled her nose. "My birthday's on a Sunday this year. I looked it up."

Shaun had started closing the bar on Sundays. Libby blew out a breath. "If that's what you want."

"Thanks," Kiwi said. Then she entered her fantasy world at the bookmarked place, leaving her mother behind.

Summer came early to the Mojave. Kiwi's birthday dawned hot and dry, the sky pale and cloudless from horizon to horizon. At two-thirty, half an hour before the party, Libby heard Shaun working inside the bar kitchen. She gathered up the supplies she'd bought—confetti-patterned plates and napkins, crepe-paper streamers. She had tried to choose decorations that didn't look too childish.

When Libby unbolted the door from her apartment and entered the kitchen, Shaun looked up from grating cheese and smiled. "Where's the birthday girl?" He had loved the idea of hosting Kiwi's party in the Sleepy Iguana. He was providing the drinks and nachos.

"She's in the shower." Libby leaned close to receive his quick kiss. They had been lovers for several weeks now, although it was hard to find time alone. When she and Kiwi stayed at his house, Kiwi was blatantly uncomfortable, so it didn't happen often. Mostly, though, Kiwi and Shaun got along okay, and Shaun went the extra mile to be patient with her. Libby had told him the whole sordid story of Rocket and about her agreement with the officials in San Jose. He'd told her about his former life as a video-game designer, and they talked about her Army life. But he had never asked about Deacon, and she had never asked about the wife he'd lost. It seemed to be the best way to move on.

Libby left him to his nacho preparation and passed through the kitchen to the main room of the bar. She strung crepe paper around the long oak bar and one table, set out plates and napkins. On her way back to the kitchen, she noticed a large white box on the backbar. It wasn't wrapped or sealed, so she lifted the lid and peeked inside.

Shaun had bought Kiwi a birthday cake. It was three layers tall, frosted white with pink roses around the edge and *Happy Birthday, Kiwi*! spelled in lime green, Kiwi's new favorite color. Libby lifted the cake from the box and placed it on the center of the table. Then she went into the kitchen and gave Shaun an enthusiastic hug.

He laughed. "You think she'll like it?"

"I have no clue. But I think it's terrific. Thanks."

"A girl's twelfth birthday ought to be special," he said.

Myra arrived at the front door of the Sleepy Iguana right on time, bearing a wrapped gift. They shook hands like a couple of idiots and laughed at their awkwardness. Except for the phone call when Libby had invited Myra, it had been weeks since they'd talked. Myra had been promoted to shift manager at the warehouse, with a good raise. Libby was happy for her. She wished Myra could find a gentle partner but suspected she might always be alone.

She showed Myra to the decorated table and brought her a cola. Kiwi still hadn't come over from the apartment.

"I'll go tell Kiwi you're here," she said. "I guess she's still primping." Which was absolutely an untruth; the girl didn't primp.

Libby stuck her head through the doorway to the apartment. "Kiwi, where are you? Your company's here!"

"What time is it?" her voice yelled back from the upstairs.

"Three o'clock! Come on over."

"Be there in a sec."

Libby went back to the bar, where the jukebox was playing a song Kiwi probably liked. Shaun kept up with the new music better than Libby did; to her, it all sounded the same. Shaun and Myra were talking sports. When Kiwi came in, they chorused, "Happy birthday!"

Kiwi grinned. "Thanks. Hi, Myra. Long time no see." She high-fived with Myra and looked toward the front entrance, then at the clock, as if she were waiting for something. Finally her glance fell on the decorated table. "Presents! Awesome. Oh my gosh, look at that cake!"

Libby watched her daughter examine the fancy birthday cake. "Shaun brought that for you," she said. Kiwi offered Shaun a high-five, and Libby relaxed. Maybe this day would actually be fun.

Kiwi was wearing her favorite ripped jeans and a black tank shirt with yellow screen printing on the front. She had combed her hair long and straight with the aid of a flatiron. Beneath the bar's track lighting, the long layers shone making her look older. Kiwi's cheeks and arms had lost some of their childish roundness. Libby realized with a jolt that she ought to talk to Kiwi about menstruation, and soon.

Shaun served Kiwi a diet Coke, her usual. "Want to have the nachos now or after you open your presents?"

"Ummm, presents first." She glanced again toward the front door. "Can we have the door open?"

"Sure. Some fresh air would be nice," Shaun said. He propped open the heavy door to the gravel parking lot. Hot air flowed through the opening. What's up with that? Libby thought.

Myra pushed her gift across the table. The package was obviously a book, and Kiwi smiled. She ripped open the colored paper. "Wow, it's the next one in the series I'm reading. Thanks, Myra! How did you know I wanted this book?"

"I cheated and asked your mom," Myra said. "Glad you like it."

"I love it. Now I don't have to put it on reserve at the library and wait in line, like, forever!" To Libby's astonishment, Kiwi got up and gave Myra a hug. Myra looked equally surprised, but pleased.

Kiwi reached for the present from Shaun, but he put a hand on it. "Mine won't make sense until you open the one from your mom."

So Kiwi opened Libby's gift—a lime-green iPod and earbuds. She looked truly shocked. "Awesome! I can't believe it." She knew what those things cost. She broke the earbuds out of their package, tried them on, and pantomimed grooving out to music. Everybody laughed. "Thanks, Mom. It's terrific." But Libby didn't get a hug.

"Now mine," Shaun said.

She opened the box and found a gift card to iTunes. "So you can download music onto your iPod," he said. Shaun had installed parental controls on his home computer and given Kiwi access to the internet.

"Cool. I can pick out my own songs. Thanks!"

"There's something else," he said.

But before Kiwi could dig beneath the tissue paper in the box, the noise of tires on gravel drifted in from the parking lot. They looked up as a dark wine SUV parked by the front door.

"Uh-oh," Shaun said. "Somebody thinks we're open for business." He started to get up, but Kiwi was ahead of him

"No, it's the other guests I invited." She hurried to the door.

Libby squinted toward the rectangle of sunlight. "What other guests?"

A man and woman got out on opposite sides of the SUV, each holding a wrapped package. Libby recognized the stocky form of Jeremiah Redbone Summernigh. With him was an older woman, her hair mostly gray, her face partly hidden behind sunglasses.

"Hi, Jeremiah," Kiwi called, waving. Then she stopped in the doorway, her posture uncertain. "Hi, Grandma."

Past Kiwi's shoulder, Libby saw the woman approach the doorway and remove her sunglasses.

"Justine?" Deacon's mother had come here from Alabama? Libby moved quickly to stand behind her daughter.

Justine Seager smiled. "Happy birthday, Kiwi. My stars—look at you. You're a beautiful young lady!" She held out her arms and Kiwi gave her an awkward hug.

"Justine?" Libby said again.

"Hello, Libby."

Justine had aged more than Libby would have guessed, but there was still something of Deacon in her smile. Libby had trouble drawing breath. "I didn't know you were coming," she said lamely.

Justine raised her eyebrows and looked at Kiwi.

"I wanted it to be a surprise," Kiwi said, not meeting Libby's eyes.

"That's more like a shock," Justine observed.

Jeremiah stepped forward then and handed Kiwi his package. "Sorry we're a bit late."

"No problem," Kiwi said cheerfully. "Come on in!"

Now she was the little hostess, leading Justine into the dim bar, which suddenly looked cheap and dusty. "Jeremiah, you're gonna love Shaun's nachos. We can put extra jalapeños on yours."

Jeremiah laughed. "Sounds great." He turned toward Libby. "How are you doing? You look good, not so skinny as last time I saw you."

"Thanks, I think," she said, and tried to smile. "It's nice of you to come all this way."

"Glad to help her celebrate."

In the ambush, Libby forgot her manners. But Kiwi introduced Myra to both guests and her grandmother to Shaun. Shaun and Jeremiah shook hands; they'd already met. Shaun moved two more chairs to the decorated table, and Kiwi brought drinks. "Let's have the nachos now," she said to Shaun. "Can we? I'll help you."

"Libby can help," he said. "You stay and visit with your guests."

God bless him. Libby followed him into the kitchen, her armpits slick. "Holy shit," she said, when they were alone.

Shaun turned around and held her. "Calm down. She invited her grandmother for her birthday, and you know how she idolizes Jeremiah. It's okay."

"But she didn't say a word to me! Is Justine planning to stay a while? Where will I put her in that little apartment?"

"I guess she could bunk at my house," he said, his smile crooked. "She's not bad looking."

Libby punched him in the ribs. "How did Kiwi organize this? The internet?"

"No doubt. Take a deep breath," he said. He started setting up trays of tortilla chips for the nachos. "We'll figure things out."

She loved him for saying *we*. But she couldn't dispel a sense of foreboding, like something important was slipping away.

Chapter 27

Kiwi's Journal

15 May 2009—Happy birthday to me!

TODAY IS MY TWELFTH birthday—until midnight, which is only an hour away. Mom's asleep, but I'm on a sugar high from all the birthday cake. I haven't written in my journal since we came home from San Jose three months ago. But tonight I feel like writing again, so here goes:

Mom and I are keeping our promise to see a shrink. He's nice, but if he's trying to fix my brain, it's not working. We still haven't talked about You-Know-What, and I thought that was the whole point.

We practically live with Shaun now, although he doesn't stay at our apartment. We stay at his house sometimes. It's weird to go to sleep in his spare bedroom with Mom, then wake up in the night and she's gone. Like I'm a total idiot and don't know what they're doing. Why don't they just sleep in the same room and quit pretending? It's so lame.

I have to admit I was wrong about Shaun. He's turned out okay, tats and all, but it irritates me that Mom wants to spend *all* her free time with him. I get that's not his fault. That's just Mom.

Shaun's Good Points:

1. He doesn't talk bad to Mom or bring gross friends around. Actually I don't think he has friends except for his customers. He's kind of a loner, like me.

2. He doesn't do drugs and hardly ever drinks, which is kind of surprising for a guy who owns a bar. Believe me, we spend so much time with him that if he had bad habits, I would know.

3. He never talks loud or yells, and he doesn't hit.

4. He lets me use his computer. This is lucky because all the kids at school have a computer at home. It's almost a requirement for getting your homework done. Shaun sets rules about what I can use it for, but that's okay. I'm not interested in meeting some creep on the internet.

He did let me bookmark the video of the little kiwi bird who gives up his life for one chance to fly. But I had to let him watch it before he agreed. He stood behind me, looking over my shoulder. When it was over, he said, "Wow. That's a downer."

"But it was worth it to him," I said. "He'd spent his whole life longing to fly, like the other birds."

"Yeah, well. I recommend finding a way to do it that won't get him killed," he said. Then he thumped me on the head, but not hard.

5. I think Shaun likes me, and not just because of Mom. He calls me Kee. I've never had a nickname before.

Shaun's Bad Points:

1. There's only one, really: He'll never be my dad, even if he tries. No matter how hard he tries.

Again, not his fault. And obviously, the good points outweigh the bad. But for a long time, I wasn't sure I could trust him. So about a month after the Five Days in San Jose, I devised a test of his character. I asked Shaun to help me capture a zebra-tailed lizard for science class on Sunday when the bar was closed. We took an empty mayonnaise jar and put holes in the lid and went walking in the desert behind his house.

I think he knew something was up because I usually go exploring in the desert by myself. But he didn't push it. We hunted quietly, watching for movement beneath the scrawny bushes. After a while, I said, "Remember when we were in Jeremiah's backyard in San Jose? You told me you'd stick with Mom through our trouble with the police, and then if I still thought you were bad for her, you'd walk away."

Shaun kept his eyes on the path. "I remember."

We walked a little farther, and he said, "I also promised I'd never do anything to hurt her. And I haven't."

"*Never* is a long time," I said. I glimpsed something under a bush and stopped, but it was only a shadow.

"You don't still think I'm bad for her, do you?" he said.

The truth was that being around Shaun put Mom in a good mood. She didn't look like a skeleton anymore, and sometimes she sang in the car like she used to do when I was little. But I said, "I don't know. What if I do?" I balanced the mayonnaise jar on my head so I wouldn't have to look at him. "Would you keep your promise and break up with her?"

He exhaled loudly. He didn't answer for awhile, and when he did, his voice was sad. "I'd have to. I gave you my word."

Wow—that stopped me in my tracks.

We heard a scuttling in a patch of dry grass, and Shaun bent down and scooped up a lizard, quick as a frog's tongue. I opened the jar, and he dropped the skinny reptile inside.

"The trouble is," he said, "if I leave your mom now, that will hurt her too. Then I'll have broken my other promise." He put the lid on the jar and handed it to me. The low sun made our shadows long. "It looks like my reputation is in your hands, Kee. I can't keep both promises unless you let me stay."

I looked down at the little zebra-tailed lizard in its plastic prison. It stared right back at me with hard black eyes. Mom would be wrecked if Shaun left her, no question. Any moron could see she was in love with him. As for me, I couldn't know whether Shaun would stick with Mom forever, and neither could she. But if she was brave enough to risk it for a chance to be happy, I wasn't going to be the one to mess this love story up. So I told Shaun, "You're off the hook. You can stay."

But I couldn't hang around to watch.

The next day I put a plan into action. Now that I had computer privileges, I'd been keeping in touch with Grandma and Jeremiah by email. Perry, too, sometimes, but he was so busy with sports I didn't hear from him often. Grandma said she'd had a computer for years and even paid her bills online. Techno-Granny! Who knew? She didn't seem as old as she used to be.

So unbeknownst to Mom, I invited Grandma and Jeremiah for my birthday party. I wanted Grandma to stay a few days, so I told her about the nice motel up on the highway. I figured that was better than making her sleep on our lumpy sofa, and Mom wouldn't be so stressed. Grandma hates airplanes, but she said for me, she'd get brave. She flew to San Jose and rode down with Jeremiah. Perry couldn't come because he had a baseball game.

All in all, it was one of my best birthdays. Shaun fixed his amazing nachos and brought me a genuine bakery cake. And I got killer gifts! The most surprising was a new journal from Shaun. It's black with gold swirls and has the words *My Journal* written on the front cover in cursive. Grandma brought me headbands and scrunchies, a fingernail art kit, and perfume named after a rock star. I'm not that into girlie stuff, but I pretended to be excited.

After Jeremiah went home, Shaun and I drove Grandma up to the motel with her suitcase. She said she had jet lag and was going to sleep late, but after school, I should come up and swim in the motel's pool and spend the night. We could hang out together while Mom was at work. I can't wait! I need to talk to Grandma alone.

More later,
Kiwi

The Spiderling

Four days later (I've been busy.)

I aced my math test on Monday and fidgeted all day until school was out. Mom picked me up, and I dropped my backpack at home and grabbed my swimsuit and the nail-art set. Then Mom drove me up to Grandma's motel. I had hoped Grandma would go swimming with me, but she said she didn't bring a suit and there was a good reason for that. When I asked what the reason was, she said, "Nobody wants to see a plucked chicken in the swimming pool."

I had to agree. Grandma is pretty funny. She did take off her shoes and roll up her pants legs and sit by the pool in a lounge chair. She doesn't look like I remember her, but then I don't look like she remembered, either. I like the little wrinkles in her cheeks when she smiles.

I'm not a good swimmer because I haven't practiced much. But Grandma bought me a "noodle" at the motel gift shop so I could hang onto it and jump off the diving board. I dog-paddled to the edge and jumped again, over and over. Grandma would call out my score each time—8.5, 9.0, and finally a 10! I stayed in the pool until dinnertime.

We ate in the restaurant at the motel. Grandma coached me on how to use a napkin in my lap and which fork was for the salad. For dessert, we shared a double-chocolate brownie with ice cream. Yum!

Afterward, we set up the nail-art kit on the little table in her motel room, and I got the chance alone with her that I'd been waiting for. "I've been thinking about your invitation to come to Alabama," I said.

She was painting my left fingernails white. They looked like I'd dipped them in liquid paper.

"I wish you would, honey," she said, in her round Alabama accent. "Maybe this summer when you're out of school. Do you think your mama would come?" She moved to another finger with the nail polish.

"I was thinking I'd come by myself," I said, acting casual. "And stay."

Grandma stopped painting and looked at me.

"You said they have a good school there," I reminded her. "I wouldn't be any trouble, and I could help with the cleaning and cooking." (I didn't mention blowing up Myra's kitchen. I figured that was too much information.)

227

Grandma turned the blow dryer on low and aimed at my fingers. "You want to come live with me?" She said it tentatively, as if she was making sure she had heard me right.

"Yes, I do."

"You're not happy at home?" She went back to work on my fingernails, but I could tell she was paying close attention to what I said.

"Actually things are pretty good. Shaun's nice to Mom."

"What about to you?" she said.

"Yeah, he's nice to me too. But you know." I shrugged. "He's not my dad."

"Well, no," she said, with a sigh. "Nobody is. Nobody could be. It's not fair to compare them. But if you're getting along fine at home, why do you want to leave?"

"I think Mom and Shaun are in love," I said. Saying it out loud I got a big lump in my throat. "I'm like a third foot, you know? Kind of in the way." Suddenly I got a cold little idea: Maybe Grandma's invitation had a time limit. "If you've changed your mind, I understand. You're not used to having a kid around, either."

"Honey, I would absolutely love to have you." She smiled at me and I could tell this was true. "I just wondered . . . Have you talked this over with your mom?"

"Not yet."

"Do you want me to talk to her?"

"No—I should probably do it myself," I said.

"I agree. Let me know how that goes."

"I will," I promised. I spread out my hands and admired her work. Ten little rainbows were stenciled on my fingertips.

The rainbows wore off in three days, and by that time, Grandma was gone. She left me a plane ticket to Alabama, which she had bought on the internet, for the day after school was out.

Mom went ghost white when I told her my plan. We were driving home from school, and she sat at a stop sign and just stared at me. I could read her mind: She wanted to talk it over with Shaun. That's how much she depends on him now. Sometimes I wonder if she has a thought of her own anymore.

I reminded her that Grandma had invited me a long time ago, and then guilted her about having hidden those letters. I felt kinda bad about doing that, but in the end, she didn't argue very hard, so I figured I had done the right thing.

But then as she took her foot off the brake, she said, "It's only for the summer, right?"

I didn't make any promises I couldn't keep.

This is the last page in my lavender notebook. Definitely the end of something.

A minute ago, I had a sure feeling that Bones was in the room, but when I looked, he wasn't there.

Last time I left home he couldn't go with me. I have another sure feeling that I've seen him for the last time. But that doesn't mean he isn't here with me.

Love,
Kiwi

Chapter 28

Kiwi's Journal

25 June 2009—Over the rivers and through the sky, to Grandmother's house I go. (You're supposed to sing that part.)

THIS IS MY FIRST ENTRY in the journal Shaun got me for my birthday. A new journal for a new chapter in my life. I'm on an airplane flying into the sun. The pilot just got on the speaker and said we were passing over Death Valley. I didn't like the sound of that.

Last night I was so excited I couldn't fall asleep. Living with Grandma will be an adjustment—for both of us. When you think about it, we've really known each other only a few days. I'm going to try my best to help around the house and be more like a roommate instead of a kid she has to worry about.

Mom and I got teary-eyed when we said our good-byes at the airport. Even Shaun looked kind of runny.

As for me, I'm excited and sad and nervous all at once. Grandma got me a direct flight from Los Angeles to Atlanta so I don't have to change planes somewhere and maybe get lost. All I have to do is sit here for four hours and nineteen minutes!

The airline designated me an Unaccompanied Minor and assigned me two handlers. One took me through the security checkpoint in the LA airport and got me on the plane, and another is supposed to meet me in Atlanta and help me find Grandma. The flight attendant said I'm the only UM on this flight, so I get all the attention. She stops by every so often to see how I'm doing. But I brought plenty to keep me busy. Besides my new journal, I have a book, my iPod, sudoku puzzles, and even some snacks. Snacking is always a good way to pass the time.

Yesterday was my last day of school. I'm now officially a seventh-grader. When I went back to school after the Five Days in San Jose, hardly anybody would talk to me. It was like I'd become invisible. But I didn't care. I knew I'd be gone soon. I emailed with Perry for a while, but he's too far away to be a close friend. I hope I can make at least one new friend in Alabama.

I'm glad school doesn't start for a couple of months though, so I can get used to things. Part of the deal was that Grandma has to find me a new shrink in Monteverde, where she lives. I dread that because shrinks are like a box of chocolates—you never know what you're going to get. (I loved *Forrest Gump*.)

We're passing over more mountains now and dark green patches that look like forests. I can see cloud shadows on the ground, and the lakes look like squashed silver coins. It's a different world up here, the earth looks so beautiful and quiet. Maybe this is what heaven is like.

Maybe I'm crazy, but I'm feeling lucky. I'm not like that little kiwi bird after all—I get to fly!

I may go to hell someday, but I refuse to feel guilty and scared for the rest of my life. What's the point?

Kiwi the UM

1 July

The South must be the original Garden of Eden. You can't see a bare spot of ground that isn't green. There are huge trees with vines and moss hanging from the branches and flowers everywhere. Grandma says if you left your car in the woods overnight, by morning, the kudzu vines would cover it up. Plants are taking over Alabama!

It's beautiful, and it's also *hot, damp sweaty hot.* That was a little disappointing. I thought I was leaving superhot weather behind in the desert. The air here is so muggy it's like breathing a living organism. Grandma says the fall and spring are much more comfortable than summer, and winters are mild, but once in a great while, they do get snow. I sure hope I get to see that.

Grandma's house is two stories high with even taller trees all around it. The house is pale yellow with white trim and tall white columns. It has a balcony on the front and a covered porch that wraps around three sides of the house. There are bathrooms upstairs and down and four bedrooms. Grandma uses one of them for storage. Her house is on the register of historical places.

This week she's been showing me around town. Here's my report on Monteverde, Alabama: Monteverde has a population of about five thousand. The main industry is making furniture. They have a huge plant outside of town and a furniture showroom. Main Street is short and sweet, with rows of little shops, and there are three schools—an elementary, middle school, and high school. In seventh grade, I'll be in the middle grade of the middle school. Not the youngest, and not the oldest—perfect. There's also a university in town. The whole community is shaded by live oak trees so big it would take three kids my size to lock arms around one trunk. I'm becoming a tree hugger!

One of my favorite places—surprise!—is the public library. It's less than a mile from Grandma's house, and I already have my library card. The library is in a historic building with squeaky wood floors and high ceilings. I'm going to check out and read *Gone with the Wind*. Grandma says the movie was fine, but if I read the book, I will understand the South.

Grandma gave me my own bedroom upstairs, right next to the one that was Dad's when he was a boy. His old baseball bat and mitt are still in there along with all his school pictures. I can go in whenever I want and look around. But I wouldn't want to sleep there. My room has a wood floor covered by a paisley rug that smells like history.

There's a huge magnolia tree outside the window. Grandma calls the bed a "four-poster," and it's so tall I have to climb onto it. The four-poster once belonged to Grandma's grandmother, which makes the bed at least a hundred years old. (Not the mattress, though, thank goodness.)

I didn't know it before, but I like old furniture. I run my fingers over the little dents and scuff marks and try to picture the people who made them. Just think: A hundred years ago, my great-great-grandmother slept in this bed. I never even knew I had a great-great-anything.

I've been here one week as of today. We've been so busy I haven't had time to miss Mom except at night in that valley of time before I fall asleep. I picture her in our little apartment alone, but of course she isn't alone. She has Shaun.

I may be a little homesick for Mom, but I do not miss the desert. I like this green world where everything either grows and grows in every shade of green you can imagine or has been here forever.

Nothing here is temporary.

This is the house my dad grew up in. When I close my eyes, I can feel tendrils growing from my fingers and leaves opening up from my head. I become a tree with long, hidden roots.

Night,
Kiwi the Southern Belle

4 July

Our nation's birthday is a big deal in Monteverde. They had a parade downtown this morning, with horses and kids and dogs all dressed in red-white-and-blue. Girls in Southern Belle dresses rode in convertibles, holding ruffled parasols to keep off the sunshine. (New word: *parasol*.)

The high school band played "The Stars and Stripes Forever" and followed right up with "The South Shall Rise Again."

There was a big picnic in the park—everybody brought big wicker baskets full of homemade pies and fried chicken . . . and I thought of Dad. After dark, they set off fireworks over a pond. I would have stayed outside forever except for the mosquitoes. Note to self: Use more bug spray! I looked like a pincushion when we got home. Grandma told me to dab bleach on my bites to stop the itching.

I may end up with white polka dots.

Love,

Kiwi the Much Bitten

15 July

This week Grandma and I drove to Birmingham for a day of shopping. We were looking for stuff to make my bedroom feel more like mine. Grandma goes to church, so she wanted me to have a couple of summer dresses to wear too. I haven't worn a dress in, like, years.

We had lunch at a fancy place Grandma said was famous for its southern hospitality. It was a tearoom, which made me think of hot tea in a teapot, but come to find out, they serve all kinds. We had iced sweet tea. The food was so pretty: little cucumber sandwiches with no crust, and cold chicken salad with melon slices on the side. Delicious too! But I was hungry again in an hour.

The big surprise came after lunch. I had decided to keep the bedspread and curtains that were already in my room, and Grandma said we saved so much money with that decision we could get me a bicycle! The bike is candy-apple red with whitewall tires and white racing stripes—and all mine!

Now I can ride my bike to the library and to school in the fall. Grandma asked the man for the display bike so we wouldn't have to put it together ourselves. He took it right out of the window for us and put it in Grandma's hatchback. As soon as we got back home and unloaded it, I climbed on and took off. I was wobbly at first, but now I'm a speed demon on two wheels.

Mom called this week.

I'm still not used to talking to her on the phone, like we were friends who haven't seen each other in a while. I asked if she'd kept up her visits to Dr. K, and she said she'd gone every Friday. He gave her some medication to help her not feel so depressed, and she said it was working.

She wanted to know if we'd found me a psychologist yet, and I told her Grandma had lined me up an appointment in two weeks. Then I said, "So have you moved in with Shaun?" Only half kidding.

"No, I still have the apartment," she said. "But I spend a lot of time at his house. It's too quiet around here. I wish you were home."

After that we ran out of things to say. When I hung up, I felt lonesome and sad. Grandma brought me a glass of sweet tea and said, "Let's go sit on the front porch."

She took the Adirondack chair and I sat in the glider so I could stay in motion. We watched fireflies come up from the grass the way we did when Dad and Grandpa were alive. I was glad it was dark underneath the porch roof in case the tears ran down my face.

"How's your mom?" Grandma said.

"Okay, I guess."

"Hmmm," she said.

We sat there and sipped our tea.

"Actually," I said, "she sounded good."

Grandma smiled but didn't say a word.

Just then, a whippoorwill started up a lonesome song, and I started to snivel. "Grandma, I'm a horrible person! Why is she happier without me? Why is she happy with Shaun when she never was with me?" My voice squeaked. "I'm so jealous of him, which is stupid, I know. I'm the worst daughter in the world."

"No," she said. "You're a twelve-year-old girl who's been through a lot, including some difficult things with her mother."

I strained to hear the end of the whippoorwill's sad song.

Grandma patted my knee. "There are two kinds of women, Kiwi," she said, her drawl more Southern than usual. "Those who need a man to be happy, and those who can be happy on their own. Libby is the first kind, and there's nothing wrong with that. I recognize it because I'm that kind of woman too."

I looked across at her in surprise. She was looking out at the fireflies in the yard. "But you lost Grandpa. Are you an unhappy woman?"

"I was for a long time after he died," she said. "But I'm a lot older than your mother, and things change as you get older. I also had your grandfather for thirty-nine years. That's a lot of memories. Your mom's still young, and she still needs somebody. It seems to me that Shaun could be that someone. He's a good person."

"I know he is, but sometimes I felt like she's cheating on Dad. That's why I had to get out of there."

"At your age, I'd probably have felt the same way," Grandma said. "But the truth is your dad's gone, and your mom is doing what she needs to do. Not only for her, but for you. I understand that you need some time to get used to that idea. When you do, I know you'll be happy for her. Because, my dear girl, you are not a horrible person. You are good-hearted and strong, and pretty darned amazing."

In spite of the tears dripping off my chin, I felt like laughing.

"You have to say that," I said. "Because I'm the only grandkid you've got."

"And the only one I need," she said.

Who needs a shrink when I've got Grandma?

Luv,

Kiwi the Crybaby

Chapter 29

Kiwi's Journal

5 August 2019

I AM SITTING HERE bawling (again), but this time the tears are because I just finished *Gone with the Wind*. The book has 1,037 pages, and it took me two weeks to read it, but I *loved* it. The story is about this girl named Scarlett whose family owned a plantation during the Civil War. It's sad and romantic, and Scarlett ends up alone. I sure wish the author had written a story about what happened after that, but Grandma said she never did.

I think southern accents might be contagious because I'm getting one. I can't help it—everybody around here drawls. The g's keep dropping off the ends of my words. Only one thing will keep me from being a true southerner: I'll never learn to like grits. No matter what you pour over them, gravy or syrup or sugar and milk, they taste like sand mixed with wallpaper paste.

Speaking of wallpaper, Grandma and I redid my bedroom. We had to steam off the old paper with a machine we borrowed from the store. But it didn't peel off in long strips like the man said. We had to scrape it off in tiny pieces that got in our hair, our ears, and under our fingernails. It was hard and messy and also funny. Then we textured the walls with a white goop to hide the dents we'd made. At that point, I thought the project was a disaster. But when the goop dried, we painted over it with an apricot color, two coats, and the walls look great. We added a wallpaper border right below the ceiling. Wallpaper paste looks like snot.

Now my room feels clean and fresh, but still old-fashioned like the house. Grandma gave me a bookcase she had in the storage room, and I'm going to start my own personal library. The public library has an annual book sale, and you can buy their extra books for fifty cents apiece. I hope they have a copy of *Gone with the Wind* in the next one.

Lots of other stuff has happened too. School starts August 13—less than two weeks away. Grandma and I went to the Board of Education to get me enrolled, at least temporarily, until they can get the paperwork from Sand Flats. Then we went to the middle school and looked around. It's bigger than my old school, but not too big. I'm nervous and excited. A new school year always feels like a new adventure.

When Mom called last week, I told her I had enrolled for school, and the line went quiet so long, I thought we'd been disconnected. I was about to hang up and call her back when she said, "I thought you would come home before school started."

I tried to sound casual. "School starts early here. I've decided to stay."
More silence. "Kiwi," she said, but I didn't let her finish.
"Gotta go!" I said. "Grandma and I are painting my bedroom."
I heard a big sigh. "Okay," she said. "I'll call again soon. I love you."
I wanted to say, "Really? Or are you just being polite?" But I didn't.
"Love you, too," I said, and then I went back to painting.
Confused,
Kiwi the Seventh-Grader

10 August

Donna Medina doesn't mess around. She's my new psychologist. Grandma thinks it's disrespectful to call her a shrink. Donna said I could call her Donna because she isn't a doctor. She has a master's degree in counseling or child psychology or something like that. I asked what the difference was between her and a doctor, and she said she doesn't hand out pills like they're jelly beans.

Donna's round, with black hair and black-rimmed glasses. The other two head doctors I went to were afraid to bring up the Big Issue. Not Donna. I sat down in her office, and we talked about Monteverde maybe three minutes before she told me she'd been in touch with Detective Nick in San Jose. Shrinks are supposed to keep your secrets, but apparently police detectives have no such rules. He told her everything.

Donna looked me right in the eye.

"So tell me about this man you shot," she said.

Bingo! Okay, I thought. If she wants straight talk, I'll give it to her.

"Rocket was a perv and a druggie," I said. "He treated my mom awful and got her hooked on pills. I'm not sorry he's dead, but I wish I hadn't shot him because that caused a whole bunch of other problems. We had to hide out in the desert, and now my soul is doomed to hell, and Mom can't love a creepy kid who shot somebody in his sleep."

Donna nodded as if all that was logical. "I see," she said. "Go on."

The avalanche started down the hill. I told her about all the other towns Mom and I had lived in after Dad died and her other boyfriends, Before Rocket. I told about Dad's funeral and the roadside bomb and the things Jeremiah had told me when I saw him in San Jose. I explained how I went back to San Jose, trying to do the right thing, but nobody would let me. And about meeting Jack and Birdie and Stanton. I told her how the Army is your family, and after we left, we didn't have a family, and how I thought Mom was still looking for that.

Basically, I talked the whole hour. At the end Donna said, "Kiwi, you've got some screwed-up ideas, but we can fix that. You're a smart cookie and you're gonna be okay."

I felt shaky but better, like when your stomach's upset and you finally vomit. Donna gave me a big smile.

"You need a hug?"

"No, I'm good." I didn't want to get smothered in those big boobs. Donna is no lightweight.

"Fair enough," she said. "Next time it'll be my turn to talk."
That ought to be interesting.
Bye-Bye,
Kiwi the Smart Cookie

13 August: First day of seventh grade, Monteverde, Alabama

In the South, even the kids are friendly. My homeroom class has twenty-five kids; most of them have lived in this town their whole life.

But instead of me being an outsider, I felt like their guest.

I'd met one of the girls at Grandma's church, and she invited me to eat lunch at her table. Her friends were nice, and one of them is actually named Tara, like the plantation in *Gone with the Wind*. Another kid, a boy, talked to me after math class, and I think he was flirting.

I looked pretty good, if I do say so myself. I was in my favorite jeans and a lime-green top. Grandma had helped me get my hair up in a ponytail. In this humidity, my hair kinks like Spanish moss if I don't use the flatiron. I saw another girl with the same problem, and she just wore it frizzy. That sure would be easier.

I think school's going to be harder than I'm used to. Grandma says seventh grade separates the women from the girls. I need to get busy right now on a writing assignment for language arts. Homework the first day! I'm supposed to write about "The Person Who Is [fill in your own name]." The teacher wants to "assess our grammar and writing skill" and learn something about us at the same time. I'm considering fiction because there's no way I can tell her who I really am.

Kiwi the Storyteller

7 September

We're out of school for Labor Day, and so I have time to catch up in my journal. I've been so busy, I keep forgetting. I have homework every evening, and on weekends, I help Grandma clean house. I've also signed up for a girls' basketball league. Grandma says exercise is good for the brain. That remains to be seen.

Anyway, we practice Tuesday and Thursday after school as well as on Saturday afternoons. It took two weeks before I could dribble the ball down the court and back without hitting my foot or tripping. I'm the second shortest one on the team, but in wind sprints, I'm the fourth fastest. There's a girl named Alexandra who isn't any good either, and we have a lot of fun together. The other night I went home with Alex after practice and slept over. She has a big family—one brother and two sisters, all younger. The littlest is a baby named Tess. Alex carries her around like a sack of potatoes.

Donna the Shrink—sorry, Grandma—has become my friend too. She talks to me as if I was an adult. We discuss all kinds of things like where guilt comes from, what it's good for, and what it's not. We talked about God and heaven and hell. She said if you believe in the concept of hell, then you have to accept the other basic beliefs of organized religion, and one of those is that God is love. Would a God who loved all people send a child to hell for defending her mother's life?

I said, would a God who loved all people let a little girl's daddy get killed by a roadside bomb?

She said, "Good question." I don't think Donna's religious.

Donna also told me about the battered-wife syndrome. She says some women who've been abused by their husbands are so scared of them they can't escape. If they try, the husband comes after them and beats them up again—or they think that's what will happen because the husband tells them what he'll do if they ever leave. Sometimes these women get so desperate, they feel the only solution they have is to murder the husband in his sleep. The law recognizes this as an act of self-defense. She said that's basically what I did when I shot Rocket. He was killing my mom and threatening my life. Shooting him was a bad choice, but also self-preservation. We talked about other options—what I could have done instead.

One session we even talked about sex because nobody had ever talked to me about it, and I'll probably start my period soon. There was stuff I should know.

The other day, Donna said I was saner than most adults she knew, and then she cut my visits to every other week.

I almost regret that, but I can use the time off.

Kiwi the Harlem Globetrotter (Not!)

P.S.

I talked to Mom again. She's moving in with Shaun. Big surprise.

21 September

Not much time to write before ball practice. Big News: Mom and Shaun are coming for a visit! I cannot believe it. Mom said she was lonesome and needed to see me.

I have the feeling she wanted to tell me something, and not over the phone. I talked to Grandma about it, and she didn't have a clue what it could be about, either.

They're supposed to arrive Friday, October 9, because that following Monday, I'm out of school. That's eighteen days away. I'll be a nervous wreck until then.

Before then, Grandma and I have to clean out the bedroom she uses for storage. No way can we put Mom and Shaun in Dad's old bedroom.

—K

Chapter 30

Once upon a Time

LIBBY FOLDED SHAWN'S briefs into neat squares and packed them in a pocket of his oversized duffel bag. The sight of them next to her cotton panties amazed her. How had she become this intimate with another human being? She had never expected it to happen, but now she couldn't imagine a future without Shaun. Sometimes when they were apart and she thought of him, the intensity of her emotions was overwhelming. It was different from her love for Deacon, but no less strong.

What if she lost Shaun, too? She had talked about this fear of hers with Dr. Kelvin. His response was predictable, but also true: Love was never without risk, but the potential rewards were so much greater.

Shaun wanted to get married and she had agreed. No, not just agreed; she was thrilled about it. She was happy. They were packing so they could go tell Kiwi and bring her home.

Shaun came into the bedroom where Libby was working. "You look as if you're in shock," he said.

"I guess I am. About everything."

He pulled her in close, and she laid her face against his chest to feel the heartbeat that was no longer distinguishable from her own. His smell was calm, certain. She tipped her head back and kissed his stubbly chin. "No time for that," he said, grinning. "We need to leave in ten minutes. This bag ready?"

"Almost." Libby fit plastic bags of toiletries on top, along with the GPS for the rental car they would take from the Atlanta airport. Shaun was a gadget person.

He carried the bag to the front door, where their carry-on was already zipped and waiting. Libby glanced around the bedroom for anything she might have forgotten. In her travel tote, she had the boarding passes, paperback books, hand lotion, and lip gloss in a tiny plastic bag. Cell phone. A packet of chocolate candies with peanuts. It seemed as if she couldn't do without those after 10 a.m. Before that, nothing stayed down.

Shaun did the driving. It was a luxury, getting to watch the landscape float past instead of paying attention to the road. She liked to watch his hands on the wheel, the long fingers, tanned forearms she'd learned to trust. He wore a bronze bracelet engraved with the name of a friend who had been killed in Afghanistan. One night, under cover of darkness, he had told her he felt guilty because he hadn't enlisted. At the time of 9/11, his wife was in chemotherapy, and after she died, he hadn't been fit to serve. Libby was indecently glad he hadn't gone.

He noticed her watching him and squeezed her knee. "Are you more nervous about flying or about telling Kee?"

"Yes," she said, and he laughed. She thought about the extra plane ticket they had optimistically bought for Kiwi's return. "What if she doesn't want to come home?"

It was the third time she had brought this up. "You're the mother," he reminded her.

"I know, but if I have to order her to come home, we'll all be miserable."

"Probably. She's going to be getting a lot of news at once, remember. We have to be patient, give her some time to come around."

Libby sighed. Patience was Shaun's answer to so many things, and it did work. But she had always had trouble being patient.

A lot of news at once. There was an understatement. Shaun had accepted a job offer in Sacramento; they would be moving next month.

His former business partner had made a success of the video-game company they had founded together. He wanted Shaun to come back at an astonishingly good salary. When they'd discussed the offer, Shaun said he wouldn't take it unless she would go with him.

She hadn't had to think about it long. Sacramento was less than two hours from the ocean. He had enough savings to get them by until his paycheck started and the bar sold. In fact, Myra had expressed an interest in buying the Sleepy Iguana and hiring Denise and her husband to run it. "Myra doesn't want her favorite watering hole to fall into the wrong hands," Shaun said, grinning.

A week after that discussion, Libby learned she was pregnant. It was an accident, but Shaun was elated. He couldn't wait to be a dad.

How would Kiwi react to all this? What if she had formed such a bond with her grandmother that she refused to leave? Kiwi was both her baby and her hero, and Libby missed her terribly. She had never told Kiwi any of this, hadn't recognized it herself until Kiwi was gone. Libby had to fix that; she had to convince Kiwi that things would be better if she came home.

At the Bakersfield airport, Libby bought juice and nibbled on a handful of chocolate-covered peanuts, then felt queasy. Shaun shook his head as he watched her run to the restroom. By the time she returned, it was time to board.

Two plane changes later, they arrived that afternoon in Atlanta, secured a sedan with plenty of trunk space, and set their clocks on Alabama time. The female voice of the GPS guided them smoothly to Monteverde and then to Justine's address, and Shaun parked in the driveway.

"Wow! What a great old house," he said as he climbed out of the car.

Libby sat for a moment, staring at the home she and Deacon used to visit. She hadn't prepared for such a visceral reaction. Then the front door opened, and Kiwi bounced down the steps. Justine emerged behind her.

Shaun was busy unloading their luggage. He greeted Kiwi with high fives and a hip bump, a ritual they'd devised when Kiwi was home. Shaun gave her a one-armed hug and pointed her toward Libby.

Libby smiled at her daughter. "Look at you. You're almost as tall as I am." She opened her arms and felt a rush when Kiwi came to hug her. Her hair smelled like citrus, and Libby's eyes filled. "I sure have missed you," she whispered.

"Me, too," Kiwi said. And she didn't pull away.

Justine gave Libby a quick hug. "Are you exhausted from your flight? I have some iced tea ready."

"I am a little wilted," Libby admitted. "Iced tea sounds great."

Shaun carried the big bag and Kiwi lugged the carry-on. Libby followed them up the steps, looking up at the white columns, remembering the glider on the wide front porch. It felt strange to be here, even stranger to be here with Shaun. She pushed the old memories aside.

The house was cool and breezy. Although the day wasn't hot, Libby was perspiring from the unaccustomed humidity.

"I'll show you your room," Kiwi told Shaun, and he followed her upstairs with the bag. They disappeared where the staircase made a perpendicular turn. Libby could hear their voices but not the words. She found her way to the bathroom and felt better once she had washed her hands and splashed cool water on her face.

Justine was in the kitchen, pouring tea over ice. "Has Kiwi worn you out?" Libby asked.

Justine smiled. "I won't pretend it's no trouble having a youngster around, but it's been good for me. We have a lot of fun."

Fun—how long had it been since she and Kiwi had fun together? Except for brief moments, a long time. But that was a result of circumstances which no longer existed. She and Kiwi could decorate the new house, hit the seashore on weekends. Shop for the new baby. At that thought, her stomach rolled like a red tide. She rose to run for the bathroom, but the sensation passed. She sat back down.

"You seem nervous," Justine observed.

"We have some important news to tell Kiwi. And you." Libby hoped to make her former mother-in-law an ally.

Justine's eyebrows lifted behind the rim of her glasses. "Can't wait to hear it." She turned to adjust a dial on the oven. "I hope it will hold until after dinner. Kiwi and I spent a lot of time cooking this afternoon."

Libby got the message: Don't spoil dinner with controversial conversation. She sipped her too sweet tea.

Shaun and Kiwi entered the kitchen, both smiling. "Lemon?" Justine said to Shaun.

"Yes, thanks." He took the glass and leaned against the refrigerator. "It's good to stand up a while."

"Did Kiwi give you a tour of the house?" Justine said.

"A quick one. It's amazing. Do you know who the architect was?"

"Shelby Wittenmore," Justine said, smiling. "Are you familiar with southern architecture?"

"A bit. I studied architectural drafting in college." He winked at Kiwi. "Mostly because I liked to draw buildings, and that gave me an excuse."

Libby looked at the stranger she was in love with. Architecture? There was so much about him still to be discovered.

"What was your major?" Justine asked.

"Computer systems." He shrugged. "Great training for tending bar. Actually, though, I've accepted a job offer that will put me back in my field." His face was practically shining as he grinned at Kiwi. "We're escaping from the desert, Kee. Ever been to Sacramento? You'll love it. Beautiful city, lots of things to do—less than two hours from the ocean."

Libby stared at him, mouth open. He saw her face and looked sheepish. "Sorry," he said. "I'll leave the rest of the news to you."

Kiwi and Justine turned toward Libby, waiting. Her face flamed.

"Okay, what?" Kiwi demanded.

This wasn't how she'd planned it, but there was no escape. "Shaun and I have decided to get married," she said, almost as if she was confessing a weakness. "We'd like to do it while we're here, so you both can be with us."

"Well," Justine said dryly. "So much for waiting until after dinner."

Kiwi was watching Libby's face. Silent.

"Kiwi?"

The kitchen was malignantly quiet. Libby looked in her daughter's eyes and saw a fleeting glimpse of a much younger Kiwi who was still afraid of the dark. But in less than a second, that little girl was gone, replaced by preteen bravado. Kiwi lifted her glass of iced tea like a toast. "Go for it!" Then she got up and left the room.

"Congratulations," Justine said, and this time her voice was warm. "I'm sincerely happy for you. Kiwi will come around."

"I'm not so sure," Libby said.

"Maybe I should go talk to her," Shaun offered.

"No, let me." Libby struggled to her feet as if she were nine months pregnant instead of two. She followed the echo of Kiwi's footsteps to the backyard, where impossibly tall trees enclosed the grassy lawn, swaying long arms in a welcome breeze. The air felt heavy in her lungs. She found Kiwi sitting in a white gazebo that was on the verge of needing paint.

Libby approached slowly and took a seat beside her. And waited.

"I'm okay," Kiwi said. "Actually, I was kind of expecting this. Shaun is good for you."

"What about for you?" Libby said. "We want to be a family, and you're an important part of that."

"I don't know." She shrugged.

"Kiwi, please look at me. I've missed you something terrible. I love you more than my life. And I want you to come home."

"Home?"

"We can make one together. In Sacramento. You never did like the desert."

"That's a fact," Kiwi said. "But to tell you the truth, I've felt more at home here at Grandma's than I did with you and Shaun. This is where Dad grew up. I like the school and I've made friends. I'm starting to feel like . . . like I know who I am."

Libby wiped her eyes. "I'm glad. I'm glad you've been happy here. But couldn't you learn to be happy with me and Shaun? I know he's not your dad, but he's a good person. And I love him."

"I know," Kiwi said. "It's nothing against Shaun. I'm glad you've found somebody you can love."

"I love you."

"But you didn't love me for a long time, and I don't know if I can get over that. It really, really hurt."

"Sweetheart, I always loved you. I never stopped, but I was so messed up inside that I couldn't give you what you needed. I'm truly sorry for that. I'm better now, and I'm asking you to forgive me and try again."

Kiwi let out a breath that shook her shoulders. Libby gathered her daughter in her arms and hugged her tight, rocking like the trees in the wind.

That night Libby slept as if drugged. When she awakened, it was midmorning, bright sunshine in the bedroom, and Shaun was not there. She pulled on her clothes, brushed her teeth and hair. Voices from the kitchen floated up to her as she came down the stairs. She heard Kiwi's laugh and immediately felt brighter.

Justine and Shaun and Kiwi were sitting around the antique kitchen table. In the center sat a pan of homemade cinnamon rolls. The aroma made Libby hungry and nauseated in the same instant.

"Morning," she said, and they repeated her greeting in unison.

"Black coffee, right?" Justine said, and got up to pour.

"Right—thanks." She sat next to Shaun, who reached out to squeeze her hand. If Justine had objections about their sharing a room, she'd kept them to herself, and Libby was grateful for that. "So what have I missed?"

"We've been planning the wedding," Kiwi said, mischief in her eyes. "You have nothing to do with it. You're just the bride."

"Nothing fancy," Libby warned. "I brought one simple dress." She had in mind a brief ceremony at some municipal building. Shaun had researched the license requirements online.

"We'll have it in the backyard," Kiwi said. "The weather's perfect, and we can get Grandma's pastor to officiate."

Officiate. Kiwi's vocabulary never ceased to surprise her. "Are you sure?" she asked Justine. "I don't want to make any trouble for you."

"No trouble at all," Justine said. "Reverend Beasley is a longtime friend, and if you don't mind, we'll invite his wife too. There's a wonderful little bakery here that does pretty cakes. And Kiwi can make plantation punch, without the rum."

Libby looked to Shaun for backup. "Can't we just exchange vows at the courthouse?"

He shrugged, obviously in on the conspiracy.

"I repeat," Kiwi said. "You're the victim. Er, bride. Your vote doesn't count."

Libby sighed. "Okay, then, but no more guests. This is a family thing."

The word *family* effectively stopped the conversation. We're an odd group, Libby thought. My daughter, former mother-in-law, and new lover. Can we really be a family?

They spent Saturday touring Monteverde. They visited the furniture factory outlet, did a drive-by of Kiwi's school, and then had dinner at a quaint little restaurant on Main Street.

On Sunday, while Justine and Kiwi attended church, Libby and Shaun took a walk in the neighborhood. The weather was pleasantly cool, and a few yellow leaves tumbled onto their shoulders.

"When are you going to tell Kiwi about the baby?" Shaun asked.

"I thought I'd wait until we got married."

He shook his head. "She's way too smart to believe the ceremony made you pregnant."

She laughed. "Silly—I just thought we'd jump one hurdle at a time."

"So getting married is a hurdle."

"You know what I mean. For Kiwi it is."

Shaun was quiet. Libby looked sideways at him. "You think we should tell her now?"

"I think the sooner the better. But that's up to you."

Justine arranged with the Reverend Beasley for a ceremony at 4:30 p.m. on Thursday. When Kiwi didn't ask to miss school that day, Libby tried not to feel disappointed.

The reverend and Mrs. Beasley, a merry couple in their sixties, arrived at 4:15 p.m. to meet the bride and groom. At 4:30 p.m., the six of them assembled in the shady backyard. The reverend stood in an arch of the gazebo, holding his Bible. Shaun and Libby faced him, flanked by

Justine and Kiwi and the pastor's wife. A bowl of bright pink punch and a white layer cake bore silent witness on a white-clothed table, while finches sang from the trees.

The ceremony was short, although the reverend digressed briefly into the sanctity of marriage. They exchanged gold bands, and Libby was taken aback to see that Shaun's eyes were shiny as he was advised to kiss the bride.

Their flight would depart from Atlanta at 1:00 p.m. the next day. They would have to leave Monteverde early to make it. Libby had put off her last bit of news until after the cake and punch, after the Beasleys had said their good-byes. She and Kiwi went upstairs to change out of their dresses. Safe in her jeans again, Libby knocked on the door to Kiwi's room. "May I come in?"

"Sure."

Libby slipped into the room and took a seat on the bed. "You looked very pretty in your dress," Libby said.

"Thanks. You, too."

Libby smoothed her fingers over the bedspread. "I have one more piece of news I need to tell you."

Kiwi was pulling a cotton tee over jeans that would soon be too small. "Okay, shoot."

Libby waited until Kiwi looked at her. "We're going to have a baby," she said. "In the spring."

Kiwi stopped dead. "You're pregnant?"

"Yes."

Kiwi's face whitened. She plopped down beside Libby.

"Holey cheese."

"Yeah, I know. It was a shock to me, too, but now that I'm used to the idea, I'm so happy about it. Shaun is, too."

"Jeez Louise," Kiwi said. Her voice turned cutting. "The poor kid has no choice, and no idea what it's getting into."

Before Libby could react, Justine's voice called up the stairs. "Kiwi? There's a phone call for you!" And Kiwi bounded from the room.

Kiwi said not one word at dinner, staring at her plate while the others pretended not to notice. As soon as the dishes were cleared, she disappeared upstairs to her room. Libby gave her an hour, then climbed the stairs. She found Kiwi spread-eagled on the bed, her iPod hooked to her ears.

"I've come to help you pack," Libby said. "We'll need to leave by nine at the latest tomorrow."

Kiwi didn't remove the buds from her ears or her gaze from the ceiling. "I don't want to go," she said. "I like my school and living with Grandma. You and Shaun don't need me around to start your new family."

"Don't be a drama queen," Libby said. "We've made it abundantly clear that we want you to come home. Not just me; Shaun wants you there. You belong with us."

Finally Kiwi looked at her.

"No, I don't. I belong here."

She rolled over and faced the wall.

Chapter 31

Kiwi's Journal

21 October 2009 : After math (It's a pun, get it?)

MOM AND SHAUN RETURNED to California. Mom was crying when they drove way. I hated that. Before they left, she told me she loved me, and I know she meant it. But I couldn't go with them.

I've been going to school and basketball practice as usual and hanging out with Grandma on weekends. But nothing is the same. I now have a stepfather, for one thing. And if that's not weird enough by itself, I'm going to have a baby sister. Or brother, I guess, but somehow that doesn't seem likely.

Before all this stuff happened, my life in Alabama felt perfect. It was filled up. Now I have a hollow place I can't pin down. It's like those little specks you see at the edge of your vision when you close your eyes. When you try to look right at them, they slide away. Since my friend Alex has a baby sister, I decided I would tell her. She also has two other rug rats at home, who are three and five. Her house is a zoo.

We rode our bikes to her house after basketball practice this week, and I stayed to do homework. Baby Tess was in the room with us, of course. Alex's mom always hands Tess off as soon as Alex gets home. Tess has one soft curl on top of her head and huge blueberry eyes. She's so cute. Alex is good-natured about all of it, and you can tell the baby adores her. We were working on our pre-algebra homework, but Alex wasn't getting much done. First, Tess wanted in Alex's lap, then she wanted down, and then she climbed back up on Alex's lap and stuck her fingers in Alex's mouth.

Alex knew that my mom and Shaun had gotten married while they were visiting me, but she hadn't met them.

"I'm going to have a baby sister, too," I told her.

"Really? You have my sympathy!" she said with a laugh. But I could tell she didn't mean it. "Are they going to live here?"

"They're moving to Sacramento."

"When's the baby due?"

"In May, I think. She'll be my half sister, actually."

"Like Tess."

I stopped working and looked at her. "What?"

"Tess and Audrey and Cody are my half siblings. But I never think of them that way." She groaned as Tess made a grab for her math paper. "Tess, quit! Here, chase Teddy!" She tossed Tess's pint-sized bear across the floor. Teddy had been slobbered on so much, his fur looked shellacked. Tess took after him on all fours.

"You have different dads?" I said.

"Technically, yes, but not really. Burt couldn't be any more my dad if I had his genes. He and Mom have been together since I was itty-bitty. I hardly ever see my biological dad."

"Gosh, and you look so normal," I said.

"Looks can be deceiving." She gave me her crazy face.

Her mom hollered just then for Alex to come help her a minute. (*Hollered* is a real word in Alabama.)

"Coming!" Alex yelled.

She scooped up Tess, who was busy eating carpet fuzz, and plopped her on my lap. "Here, watch her, will you? I'll be right back."

Tess and I looked at each other with surprise. She knew me, of course, because I'd been to Alex's house a lot. I smiled at her, and she gave me a two-toothed grin with a good amount of slobber running down her chin. I felt like I should do something to entertain her, so I retrieved Teddy and started to play airplane with him, the way I'd seen Alex do. I zoomed him in and landed him on Tess's tummy. She cackled with delight. More slobber came out.

She felt surprisingly solid sitting on my legs. And really warm. And pee-scented. Despite the sour aroma, I wanted to give her a hug, so I did. She didn't seem to mind. I'd been feeling strange all day, but sitting there with Tess, I felt something I had never felt before.

Alex returned, and her mom came and took Tess away, and we finished our math. I rode home and went straight to the bathroom. When I came out, I found Grandma in the living room reading her book.

"Grandma, I need those feminine supplies we bought a while back."

She looked up and smiled. "Why are you whispering? There's nobody here but us chickens." She got up and gave me a hug.

Getting ready for bed tonight, I found Tess's little red hair bow stuck to the sleeve of my shirt. I taped it to the mirror in my room.

—K

31 October : Halloween, Halloween, Everybody Scream!

I can't believe it's been only a year since Mom and I landed in Sand Flats and I enrolled in sixth grade there. Halloween is still my favorite holiday, but I no longer feel the urge to dress up. I'm a lot older than I was then.

Alex and I took Audrey and Cody trick-or-treating in their neighborhood this evening. It's safe enough around here you can actually do that. Their front yard is decorated with fake spider webs and skeletons and pumpkins with crooked faces the kids helped to carve. When you step up on the porch, a corpse raises its head and gives a wicked laugh. It's awesome.

On the way to Alex's house just before dark, I turned a corner on my bike, and something amazing happened. The sun had dropped below a mound of clouds on the horizon and turned the sky a golden orange. I looked up against that glowing sky and saw hundreds, no thousands of tiny silver threads floating in the air. The sky was full of them, as high as I could see. Teeny, wispy sparkles catching the light.

All day long, I'd been feeling tickling sensations on my arms. I kept brushing at them, but I couldn't see anything there. Now I understood. I'd read about this in a science book.

October is the time of ballooning spiderlings. Baby spiders hatch by the thousands, and there are too many in one place to find food. They're no bigger than a dot, but they spin a silk thread that catches the breeze, and they fly away. Sometimes short distances, sometimes hundreds of miles. With no control over where they land to start their new lives.

I stopped beside the street and watched them glisten in the sky. Thousands of baby souls, sailing on the whims of the wind. Some would be lucky and land in a safe place. Some would be unlucky and die.

That's when I knew I had to go live with Mom and Shaun in California. A baby soul has been cast out on the wind, with no control over where she might land. I have to go home and make a safe place for my little sister. If I don't watch out for her, who will?

Love,
Kiwi

Acknowledgments

This book was many years in process, and I fear it is impossible to list every person who assisted in its writing. If I have left anyone out, my sincerest apologies. Particular thanks to Sergeant Ronnie Lopez of the San Jose Police Department for his patient explanation of how juvenile suspects are processed and to Anne Early, a licensed clinical social worker and member of the Academy of Clinical Social Workers, for insight into the psychology of children who commit violent acts. Much gratitude to the FCG group—Linda, Inez, Gail, Rakell, and Shelley, as well as Jeff, Ann, and Suzanne for cogent discussions over pizza and wine. Appreciation and love to Carolyn Wall, writing guru and beta reader extraordinaire.

Discussion Questions for The Spiderling

1. Who is the spiderling in this story? Why do you think the author chose this title?

2. In what way is Kiwi more of a parent than her mother?

3. Why would Libby revert to her old behaviors after losing her husband Deacon?

4. Have you ever lost someone you considered essential to your happiness? How did you cope? Did it change your behavior?

5. In what way is the "traffic game" a release for Kiwi's emotions? Why does she keep putting herself in danger?

6. Kiwi meets "interesting people" on her trip to San Jose. How does she grow from her contact with Birdie, Stanton, and Jack?

7. Have you met any interesting characters in your travels? Who and where?

8. What role does Jeremiah Redbone Summernigh play in Kiwi's struggle to accept her father's death?

9. How do you explain the appearance of Bones?

10. What kind of relationship do you think Kiwi and Shaun might have in the future?

11. What kind of older sister do you see Kiwi becoming?

12. Do you think Kiwi will ever learn to trust her mother again? Would you?

About the Author

Marcia Preston is author of *Song of the Bones*, which won the Mary Higgins Clark Award, and the novel *The Butterfly House*. The mother of a career military son, the former magazine writer and teacher makes her home in Oklahoma.